A Reckless Courtship

A CHRONICLE OF
MISADVENTURES

A Reckless Courtship

A REGENCY ROMANCE

MARTHA KEYES

To all those both seeking and avoiding love:

Sometimes love is found in the most unlikely of places

1

SILAS

In retrospect, moving directly to one of London's most bustling areas after being hidden away in the countryside for nearly a year might not have been the most prudent course of action.

But when had Silas Yorke ever been accused of prudence?

He stared through the window of the sitting room in St. James's, watching the constant flow of traffic with anticipation that made his skin tingle. He had only ever spent a few days in London, but this time, he would remain until his name was cleared. And cleared it would be. Of that he was determined.

A hand grabbed Silas's shoulder and squeezed it. "Electrifying, is it not?"

Silas glanced at his brother Frederick, who was staring through the window with a large smile.

"It is," Silas agreed, his eyes returning to the scene. It might have been silly to be amazed by all the people and chaos, but amazed he was.

Frederick watched with him in silence for a moment. "Are you busy concocting a plan?"

Silas chuckled. "Have you ever known me to have such a thing?"

"No, I suppose not. But the stakes being what they are, I thought you might make an exception."

Silas turned toward his brother. "Is he in Town?" There was no need to clarify to whom he referred. There could only be one person.

Frederick shook his head. "Not expected for some time, either, based on what I heard from Lord Banister. Evidently, Drayton has important business interests to see to up north."

Silas gave a little scoff and turned back to the window. "As opposed to his entirely *un*important duties in the House of Lords. Not that I am complaining. It will be much easier for me to make headway without him in London. He is the one person who would recognize me."

"You truly think no one else will?" Frederick regarded him with a hint of skepticism.

Silas smiled. "I truly think that. Unlike you, I have not spent every waking moment of my life attempting to be noticed by the entirety of Parliament. If I am discovered, I rather think it will be you"—Silas poked him in the chest—"who is responsible."

Frederick scoffed. "Me?"

"You."

"You think I shall forget to refer to you as Hayes?"

"I think you have spent a lifetime calling me something other than that—"

"It has been years since I called you *idiot*."

"And..."—Silas ignored this little quip—"you are likely to slip up, particularly when you have had too much to drink."

Frederick adjusted the sleeves of his tailcoat. "I always have just the right amount to drink."

"No doubt," Silas said with a hint of amusement.

It was pure good fortune that the two of them did not resemble one another. Frederick's hair was lighter, his face more square. He favored their mother.

Silas, on the other hand, not only favored their father but had spent a miserable year hiding in France to evade being hanged for a murder he had not committed. It had aged him, making his face even more angular and narrow. This only served to heighten the difference between the brothers.

Just now, Silas wore his hair longer than was fashionable, and he had taken to parting it on the opposite side. These were small details, certainly, but they mattered. It was possible he might stumble upon an acquaintance from Oxford somewhere in London, but he would choose his public appearances wisely.

"There you are, Yorke," said a voice from behind them.

Instinct had Silas turning in response, but he reminded himself he was not Silas Yorke here. He was John Hayes from Devonshire, in Town on his father's business.

He and Frederick turned toward the two men entering the sitting room: Benedict Fairchild and Sebastian Drake. They were the other bachelors staying in the townhouse, which was owned by Fairchild's father. Silas had only met them yesterday upon his arrival in Town. His oldest brother William and William's wife, Clara, had brought him before making their way to their own townhouse—but not without attempting to convince Silas to stay with them instead.

Silas knew, however, that William would not approve of some of the things he would choose to do in the quest to clear his name. Frederick, on the other hand, was younger than Silas and had always looked up to him. He was much less likely to try to reason with Silas.

Silas needed the freedom to go about things in his own way, and living with a group of unmarried men was much more conducive to that than living with a duke who already mistrusted Silas's decision-making.

"Are you coming tonight?" Fairchild was blond and built along stockier lines than the other three. Like Frederick, he hoped to pave his way in the world through politics.

"Coming?" Frederick repeated. "To what?"

"The masquerade," Drake said, using a piece of post to cover his eyes for a moment. Drake was the most handsome of the four of them, with dark brown hair, a sharp jaw, a charming smile, and eyes full of wit and amusement.

"At Vauxhall?" Frederick asked, his face screwing up a bit.

Fairchild nodded. "My aunt has arrived in Town and all but begged me to accompany her and my cousin—and some other chit as well, apparently."

Drake's head turned toward him, eyes alight with curiosity as he set the piece of post down. "You failed to mention *that* detail. Pray, who is this cousin of whom you speak?"

Fairchild shot him a look of impatience. "Stay away, Drake."

Drake took this in good spirits. "Fair enough. And the chit?"

"I haven't the faintest idea. But you can stay away from her too."

"Spoil sport," Drake said without rancor.

Fairchild returned his gaze to Frederick. "Do you mean to come, then?"

Frederick considered the offer, hesitating far longer than Silas could comprehend. "Will anyone of note be there?"

"Undoubtedly," Fairchild responded. "I heard it being discussed at White's last night."

Frederick's interest grew more visible, and Silas suppressed a smile. His brother regarded every social event as an opportunity to expand his connections. His goal was to obtain a seat in the House of Commons, and it was one he took seriously.

"Very well," Frederick said.

"Capital!" Drake replied. "What of you, Hayes?"

Frederick's head turned, and Silas could feel his eyes boring into him.

"I wouldn't dream of missing it," Silas said, ignoring the pointed look. "One of you wouldn't happen to have a spare domino and mask, would you?"

"I saw one in a trunk upstairs." Fairchild's brow furrowed in an effort to remember. "I believe it was in the Blue Room if you wish to go see."

"Thank you. I shall do so immediately," Silas said, making his way for the door.

Frederick followed, just as Silas had suspected he would.

It wasn't until they were halfway up the stairs that his brother spoke, though. "Are you certain this is wise?"

"It is a masquerade, Frederick," Silas said. "There is no place I could go where my identity could be safer."

Frederick gave a non-committal grunt.

"You are beginning to sound like William, you know."

Frederick's brows snapped together. "I am not."

William was the eldest and most proper amongst them—and a duke to boot. Although his decision to marry a maid had put a considerable chip in the pedestal he sat upon.

Silas stopped to face Frederick as they reached the Blue Room. "Freddie, tell me something: do you mean to be forever attempting to convince me to stay within the walls of this townhouse?"

Frederick regarded him for a moment. "No."

Silas smiled and squeezed his brother's shoulder. "Good. We shall get on famously, then." He went into the room and straight to the trunk at the foot of the bed. It took only a few moments until he found the domino in question.

He chuckled softly as he pulled the heavy cloak from the trunk.

Standing nearby, Frederick's mouth turned down in disgust. "You cannot truly mean to wear that thing."

Silas held it out in front of him, admiring the old-fashioned garment with a smile. It was made of black brocade with gold threaded detailing. The hood was almost comically large, not to mention the ornate trim—gold, of course. It would have been the height of fashion forty years ago. "I have every intention of wearing it."

Frederick stared at Silas, a hint of resignation in his eyes. "You mean to make a fool of me this Season, don't you?"

Silas draped the domino on the bed and began searching for a mask to go along with it. "It is not my primary goal." He grasped a glittery black mask with satin strings hanging at each side and held it up in victory. "But I can make no promises."

Frederick sighed.

A cacophony of sound filled the night air as their carriage slowed on the street near Vauxhall, taking its place in the line of equipages. There was music from within the gardens, carriage wheels on cobblestone, the chatter of masqueraders, coachmen yelling, and the clopping of horse hooves.

Silas had never felt so invigorated.

He had rarely heard such magnificent sounds nor seen so many people in one place. For so long, he'd had only his own mind to keep him company, with staggered visits from William and Clara. The majority of the time, he had been entirely alone, with only the odd mouse to talk to. They had generally not cared to listen.

The prospect of rubbing shoulders with so many other people and without having to worry he might be recognized? It was a gulp of cool, fresh water after wandering in the wilderness for months. It was freedom—or as near to it as he had come since his escape to France.

The four gentlemen descended from the carriage and walked to the entrance of Vauxhall to pay their fee.

"I will repay you," Silas said in an undervoice.

Frederick put away his coin purse. "You can repay me by shedding that hideous domino."

"Never," Silas replied genially, his eyes already exploring the area ahead. He had heard of Vauxhall, of course, but he had never attended an event there.

The doors ahead were open and offered the view of a large path and the trees that lined it on either side. The sound of music grew louder as they approached, and Silas's own heartbeat seemed to strengthen and quicken with each step.

"Are you meeting your aunt?" Frederick asked Fairchild.

Fairchild glanced at his pocket watch. "In an hour or so."

"A bit of time for your own entertainment, then," Drake said. "Where shall we go first?"

Fairchild thought for a moment, his eyes searching the scene before them. "The Rotunda."

Drake nodded decisively, and the four of them passed through the doors and outside again. The wide path twinkled with the light of lamps, while a large building with a conical roof loomed on their left behind a long colonnade.

Silas's shoulders bumped against those of other attendees as they fought their way to the Rotunda, a powerful feeling of anonymity coursing through him.

"Not a foot of space to oneself," Fairchild lamented.

Silas could not keep from smiling, though. Everywhere he looked there was gaiety and laughter, all behind masked faces in flowing dominos of varying colors. A few of the women who passed smiled coyly at him, and his heart stuttered. It had been some time since he had received attention from a woman.

It was not a distraction he could afford while in London, however. He had one goal and one goal only: pin the murder he was accused of on the man responsible.

It would be a tall order in any situation, but the power and position that particular man held made it into more of a *towering* order. Lord Drayton was only a baron, but he may as well have been a Royal Duke. Everyone either revered him or feared him, which would make Silas's task all the more difficult.

The Rotunda was a magnificent structure, vast and circular within. A host of ornate columns held up the high roof, while the walls were covered in vibrant murals lit by lamps and lanterns. In the center, a raised stage housed the orchestra, whose music filled the enormous space and filtered out through the open door.

They listened for a few minutes, but Silas's gaze flitted away from the orchestra again and again, taken up with the myriad people to observe. Did they realize how fortunate they were to take up a mask for entertainment and dispose of it at their leisure? To live life without fear of recognition or false accusations following them like a shadow?

When the others had had enough of the music, the four of them made their way outside again, and Drake led them to the Turkish tent. Outside of it, three acrobats were performing. Dozens of people had gathered around, but most seemed more intent on talking and laughing than in watching the feats of movement taking place before them.

They passed by the acrobatics and into the tent, warm air

enveloping them. Silas blinked at the astounding burst of color and the smell of burning incense, which left trails of smoke creeping into the air. It created a haze, diluting the vibrance of the colorful drapes, the elaborately patterned rugs, and the low tables, which were adorned with refreshments and hanging lanterns. Dancers occupied the space in the middle, tapping on tambourines as they moved in ways Silas had never before witnessed.

Frederick, Drake, and Fairchild laughed and tended to the drinks in their hands, while Silas's own glass sat in his hand, untouched. Perhaps it was the incense that was making his head begin to ache.

Fairchild took a pocket watch from inside his domino and cursed. "I must meet my aunt at the entrance."

Silas forced himself to take a sip from his drink as Fairchild wound his way through the crowd and out of the tent.

Frederick grasped his arm suddenly, jolting the drink.

"What?" Silas brushed off the drips that had landed upon his coat.

Frederick squinted, shifting his head as though trying to obtain a clearer view of something. "I believe that is Bence."

Silas's muscles went taut, and his alert eyes searched the direction in which his brother was looking. It was full of haze, which was thickest near the tent's roof. Sir Walter Bence was the business partner of Lord Drayton, but according to gossip, the two were at loggerheads now. If anyone might have information Silas could use against Drayton—or might know where to find it—it would be Bence.

"In the gold domino," Frederick said. "I can't be certain, but I could swear..."

Spotting a flash of gold, Silas wrested his arm from his brother's grasp and started to wind his way through the crowds.

Frederick's hand snatched at his arm again. "What are you doing?" he hissed.

Silas forged ahead. "I need to speak with him."

"And say what?"

They reached the exit through which the golden domino had left, and Silas searched the area for it.

He swore under his breath. There were simply too many people and no gold dominos in sight.

"You think Vauxhall the proper place for that conversation?" Frederick asked.

Silas did not respond. His brother was undoubtedly right, but when *would* the proper circumstances present themselves? "I have been waiting nearly two years for an opportunity, Freddie."

"Which is precisely why you must take care not to bungle it. Yes, Bence might be at odds with Drayton, but that does not mean he will take kindly to a stranger accosting him and casting aspersions on the character of an old friend."

"I am not a fool, Freddie. I did not intend to *accost* him. I merely wished to cultivate the acquaintance. But it makes no difference. He is gone now." Resigned, Silas turned back to the tent, and they returned inside.

It felt even more stifling somehow.

"Ah," Frederick said, craning his neck. "Is that Mr. Parker? In the scarlet domino over there?"

Silas gave no response, for he was unlikely to recognize anyone here, even without the masks, and he was taken up with frustration at losing the chance to speak with Bence. He was the one man who might know that Drayton was responsible for the murder with which Silas had been charged.

"I am certain it is Parker," Frederick said. "Stay here. I won't be but a moment." And with that, he was gone.

Silas turned toward Drake, but he was obtaining a drink for

a young woman in a blue domino. Based on the smiles both of them wore, he was unlikely to return from the encounter anytime soon.

One of the dancers drew near Silas, looking at him fixedly, a provocative smile on her face as she slapped her hand against a tambourine. She came closer, her hips swaying with each beat of the drums, the coins on her costume jingling. Her arm brushed his as she danced around him in a circle, her kohl-lined eyes finally reappearing before him again, nearer than ever as the scent of jasmine enveloped him.

He kept still, unable to move, unable to blink until, finally, she spun away with a musical laugh, never losing the beat of her tambourine.

His stomach tight with anxiety and discomfort, Silas forced himself to breathe, but the result was a fit of coughing. His lungs had grown sensitive since a bout of consumption in France, and a room full of incense was simply too much.

Covering his coughs with his free arm, he set down his drink and hurried toward the exit. His coughing subsided slowly but surely once he had emerged into the fresh air. A number of people looked at him with a mixture of concern and wariness. It was even more crowded than when they had arrived at the tent, and despite the fresh air surrounding him, Silas felt a sense of oppression.

He shouldered his way through the hordes, determined to find a place less crowded. He had so anticipated being encompassed by people and conversation, but perhaps he had become more accustomed to solitude than he had thought.

He spotted Fairchild walking down the main path from the entrance. Beside him was a middle-aged woman in a violet domino whom Silas took to be his aunt. On the other side of her was a young woman in a green domino, while Fairchild was flanked by one in a vibrant indigo domino. It was her mask, however, that drew Silas's eye, for it was large, colorful, and shaped like a butterfly. It gleamed with each slight movement of her head.

He tore his gaze away and continued in the opposite direction, the crowds thinning as he went. He turned abruptly onto one of the paths that led into the trees, for there wasn't a soul in sight. He would take a few moments' respite there, clear his head, then return to find Frederick and the others, ready for more merriment.

2

ARABELLA

"Come, sit down, Aunt." Arabella Easton gently guided Aunt Louisa to a chair at the tables under the colonnade, watching her nurse her ankle with a gentle hand.

Arabella's eyes darted to the multitude of people passing by, each attired in a domino and mask. The astounding variety of fabrics on display pulled at her like a magnet, but she forced her focus back to her aunt. "Perhaps we should not have come."

"No, no, no." Aunt Louisa waved away her niece's concerns even as she winced. She had twisted her ankle on a loose stone on the way in and was finding it difficult to walk. "I shall be well directly. The true tragedy would be if no one was permitted to see that marvelous creation of yours."

Arabella ran a hand down the velvety fabric of her indigo domino, underneath which was a satin emerald dress. "I would much rather your ankle be seen to properly." She had spent a great deal of time embroidering the domino and making the mask, but she took such joy in the creation that it was no trial for them not to be seen—or at least not too great a trial.

"It truly is a wonder," her cousin Felicity said, admiring Arabella's ensemble. "How on earth did you devise such an idea?"

Arabella touched her mask, and her fingers brushed the beads and sequins that lined the wings. She had created it in the shape of a butterfly, and the wings extended well past her cheeks. "That is one advantage of living in the country year-round, I suppose. I have had a great deal of time to imagine up any number of silly things. Can I fetch anything for you, Aunt?" Her gaze caught on a man walking past on stilts, towering over them. She had seen pictures of such things in books, but to witness it in person was something else entirely.

"Oh, no, child," Aunt Louisa said. "Benedict has that well in hand."

And indeed, just then, Mr. Benedict Fairchild came hurrying up with a drink, which he gave to his aunt. He was related via her husband, making him no relation at all of Arabella's, whose mother had been Aunt Louisa's sister. But it was Mr. Fairchild's willingness to attend the masquerade that had made Aunt Louisa relent to Felicity's pleas to come.

"Ah," Aunt Louisa said after taking a drink. "Much improved already." But as she adjusted her foot, there was a flinch in her smile.

Felicity was trying valiantly not to look disappointed at the unfortunate turn of events. Arabella sympathized, for she herself was full of tingling anticipation to see more of Vauxhall Gardens. Not only had she never been to a masquerade, but she had never been to any public party—and certainly not one in London.

"Perhaps you and your cousin could take a stroll, Felicity?" Arabella suggested. "I will gladly sit with my aunt."

"I won't hear of it," Aunt Louisa said firmly. "I need no chaperone. Felicity, on the other hand..." She cocked a brow at her daughter, then looked at Arabella again. "Go on with them, my dear. I shall be quite comfortable here. Ah! Only look. There is Mrs. Gilbert. She will sit with me a while."

"Are you certain?" Arabella felt a twinge of guilt, not just for abandoning her injured aunt but because she was not sure Papa would approve of her wandering here without her chaperone. But if the alternative was not to see any of Vauxhall, there was no question what she would do. She had made her domino and mask without a real prospect of putting them to use, and now that she had just such an opportunity, she was eager to make use of it.

For years, all she had wanted was to see London, and finally, she was here. Now that she was, she was torn between a desire to see and experience every bit she could and the weight of being a model of decorum, as Papa expected. If she was not, there was no chance at all he would agree to any of her future requests.

"I am perfectly certain." Aunt Louisa smiled kindly and stretched out a hand to Arabella, who took it. She did not release Arabella after squeezing it, however. Gentle but firm, it summoned Arabella closer. "You will help look after Felicity, will you not?" her aunt said in an undervoice.

"Of course."

She patted Arabella's hand. "I know I may trust you." Her eyes searched Arabella's, brimming with sympathy. "You deserve a bit of freedom after being kept in that out-of-the-way estate all these years. But for heaven's sake, do not do anything that will land me in a scrape with your father."

"You may rely upon me, Aunt." Arabella gently pulled at

her hand, for Felicity and Mr. Fairchild were waiting. Now that she was confident her aunt would not be alone, her curiosity was waxing.

"Wait a moment," her aunt said, still not releasing her hand. "I would be remiss not to warn you, child, before you delve deeper into the gardens."

Arabella's brows went up. "Warn me?"

"On no account must you or Felicity be alone. Do you understand? Men behave like common pigs in places like this. If you are not with a chaperone, they lose all sense of decorum. It is the most unaccountable thing. The number of kisses that have been stolen here, the number of reputations ruined..." She shook her head, eyes wide with significance. "It is truly shocking. And do *not* be fooled by pretended chivalry. More than one woman has been lulled into a false sense of security by a prettily behaved man, only to have her reputation in shreds when she leaves. And for heaven's sake, do not venture into the Dark Walks!"

Arabella nodded quickly. She had no notion what the Dark Walks were, but the name was enough to keep her away. "I shall take every care. Of Felicity too."

Aunt Louisa's shoulders relaxed, and she smiled. "Thank you, my dear. Now, go and enjoy yourself." She beckoned again to the woman nearby, and Mrs. Gilbert came to join her.

"Poor Mama," Felicity said, looking over her shoulder as they walked toward the Rotunda. "She will enjoy herself with Mrs. Gilbert, though. Do you know they had their first Season together? Mama will be enjoyably occupied."

"And you free to run loose?" Mr. Fairchild quipped.

"Hardly," Felicity said. "Though, to be sure, without her, we are likely to have a *bit* more fun. I am determined you shall have a proper Vauxhall experience, Bella."

Mr. Fairchild snorted.

Felicity looked up at him. "What?"

He cleared his throat and controlled his expression. "Nothing. Only that I am not convinced such a thing exists as a *proper* Vauxhall experience. People come here to be *im*proper."

Felicity jabbed him with an elbow. "You mustn't shock Bella, Benedict. She has never been anywhere like this."

That was true enough. Arabella's experience of the world beyond her own home had been confined to a few local assemblies and two town journeys with Papa. He had always refused her pleas to accompany him to London but had finally agreed for her to join him in Manchester.

Her desire to see London had suffered a shock as a result of the visit, so full was Manchester of thick smoke, loud machines, and people in poverty the likes of which she had never imagined.

When Aunt Louisa had invited Arabella to join Felicity and her, Arabella had nearly refused. Thank heaven she had not—and that Papa had relented as well, going so far as to invite Aunt Louisa and Felicity to make use of his townhouse. Arabella had only been in London three days, but so far, it was nothing like Manchester.

"Have I shocked you, Miss Easton?" Mr. Fairchild asked.

Arabella shook her head. "I was warned."

"Warned of what precisely?" Felicity asked.

"Excusing your presence, Mr. Fairchild, your mother warned me against the men here, particularly if I were to be found alone, which I have promised not to be, at risk of leaving with no reputation."

Felicity laughed. "Quite rich of Mama to say such things! She was very wild in her day, you know. I found an old letter—from Mrs. Gilbert, in fact—about a kiss between Mama and the son of a nabob. Besides, what is life without a bit of risk?"

"Here, here," Mr. Fairchild agreed.

Arabella's eyes roved to the statues they were passing on the left. She considered asking to go see them but decided against it. She could not stop to admire every thing that caught her interest, or they would be here for weeks. She had no desire to betray her ignorance of all things *ton*, either, so she would allow herself to be guided by Felicity.

"And," Felicity said, emboldened by her cousin's agreement, "how many young women have managed to amuse themselves a bit at Vauxhall—to flirt or perhaps even steal a kiss—*without* damaging their reputations? Far more, I would wager, then have left with their reputations in tatters. Mama is simply afraid of your father, Bella."

"Afraid of him?" Arabella asked, her curiosity roused. "Why?"

"He is so very strict. Mama has always thought it terribly wrong for you to be kept so far from Society all these years. It has made you quite old for your first foray."

Arabella felt a flash of defensiveness on Papa's behalf and, beneath it, a sliver of vexation at being called old. Felicity was but two years younger than Arabella's two-and-twenty. Felicity had been in London the two Seasons before this one, though. She was not wide-eyed and agog at every corner and stretch of Vauxhall. Indeed, she barely seemed to heed it.

"What you perceive as strictness," Arabella said, "is merely a wish to keep me safe. I assure you, I have everything I desire at Wetley—and more."

It was mostly true. Papa spoiled her and her two younger sisters, providing them with the best of everything: tutors, books, horses, food, clothing. Wetley Abbey itself was grand and sprawling, with trails and gardens aplenty. Its library was the most expansive in Staffordshire.

But Arabella had lost count of the number of times she had asked to come to London.

Papa had always refused, and she had felt a wretch for being dissatisfied with the beautiful life she had at Wetley. Arabella had sworn to herself that she would prove she could be trusted to make wise decisions and not give him cause for concern while in London. She might have lived a sheltered life, but her education and upbringing had equipped her well.

Silence followed her attempt to defend Papa and reassure Felicity she had not been living a life of depravation—even if Arabella had sometimes secretly felt that way. No one understood how deeply Mama's untimely death had affected Papa or how much assistance he had required with Arabella's sisters, Mary and Catherine. She had become somewhat of a mother figure to them, for even now they were only eight and eleven.

Their progress down the wide, lantern-strewn path was soon halted when Mr. Fairchild came upon friends. Arabella and Felicity were introduced to Mr. Frederick Yorke and Mr. Sebastian Drake, whom Arabella gauged to be somewhere between five-and-twenty and thirty years of age.

Mr. Yorke, a handsome young man with an amiable smile and confident demeanor, took the place beside Arabella as the group turned into the winding paths that would lead, according to Mr. Drake, to the much-lauded Cascade, a waterfall in the middle of the gardens.

"Are you enjoying London, Miss Easton?" Mr. Yorke inquired.

"Yes," Arabella replied. "I have only been here a few days, but it is a welcome change from the countryside." She stole a glance at him beside her, and only now did she realize how few men near her own age she knew. Papa's guests were generally twice Mr. Yorke's age.

"There is much to be said for the country," Mr. Yorke said, "but I admit that, for me, there is nothing like the tumult of London. It is ever-changing, full of opportunity."

Arabella was inclined to agree with him. London had an energy she had never experienced and was eager to explore.

The path continued to wind, and Felicity's laughter filled the cool night air. She and Mr. Drake seemed to be getting on very well.

"Are you certain this is the way, Drake?" Mr. Yorke asked.

"Of course I am," Mr. Drake replied genially. "Been here a hundred times."

"A hundred?" Felicity repeated incredulously.

"Very well. Five, then."

"I have been here just as often," Mr. Yorke said, "and I am quite certain we took a wrong turn."

"Are you?" Mr. Drake stopped and faced Arabella and him. "Shall we test your theory?"

Mr. Yorke looked at him skeptically. "Test it how?"

Mr. Drake shrugged. "Some of us go your way, the others go mine. We see who arrives at the Cascade first."

Mr. Yorke put out a hand. "Done."

Arabella listened with a hint of unease. Did they intend to send her with Mr. Yorke, and Felicity with Mr. Drake? It would doubly violate her promise to Aunt Louisa, for it would separate her from Felicity *and* put one of them alone with a gentleman—and the other alone with two.

Was two better than one?

Not that any of these men seemed dangerous, but Aunt Louisa had not qualified her warning against the opposite sex. Indeed, she had been very clear that even chivalry was to be regarded with a wary eye.

"Shall we prove Yorke wrong, Miss Fairchild?" Mr. Drake asked Felicity.

"Oh, yes! By all means."

"Yes, indeed," Arabella added, taking a step closer to them and away from Mr. Yorke.

Mr. Drake looked at her for a moment, then smiled. "We could use your impeccable sense of direction, Miss Easton."

Arabella had no such thing. In fact, more than once, she had spent an hour in Wetley's labyrinth precisely because she could not remember her way out, but she would not admit as much, and she was soon walking with her cousin and Mr. Drake.

Mr. Yorke and Mr. Fairchild followed behind for a bit, debating between them which direction to take.

The sound of the music from the Rotunda grew faint as Mr. Drake recounted a story to Felicity just steps ahead of Arabella. She glanced over her shoulder as they turned to the left and was surprised to find Mr. Yorke and Mr. Fairchild gone. Had they turned back in the opposite direction?

"Perhaps we should run," Felicity said to Mr. Drake in a conspiratorial voice. "Then we are sure to arrive at the Cascade first. Come, Bella!"

Arabella turned her gaze ahead again only to find her dress had snagged on an errant branch from the nearest hedge.

"Drat." She stooped to free herself. The nearest lantern was behind her, causing her own shadow to obscure the entanglement. It was inconceivable to her how a quick snag could possibly result in such a tangle of thread and twig. "Just a moment."

Silence met this request, and she looked up.

Felicity was not there. Nor could she hear her laughter.

Arabella's heart began to race, her fingers working quickly at the snag—too quickly, it seemed, for her efforts to free herself became more complicated still.

"Felicity!" she called, ignoring the guidance of her old governess, who had forbidden her to raise her voice. She had *also* forbidden her to be alone in public places, so Arabella had no choice but to violate one of the woman's maxims.

The twig began to loosen its grip, and Arabella looked up again, hoping her cousin would have remarked her absence by now and returned to find her.

But there was no one.

She lowered her head, but something prevented it.

"Drat *again*." It was her mask which had now caught on a branch.

Should she remove the mask and leave it hanging from the shrubbery?

The thought pained her deeply, for she had spent hours sewing on the beads.

"Might I be of assistance, ma'am?" asked a voice from somewhere behind her.

Arabella's eyes widened as the man's footsteps drew nearer. She might as well have been a hare before the hounds, for she could not escape—not without ripping her dress *and* her mask.

But the alternative risk was equally terrifying.

Men behave like common pigs in places like this. That was what Aunt Louisa had said.

Her eyes watched as the hem of a domino swept into view. Her attention fixed on it for a moment, for it was unlike any domino she had seen this evening. Rather than the taffetas and satins she had encountered, this one was of fine and heavy black brocade. The starkness of the garment, however, was countered by the glint of gold thread that had been used to embroider an intricate design all over.

The man came before her and stooped, allowing her a view of his face, which was illuminated by the lamp behind her. A black mask covered his eyes and nose, accentuating the lighter color of his eyes.

His lips spread to reveal a handsome smile. "This butterfly chose an unfortunate place to land, it would seem. No matter.

She will spread her wings soon enough." His hands rose toward her mask, the weighty brocade of his domino slipping back over his arm.

Do not be fooled by their pretended chivalry.

"No," she said.

His hands paused in mid-air, his gaze fixing on her intently and his smile diminishing.

"I can manage," she said more calmly, her cheeks warming at the violence of her interjection. She must maintain her composure.

The man's brows rose and his eyes shifted to her mask, then to her fingers fumbling with her hem.

"I can manage," she repeated, trying to keep her voice calm but firm. Did pigs respond to calmness or firmness?

His smile returned, and Arabella found herself a bit breathless as their gazes locked. He was certainly a beautiful pig, and he smelled not of the sty but of some heady and exotic scent, reminding her of some of the spices in the still room at Wetley.

"An enterprising butterfly, then." He looked at her another moment, then rose. "Very well."

Her fingers finally broke the dress free, and she set to the mask as the man's footsteps receded then stopped.

"When I see Fairchild, I shall inform him his cousin is safe."

Arabella's gaze whipped to him, and she caught a last glimpse of his smile before the black domino swept around the next corner.

He was acquainted with Mr. Fairchild? Apparently, well enough to know he had a cousin here tonight—but not to know that cousin by appearance.

Her fingers worked at the mask and finally, with a snap of a string, she was free. A few beads dropped to the dirt path, but she disregarded them, picking up her skirts and hurrying after Felicity. She would mend the mask later.

She was soon faced with a fork in the path, however, and was forced to stop to consider which way to go. If only she had the impeccable sense of direction Mr. Drake had attributed to her.

Nearby laughter caught her attention, and her heart leapt until she realized it was coming from behind, from the path she had just traversed. It grew louder, along with footsteps— shuffling, uneven ones. They certainly belonged to more than one person. Male persons, based on the laughter. And they were singing—or trying to, at least. The song was almost unintelligible, so garbled were the voices and so off-key was the crooning.

Panic bloomed in Arabella's chest just as two drunken men turned the corner. They slowed at the sight of her, their lazy gazes becoming more fixed.

"Now, who's this pretty little thing?" one of them said, his speech slurred. The string of his mask had slipped below one of his ears, making the mask sit lopsided on his face. He could only see out of one eye, but this did not seem to bother him.

"Let me have a closer look," said the other, and he stumbled toward her.

She drew back, and he smiled, revealing a mouth full of discolored teeth.

"A shy one," he said to his friend.

"My favorite kind," was the other's response.

Arabella did not hesitate a moment longer, whirling around and taking the path on the right at a run.

Behind her, the men laughed, and quick, uneven footsteps informed her that they were following.

The black domino with gold embroidery came around the corner ahead, then stopped short at the sight of her running toward him just as the two men came hobbling around the corner behind her.

If you are not with a chaperone, they lose all sense of decorum.

Arabella's hesitation lasted but a moment. Compared to the pigs behind her, this man who knew Mr. Fairchild was a veritable savior.

She ran headlong into his arms.

3

SILAS

The young woman with the butterfly mask gripped Silas's arm with two hands like a barnacle on a ship, while two inebriated men stared at him as though he had just dumped out the last pint of gin in England.

His arm was wrapped around the woman protectively, though he had no memory of putting it there.

The woman looked up at him through the slits of her mask then, without warning, she smacked the arm she held. "What sort of gentleman leaves his wife in a maze such as this?"

Silas blinked. This butterfly barnacle was apparently also his wife.

"Wife?" repeated one of the men standing a dozen feet away, swaying ever so slightly.

Silas looked at the woman holding onto him—the woman who had adamantly refused his help only two minutes ago, only to run into his arms, hit him, and call him her husband. Just now, her wide eyes looked up at him, a near-plaintive light in them.

He understood what was expected of him and cleared his

throat. "My apologies, dearest. I could have sworn you were right behind me."

"You were too busy admiring the shrubbery, no doubt."

Silas's brows raised, but he did not miss his queue. "Erm, yes. My obsession with finding the perfect topiary has become almost unmanageable." His gaze flitted to the men, who were watching this exchange with befuddlement. He sympathized. "May we help you, good sirs?"

Their slackened jaws closed.

"No," said one. "We were only..." The man looked to his companion for assistance.

"Attemptin' to help the lady find you."

The other nodded vigorously, apparently satisfied with his friend's quickness of mind, even under the influence of strong drink.

"Ah," Silas replied. "That explains why she was running from you. My cherished wife is sadly reluctant to accept help. It was very noble of you, though. As you see, I have now been reunited with my sweet...butterfly, so I thank you."

The men simply stood and smiled.

The woman's grip tightened on his arm.

"However," Silas added, "I must insist we not take any more of your precious time."

One man gave an awkward attempt at a bow, and the other followed suit. Heads held high, as though they were beacons of chivalry rather than drunken opportunists, they passed by Silas and the butterfly. She retreated into him slightly as they did so.

The men's footsteps faded, and silence reigned between them until the sound disappeared completely. Silas did not attempt to break the silence. Instead, he waited to see what would happen next in this incomprehensible sequence of events. He was burning with curiosity to find out.

The woman's grip loosened suddenly, and she took a step away from him. Her blue eyes were accentuated by the light of the nearest lamp and the colorful beading of her mask. There was a hint of wariness in her gaze as she regarded him—the man she had assigned the role of husband.

She was the strangest creature.

"You spoke of Mr. Fairchild," she said in a clipped voice. "Do you know where he is?"

Silas frowned. "I do not. I have not seen him since he went to meet you and your mother."

The woman opened her mouth as though she might speak, only to shut it again.

"Shall I help you find him?" Silas asked.

"That will be unnecessary."

The tip of his mouth quirked up. "I have been sharply—nay, violently—reprimanded by you for leaving you in these gardens, ma'am. The pressure I feel to redeem myself as a husband is immense."

It was dark, but he could swear her color was heightened as she responded. "You are not my husband, sir, as you well know."

"I do know it. I am glad to see you share this important bit of knowledge. I was unsure of that, as—if I may gently remind you—it was *you* who came tumbling into my arms and assigned me the role."

She looked the slightest bit stricken. "I needed those men to think I had a chaperone."

Silas considered this. "You might have made me your brother."

Her forehead knit just above her mask. "I have no brother."

"But you have a husband?"

Her lips pressed together for a moment as though she was considering how to respond. "No."

"May I return you to your mother, then? Or did you shake off her chaperonage on purpose?"

"Of course not," she responded with a hint of offense. "She is near the Rotunda with a friend."

"Very good. Shall we, then?" He took a step forward and put out his arm for her to take.

She did not accept it. Instead, she looked at it and then at him.

"What is it?" he asked, torn between amusement and consternation.

Her hands gripped the skirts of her domino. "If you must know, I am trying to decide whether I should trust you."

He let his arm drop to his side again, amused, intrigued, and exasperated all at once. "And this is a decision you make *after* fashioning me as your husband."

A little twitch at the corner of her mouth was quickly tamed—unfortunately, in his opinion.

"I explained why I did so."

He nodded. "And now that the threat of those men has passed, you have fashioned me into the next threat. What, pray, do you assume my designs upon you to be?"

She hesitated.

"Do you suppose me a spider who lures pretty butterflies into his web? In this case, the butterfly flew into it willingly."

"If you call desperation willingness," she said.

"Fair enough. And what do you propose to do if you venture off on your own again, and another man, more threatening than myself, were to come around the next corner? Will you pin your hopes on there being another in whose arms you can take refuge?"

She glanced over her shoulder as though only now realizing the possibility of such a thing. Apparently satisfied that the prospect he painted was not an urgent one, she turned back to him. "I can only apologize for the unpleasant situation into which I forced you, sir."

"I never said it was unpleasant. Unexpected, certainly. But I quite understand why you did it. I am merely pointing out that, if one of us has designs upon the other, anyone who had observed the last two minutes would assume it to be you."

Her brows knit. "I have no...*designs* upon you, sir."

"Nor I upon you."

She searched his face with unchecked skepticism. "You do not mean to...kiss me, then?"

A little scoffing chuckle escaped him. The woman seemed to traffic in saying and doing the unexpected. "Would you *like* me to?" His gaze flitted to her lips instinctively. They were certainly kissable.

"No," she said. "That is, I would not kno—" Her lips pressed together, stopping whatever she had been about to say. "No," she said decisively. "I would not."

He smiled at her strange way of answering. What is it that she would not know? "I am not in the habit of kissing unwilling women, and when you are not throwing yourself into my arms and calling me your husband, you have made it fairly clear you would not welcome such an intimacy."

"I would not," she repeated firmly.

"Very well, then. Shall I escort you to your mother, or would you prefer I leave you to the rough-and-tumble crowd wandering these paths?"

Her pink lips pressed together as she considered the options. She glanced over her shoulder at the sound of voices somewhere nearby, then looked at him again, more urgency in her eyes. "I believe I *can* trust you not to..."

"Kiss you," he finished for her, controlling his amusement with effort. Did she think he kissed every woman he came upon? The implied slight to his character made his tongue unruly. "At this point, the only way I would even consider such a thing is if you yourself begged me to do so."

A breathy laugh escaped her.

He raised his brows. "Is it so impossible to believe you might wish to kiss me?"

"Yes." Her smile made his heart skitter despite the bluntness of her response.

He had a sudden desire to change that answer—or to understand it, at the very least.

"I have your word, then?" she said, eyes fixed on him intently.

He put his hand over his heart and gave a small bow. "I give you my word as a gentleman, ma'am."

She seemed satisfied with this bit of fanfare. "Good. Then I accept your offer—and thank you for it. But I cannot return to my...mother just yet. I must find my...sister first." She looked around, frowning slightly. "I thought she would have returned to find me by now. Do you know where the Cascade is?"

"No. But I have heard of it, and I can find it."

She looked at him with a hint of skepticism—her preferred manner of regarding him, it seemed.

He put a hand over his heart again. "I swear I shall help you find this Cascade you speak of if it is the last thing I do." He offered his arm again.

"I sincerely hope it is *not* the last thing you do." She took his arm.

"Your concern for my welfare is touching."

She glanced up at him with a small smile, her eyes twinkling much like the beads on her mask.

His breath caught in his throat, for a more engaging face he had never seen—even half-covered.

"Perhaps you should tell me your name," he said, looking away. He would not risk scaring off the butterfly again. He had come to these tree-covered walks for peace and quiet, but he did not at all regret what he had found instead.

Silence met this suggestion, and he turned his head toward her. The wings of her butterfly mask glinted with each lamp they passed, the light gliding along the golden threads. Was she still so mistrusting of him?

"You are safe with me," he said gently. "I swear it."

She met his gaze, the weight of her vulnerability there, and he felt a swooping sensation in his chest that caught him off guard. Had the lack of women and romance for the past two years of his life made him so vulnerable to a pretty face?

"Miss Easton," she finally replied. "Mr. Fairchild is my cousin's cousin. The woman you referred to is my aunt, not my mother."

"I see." He guided them left. "And you became separated from them?"

"I was with my cousin when my dress caught on the shrubbery."

"Should we not return to your aunt, then? It seems likely your cousin might have done so once she realized you were not with her."

She shook her head. "I cannot return to Aunt Louisa without Felicity. I promised I would watch over her and assure she did not get into a scrape."

"Like being kissed by the men prowling these paths?"

She glanced up at him, and her eyes narrowed. "You are making fun of me. Does it never occur that a woman is kissed at Vauxhall?"

"Oh, undoubtedly it does. I would wager there are a few kisses being stolen even as we speak."

She seemed to consider this. "And yet you tease me. But never having been here before and having been warned against such a thing, how was I to know that kissing me had never crossed your mind?"

"Well, I never said *that*, did I?"

Her head came around, and her eyes searched his. "You are teasing me again."

"Upon my honor, I am not." Part of him wished to see how she would react to know that he *had* now thought of kissing her half a dozen times. But he had promised she was safe with him, and he meant to keep that promise, so he broke his gaze from hers with the excuse of trying to determine where to turn next. He thought he heard the faint sound of rushing water nearby.

They met two men in the path, and Miss Easton retreated into him slightly, but she pulled away once the men had passed.

"You have not told me *your* name," she remarked.

A sudden explosion had her grasping his arm just as she had when she had first come running into him. He held her to him, but his shoulders relaxed when he realized the source of the commotion. "You are safe, Miss Easton. Look."

She pulled her head back from his chest, and he pointed above them as another explosion occurred. Her grip tightened for a moment, then relaxed as she drew in a quick breath.

Her eyes were wide as she watched the bursts of light in the night sky. "What is it?"

"Fireworks."

Another blast occurred, and the tightening of her grip was almost imperceptible this time.

"Is it...safe?" she asked, her eyes reflecting the bright lights. "They look as though they shall rain down on us." She drew back as the lights fell in the sky and faded into blackness.

"Perfectly safe," he replied. "Well, perhaps not perfectly, but the danger is generally past once they are in the sky."

Her gaze was fixed on each explosion, but his was fixed on her. Rarely had he seen such wonder and amazement. It was innocent, artless.

She took note of him watching her and tore her eyes from the fireworks. Her hands dropped from his arm. "They are well enough, I suppose."

Silas smiled in bemusement. Why was she pretending not to be amazed now? "Quite so. Not worth lingering for, certainly. We should continue on."

Miss Easton's eyes shifted upward at the next explosion, then back down reluctantly. "Indeed. Lead the way."

She took his arm again, and they continued their walk toward—he hoped—the Cascade. Sure enough, the sound of rushing water, punctuated by the blast of fireworks, grew louder, and the next corner they turned opened up to a view of the waterfall.

They both stopped, searching amongst the throngs for familiar faces.

"What is your cousin wearing?" Silas asked.

"A silver domino." Miss Easton rose onto her tiptoes. "Ah! I think I see her. Yes! That is her and Mr. Drake."

"Good," Silas said absently, for his own gaze was fixed on the gold domino walking away from the Cascade.

It was Sir Walter Bence.

4

ARABELLA

Felicity and Mr. Drake were searching the area near the Cascade when Felicity's gaze landed on Arabella. With immense relief, Arabella broke away and hurried to her cousin.

She was *not*, as Arabella had feared, lost in forbidden paths, her reputation in ruins. She was safe.

"Oh, Bella," Felicity called, meeting her and throwing her arms around her. "I am so very sorry!" She pulled back, arms still around Arabella, her pretty blue eyes wide with worry and apology. "We thought you were with us! You cannot imagine the terror I felt when I discovered you were not! We went back to search for you, but we could not remember the way we had come, and you were nowhere to be found, so we came here in hopes of finding you. Are you hurt?" Her gaze searched Arabella's face and body for any sign of injury.

"No," Arabella replied. "My dress caught on a stray branch and then my mask too. And then two drunken men came along, but thankfully—" She turned toward her rescuer.

He was not there.

She turned all the way around, her eyes searching for the black domino. They found many, but none were of that elegant brocade and none embroidered with gold thread.

"What is it?" Felicity asked, following her gaze.

Arabella's brows drew together in confusion. Had he abandoned her? Had she imagined it all?

No, that was ridiculous. She would not soon forget the feeling of running away from those drunkards and into his arms. She could still smell the alcohol on the men and the contrastingly fresh and inviting scent of the black domino.

"There was a man," she said, still looking for any sign of him.

"A man?" Felicity repeated, looking at her intently.

"He protected me from the two drunkards. He escorted me here." She said the words almost to reassure herself, for the longer she searched the scene without finding him, the more like a dream it all felt.

Felicity's eyes lit with excitement. "Good heavens! That is terribly romantic! What was his name?"

"I...do not know." Arabella had asked, but then the fireworks had begun. Disappointment and confusion flickered in her chest. Why had he left without so much as a word?

Before she could ponder further, Mr. Yorke and Mr. Fairchild hurried over, both slightly breathless.

"We made it," Mr. Yorke said, hunching over and catching his breath with his hands on his knees. "Fairchild here insisted on taking every wrong turn possible." He shot Fairchild a pretendedly aggrieved look.

"If we had started at the beginning, I would have found it without difficulty," Mr. Fairchild maintained through gulps of air.

"I should have demanded a formal wager," Mr. Drake

teased. "Miss Fairchild and I have been here a few minutes already, and that was *after* returning to find Miss Easton."

"Find her?" Mr. Fairchild repeated. "Was she not with you?"

"She was too busy being rescued by her very own knight in shining armor," Felicity said with a smile at Arabella.

Arabella's cheeks warmed. "Hardly. He was wearing a black brocade domino, not armor. But he claimed to know you, Mr. Fairchild."

"Black brocade?" Mr. Yorke repeated.

Arabella nodded, eager for any information someone might have about the mystery man.

"Was it hideous beyond all belief?" Mr. Yorke asked.

Arabella frowned. "Old-fashioned, perhaps. But made of the highest quality. I thought it quite striking." Her eyes explored the surrounding area, as though she might have missed it in her previous attempts to locate him. "It stood out."

Mr. Yorke chuckled. "I should say so! No offense to your father, Fairchild."

"None taken," Mr. Fairchild assured him. "There is a reason it has been in that trunk all these years."

"You know the domino, then?" Felicity asked, impatient of these asides.

"The domino *and* the man," Mr. Yorke said. "He is my friend, Hayes."

Hayes. That was his name. Mr. Hayes.

"He is living with us," Mr. Drake offered.

Felicity turned to Arabella, her eyes alight. "How fortuitous!" She whirled right back to Mr. Yorke. "What can you tell us about him?"

He drew back slightly at her unexpected enthusiasm, as though she might pounce on him any moment. "Erm, I do not know."

Felicity merely waited.

Mr. Yorke shrugged. "He is from Devon. His father has sent him here on business, I believe."

"Business," Felicity repeated, looking uncertain. "Is he... genteel?"

Mr. Yorke laughed. "Of course. The Hayeses have owned their estate in Devon for generations. They simply choose to keep to themselves."

Felicity squeezed Arabella's hand. "A gentleman," she whispered.

Arabella shot her cousin what she hoped was a dampening look, for Mr. Yorke was watching them with a little furrow of curiosity in his brow.

"Shall we admire the Cascade, then?" Mr. Fairchild suggested.

They all agreed and drew nearer to it. Arabella's mind was successfully distracted from the elusive Mr. Hayes, for this cascade had no water at all. It was, as Mr. Drake explained, sheets of tin being moved along belts. The motion and sheen gave the appearance of a waterfall, enhanced by the sound of rushing water.

"Where is the sound coming from?" Arabella asked Felicity.

Felicity did not answer, though. She was not even looking at the Cascade.

"What are you looking for?" Arabella asked.

"Your knight, of course," Felicity said. "How strange that he should disappear so suddenly. It is very mysterious of him." She turned toward Arabella abruptly, her eyes growing large. "Tell me more of your time with him."

Arabella thought on the time she had spent with the mysterious rescuer, how he had been so willing to help her but had never insisted on doing so when she had expressed reservations. "He was very chivalrous, though he did tease me a bit."

"Teased you?" Felicity repeated, her curiosity stoked. She seemed to be reading a great deal into the word *tease*.

"He did not kiss me, if that is what you are asking. In fact, he promised he would not do so."

Felicity's eyes widened further in the slits of her mask. "You discussed it, then?"

"Briefly," Arabella said, regretting her choice of words.

This did not seem to have the effect she had anticipated.

"But to speak of a kiss is every bit as significant as sharing a kiss! Oh, Bella! I *am* sorry for leaving you behind, but you must admit, the result is very exciting. Can you only imagine what a story it shall be if you and this Mr. Hayes marry?"

"Felicity," Arabella said, pleading for reason. "You are being ridiculous."

"Am I? Stranger things have certainly happened."

"Undoubtedly, but Papa intends to choose the man I marry."

"Why can he not choose your Lancelot, then?"

"He is not *my* Lancelot. His name is not even Lancelot."

"How do you know?" Felicity smiled enigmatically.

"His name is Mr. Hayes."

"Mr. and Mrs. Lancelot Hayes," Felicity said, her eyes glazed over.

Arabella pressed her lips together and sighed. "He helped me. That is all. And he did not even stay to say goodbye. What sort of knight in shining armor would do such a thing?" Just saying the words piqued her pride.

"A very dashing, mysterious one. Perhaps he is rescuing another damsel even now."

"How very busy of him," Arabella replied, hearing a hint of resentment in her own voice. It should not bother her, but there had been something almost magical in the entire interaction that felt less so at the idea of him being constantly flitting to the aid of one woman after another.

"I am certain he will find you again," Felicity reassured her.

"He needn't bother, though I *had* hoped to thank him."

"You shall! I am determined of it."

Aunt Louisa, when informed of the turn events had taken in the gardens, scooped Arabella to her and embraced her heartily. "Bless that man!"

"It was very kind of him," Arabella agreed, submitting docilely as a few people looked on with curiosity. "But I am quite well, Aunt." She preferred not to dwell on what might have happened had Mr. Hayes not been there when she had run from the two men.

Aunt Louisa released her suddenly, her eyes round. "What will we tell your father?"

"There is no harm done," Arabella said. "We need not worry him unduly." Papa was already prone to do so, and he had enough on his plate already. Ever since Mama's death, things seemed to upset him more easily.

"No," Aunt Louisa agreed with palpable relief. "That is true. No harm done, as you say, though I think perhaps we should be on our way."

Arabella agreed to this and, surprisingly, Felicity too.

It might be wrong of Arabella to keep the night's happenings from Papa, but after all, it was through no fault of her own that she had come to be separated from the others, and it had been unintentional on Felicity's part, as well. It seemed a great unkindness to risk Papa blaming her cousin or her aunt for circumstances beyond their control, particularly when they had merely been trying to ensure Arabella enjoyed herself.

And so she had, even amidst the uncertainties. She would gladly have spent hours more at Vauxhall, taking her time to admire every last foot of it.

There was still no sign of Mr. Hayes when they left the gardens and made their way back to Papa's townhouse in Mayfair.

Arabella could not keep herself from looking for him when they attended a party the following evening to celebrate the opening of Parliament, but he was not in attendance—at least not that she could tell. Her aunt made a point of introducing her to nearly everyone who had come, and Arabella was certain she would have recognized those eyes or that smile.

The following morning, the three of them were gathered around the breakfast table when Mr. Fairchild was announced.

"Good gracious, Benedict," Aunt Louisa said. "Do you make a habit of visiting people at this indecent hour?"

He came over and kissed her on the cheek. "Only you, and only when I am starved." He took a plate from the sideboard and began filling it in a way that made Arabella's brows raise.

"Do you not have a chef at that bachelor haven of yours?" Aunt Louisa asked.

"My father took his chef with him to the countryside," Mr. Fairchild said, "so we are left with only lower kitchen staff to manage." He shot her a significant look to show what he thought of this injustice.

The door opened, and the butler appeared with a silver salver in hand. "The post, ma'am."

Aunt Louisa took three letters from atop the salver and thanked him before going through them. "For you, child." She handed Arabella a letter, and Arabella recognized Papa's script.

She slid her finger under the wafer and unfurled it.

"What does he say?" Aunt Louisa asked, a hint of anxiety in her voice.

Arabella's eyes traveled quickly over the neat, familiar script. "He hopes we are well. He regrets that he has not been in Town as soon as he had intended. Business has become more complicated than anticipated, but he has every expectation of arriving in the next few days." She looked up and smiled at her aunt, folding the short letter again without conveying the portion that inquired after their activities and whether her aunt was being the careful chaperone she had promised to be.

"How lovely," Aunt Louisa said in a determinedly polite tone. "It *is* his house, after all."

They ate in silence for a matter of minutes until Felicity spoke. "And how fares the infamous Mr. Hayes, Benedict?"

Arabella shot her cousin a look. At this point, she would be hard-pressed to say whether Felicity was asking on Arabella's behalf or her own. She was quite taken with the idea of the mysterious Mr. Hayes, and since Arabella had mentioned Papa's intent to choose her husband, she had begun to suspect Felicity might have thoughts of pursuing an acquaintance with him herself.

The sense of possessiveness this roused in Arabella was as foolish as it was unmerited, and she shoved it aside mercilessly.

"He is well," Mr. Fairchild replied, disinterested.

"I am elated to hear it," Felicity said.

Mr. Fairchild looked up at her, chewing his ham.

"As you can imagine," Felicity said, "Bella is impatient to thank him for his kind services the other night. Perhaps you could arrange for us to see him sometime?"

"Yes," Aunt Louisa said. "I, too, owe a great debt to this Mr. Hayes and would feel remiss if I did not express as much to him."

Mr. Fairchild shrugged as he scooped up the last of the ham. "I suppose we could arrange something. He and Yorke intend to make a visit to the market at Covent Garden on Thursday."

Felicity clapped her hands. "Bella has not seen Covent Garden yet. You will absolutely adore it, Bella. May we join them, Mama?"

Aunt Louisa considered this for a moment, stirring her tea. "Provided we are gone long before dark sets in, I do not see any reason against it. But do you think your father would approve, child?"

It was Arabella's turn to consider now. It was difficult to say precisely what Papa would approve or disapprove of because Arabella had never been anywhere like London, with so many opportunities for parties and excursions. He had entrusted her to the care of Aunt Louisa, though, and if she saw nothing against it, it must be harmless enough. Arabella had always wanted to go to a London market.

Besides, had Papa not raised her to be polite and express thanks where it was due? Had he not made her well-being his greatest priority? Mr. Hayes had single-handedly guarded her reputation and kept her safe. If anything merited thanks, surely it was that.

"I cannot see why he would *not* approve," she replied.

"It is settled, then," Felicity said. "We shall see the mysterious Mr. Hayes on Thursday at Covent Garden."

Arabella's heart skipped a few beats, though whether at the prospect of Covent Garden or of seeing Mr. Hayes again, she could not say with any degree of certainty.

5

SILAS

S ilas opened the door to the morning room at his brother William's townhouse in Mayfair and stepped inside.

Three heads whipped up to look at him. He smiled at the domestic scene. William had an unfurled newspaper in hand, his wife, Clara, thumbed through a periodical, and Aunt Eugenia sipped her tea.

"Thought I'd announce myself," Silas said, shutting the door behind him.

"Rascal," Aunt Eugenia said, but she put out a hand to usher him closer. "I hoped William had been funning when he said you were in Town. What in heaven's name possessed you to set foot in London when you are a wanted man, boy?"

He took her hand and kissed the back of it gallantly. "How could I possibly stay away when I knew *you* were here?"

"Toad-eater," she said, but she was visibly pleased with his flattery.

"Silas flocks to danger," William said without pulling his eyes from the newspaper, "like a moth to a flame."

"Who is this Silas you speak of?" Silas took a seat beside his aunt and reached for her tea.

She batted his hand away, and he laughed appreciatively. Aunt Eugenia's pretended curmudgeonery had always entertained him. He had always been her favorite of the four Yorke brothers—until he had been charged with murder, and she had believed the charges. Her sense of betrayal had led her to forbid his name being spoken.

Despite all the physical deprivations Silas had experienced while trying to survive in the outskirts of Paris, the knowledge that Aunt Eugenia, William, and Frederick had all believed him capable of murder had been the most wearing thing of all. It had been the knowledge they did not wish to be near him, not his fear of Lord Drayton, that had kept him away from England for as long as he had stayed away.

He owed his brother Anthony an unpayable debt of gratitude for seeing to it that they realized how mistaken they were.

"Let me pour you a cup of tea," Clara said, rising.

Silas put out a hand to stop her. "We need not stand upon ceremony. I can manage."

Clara smiled and leaned back in her chair, looking relieved as she set her hand on her stomach. She was still in the early stages of pregnancy and had slept the greater part of the journey to London.

"William tells me you are going by the name Hayes," Aunt Eugenia said as he poured his tea.

"William speaks the truth, as always."

Her lips turned down at the corners. "It is a terribly common name."

He chuckled. "I am attempting to be inconspicuous. I thought you would all be proud of my demure choice. Would you rather I chose a name like Percival FitzClarence?"

"I like a bit of recklessness," Aunt Eugenia said. "But it is true that the line between too little and too much is a delicate one, and you have never been terribly concerned with details, have you?"

He waved away the allegation. "I leave those pesky things to William. He delights in details."

William dignified this with no response.

"How was Vauxhall?" Clara asked.

Silas's mind flashed to Miss Easton and the enchanting butterfly mask. "It was...interesting." His attempts to track down the golden domino had proven futile, leading him back into the paths he and Miss Easton had walked. It had taken him ten minutes to find his way to the Cascade again, at which point she and the others had gone.

But he would see her at Covent Garden today.

"By the by, do you know a Miss Easton?" he asked no one in particular.

"I do not believe I do," William said absently.

"Nor I." Aunt Eugenia's eyes fixed on him. "Who is she?"

"Someone I met at Vauxhall," he said casually, taking a sip of tea.

Apparently, he had not said it casually enough, for all eyes were upon him.

"And your interest in her is..." William's gaze was steady.

Silas chuckled. "May a man not inquire about a young woman without all sorts of assumptions being made?"

"No," Aunt Eugenia said. "He may not."

"Particularly not a man in your situation," William said, folding the paper. "Take care, Silas."

"It is Hayes," Silas retorted. "And I *shall* take care...not to ask any of you whether you are acquainted with anyone, that is."

William regarded him for a moment, then rose from his chair. "Come. I have something for you in the library."

Silas took another sip of tea, then set it down and followed his brother out of the room and to the library, where he anticipated the *something* awaiting him there to be a lecture.

But he had wronged his brother, for William merely went to his desk, opened a drawer, and pulled out a sheaf of banknotes. He strode over to Silas and handed them to him.

"What is this?" Silas asked, not taking them.

"It is money, Silas." William pushed it toward him.

"Yes, thank you," he said ironically. "I have heard tales of it. But what is it for?"

"Generally, it is used in exchange for goods and services. If you choose to use it in place of a handkerchief, I suppose that is your affair."

Silas shot his brother an unamused look.

William reached for Silas's hand, forced the fingers open, and set the money in his palm. "It is yours. Both Anthony and I sent you money in France. You never went to the bank to retrieve it."

"I could not risk it. Drayton had people watching for precisely such a thing." Silas had hoped that once he arrived in France, he would have been able to at least live comfortably amongst the *ton* there, but apparently, Drayton's fear that he would make trouble for him even there had been too great to allow for such a thing. Silas had been obliged to make do relying on the charity of those outside the margins of genteel society and putting himself to work to earn his keep.

"Which is why I am giving it to you now," William said. "It is your share of the interest on Father's investments. I would have given it to you sooner, but I had to make a visit to my banker here in Town."

Silas looked down at the money in his hand. He had not had this much since before leaving England. He spread the bills slightly and did quick arithmetic, frowning. "This is more than it should be."

"The investments have performed well." William turned away, going back to his desk, where he organized a stack of papers.

"Will…" Silas said significantly.

It took a few seconds before his brother looked up.

"I know a bit about investments," Silas said, "and I know which ones Father made. Even if they had performed at unprecedented levels, this would be more than my portion."

William shrugged. "What of it? You must get back on your feet, Silas. We both know you would not be in this position if it were not for me."

"I know nothing of the sort."

"Then you are being purposely obtuse," William replied. "If I had not been so hardheaded and had put money toward your scheme rather than preaching to you about it—"

"Then we both would have lost the money."

"Even so, I would not have been so consumed by my own self-importance and our family's reputation that you felt you could not come to me for help."

Silas shook his head. "You were right to warn me against the investment. I chose to disregard it."

"And would you have stayed in France as long as you did if you'd known you would be welcomed home by me?"

Silas met his brother's eye, unable to counter that particular question.

William nodded. "Repay me in the future if you wish, but you *will* take that money. And you will invest it where you please."

Silas was quiet. William had never approved of his aggressive approach toward business or the riskier investments he chose to make at times. It made his gesture all the more meaningful.

"I *will* repay you," Silas said. "With interest."

"Good," William replied, but he sounded supremely disinterested. "Shall we return to the morning room?"

"No. I am for Covent Garden." He declined to tell his brother he would be seeing Miss Easton there.

Silas was not a fool. He knew he could not allow anything or anyone to distract him from his true goal in London. But he owed Miss Easton an apology.

Did the fact that she was utterly and absolutely engaging make him look forward to seeing her? Did he wish just a bit to see what was behind the mask?

Perhaps. But that was nothing to wonder at.

He had hopes of gaining an introduction to Sir Walter Bence, but how was that to happen if he was expected to kick his heels in his bedchamber? He had done more than enough of that during his time at William's estate, Rushlake, where Silas had been hidden away from all in the estate's unused hunting lodge.

Now that he was in London and operating under an assumed name, he meant to enjoy the freedom he did have, even as he sought to bring about his real freedom.

6

SILAS

The bustle and chaos of Covent Garden was muffled in the distance as Silas turned onto King Street toward the market. He stopped at the corner, where he was set to meet Mrs. Fairchild, her nephew, and her two charges. Frederick should arrive any minute, as well.

According to Frederick's sources, Lord Drayton was still not in London, which lent Silas a sense of freedom. He did not suppose Drayton was the type of man to take much joy in a place like Covent Garden—at least not until night fell and the seedier crowds made themselves at home. He had no doubt a man like Drayton, with no morals at all, would avail himself of the women on offer in the nearest brothels.

His eyes fixed on just one such brothel down the lane. If Bence refused to cooperate, perhaps Silas should try to discover whether Drayton *did* frequent any of these establishments. If so, perhaps he might have let something slip to one of those ladies of the night—not that the claims of such a person would count for much.

In his situation, he could not afford to be particular. Any information would be more than he now had.

He pulled his gaze away from the brothel and spotted Mrs. Fairchild and the others walking toward him.

His gaze went to Miss Easton, who was smiling at her aunt.

Gads, she was beautiful—every bit as beautiful as the mask that had covered half of her face the other night. Her dress reminded him of the pale blue of a robin's egg. It had cream stripes that matched both her spencer and the ribbon on her bonnet.

Mr. Fairchild spotted Silas and waved, and the eyes of the three women turned to him.

Silas strode toward them with a smile, making an effort to look not just at Miss Easton but at the others, as well. And an effort it *was*.

Mr. Fairchild introduced him to his aunt and her daughter, and Silas bowed over Mrs. Fairchild's hand.

"The famous Mr. Hayes," she said, her cheeks slightly pink as she drew her gloved hand away. She was a middle-aged woman, tending toward portliness but with a distinctly jolly expression.

"Provided I am not *in*famous," he replied, bowing to Miss Fairchild, then Miss Easton.

Her clear gaze met his with a sliver of accusation he ascribed to his impolite departure from Vauxhall. Much good it had done him. But knowing she had been safe, how could he have forgone the opportunity to speak with Bence?

"Certainly not infamous," Mrs. Fairchild said. "I am so very glad you could meet us. I have been wishing to offer you my thanks for saving my dear niece."

"It was nothing, I assure you, ma'am. The greatest pleasure." His gaze shifted to Miss Easton again, and her mouth drew into a grateful smile that made his heart stutter.

Her gaze was curious, as though she, too, was taking him in now that he was free of his mask.

"My thanks as well," Miss Fairchild said, stepping forward. "It was my thoughtlessness that put Bella in such a situation to begin with. I am indebted to you, Mr. Hayes."

Bella. So, that was Miss Easton's name.

Before Silas could respond, Frederick arrived, slightly breathless, and bowed to the three ladies.

"We are all here now," Mr. Fairchild announced. "Shall we stroll around?"

"Oh, yes," Miss Fairchild said. "Do let us."

Mrs. Fairchild leaned in and whispered something to her nephew, who nodded.

"Come, cousin." He put out his arm to Miss Fairchild, and her eyes darted to Silas for a brief second before she took it with a smile.

"Mr. Yorke," Mrs. Fairchild said, "could I trouble you for your arm? My ankle is much improved, but I would be grateful for the stability."

"By all means," Frederick said, granting it to her.

The corner of Silas's mouth twitched slightly as Miss Easton's gaze met his. Was Mrs. Fairchild purposely arranging for him to escort Miss Easton? It certainly seemed that way.

"It looks as though your choice has been made for you, and you are consigned to *my* care again, Miss Easton." He put out his arm.

"A frightful prospect," she said as she accepted it. She looked up at him, her gaze clear and intent, with a hint of a twinkle lurking there. "Shall I prepare myself in case you run away again?"

He grimaced as they walked behind the others.

"And you, so adamant about redeeming yourself as a husband..."

"Only to abandon you," he finished. "It was poorly done of me, wasn't it?"

"Very," she agreed. "Why did you do it?" There was real curiosity in her frank gaze now.

He took a moment before responding. "I have no satisfactory answer except that I am an impulsive man, Miss Easton."

She considered that for a moment as the group came to stop in front of the market entrance. "And impulse tells you to run from me?"

His eyes held hers. No doubt he *should* run. He hardly knew her, but he *wanted* to know her. She was, from what he could tell from her clothing and bearing, a woman who came from wealth. Silas might be the brother of a duke, but he personally had nothing to offer a woman but a sullied reputation, a fistful of banknotes he hoped to multiply, and the real possibility of the gallows.

Father had urged him to pursue the law, but Silas had no patience for such things. He had wanted to make his own way.

Look where that had got him.

"I think you may be calling me a coward, Miss Easton," he said.

"Are you one?"

"If I were, would I be standing here so boldly while you tear my character to shreds?"

She laughed and turned her eyes to the performers the others had stopped to watch. Three men were putting on a magic show. They made a ball disappear beneath a cup, and the surprise and delight on Miss Easton's face brought a smile to Silas's.

It was as though she had never seen a magician before. It had been the same with the fireworks. He guessed her to be three- or four-and-twenty, which made her awe at such things curious. There was a naivety to her that contrasted sharply with the wit and intellect she had shown. She was an enigma.

When the magician asked for a volunteer amongst the crowd, she stood a bit taller, then seemed to think better of it.

Silas took her hand and raised it for her.

She looked at him, half-aghast, half-laughing, as one of the magicians made his way over, a stack of cards in hand.

"Pick a card, miss," the man said, fanning out the deck.

Miss Easton kept her severe but sparkling gaze on Silas a moment longer before relenting.

"Show it to the audience," the man said, covering his face with his hat as she displayed the ten of hearts to everyone.

He returned his hat to his head and took the card, replacing it in the middle of the deck. He shuffled the cards with great fanfare as he told the audience a joke about an elephant.

Miss Easton's gaze was fixed determinedly on the cards.

"Now," said the magician, "let us see about this young lady's card." He laid the neat deck on one palm. "It must be here somewhere," he muttered as he used his free hand to push handfuls of cards off his other hand and onto the flagstone. "No, not that one. Not that one." Finally, there was but one card left in his hand.

He stared at it with a frown, then tossed the three of clubs onto the flagstones as well. He set his hands on his hips and stared at Miss Easton with exaggerated suspicion.

She stared back at him, looking torn between confusion and disappointment.

His gaze moved to Silas. "Did you steal her card, sir?"

"I did not," Silas replied.

The magician turned to Miss Easton. "Do we believe him, miss?"

She looked up at Silas, her eyes searching his. She smiled. "I do not see why we *should*."

"Nor I," said the magician, stepping toward Silas. "Sir, may I?" He nodded at Silas's right tailcoat pocket.

"By all means," Silas said, moving his arm to grant the man access.

The magician stepped toward him and slipped his hand into the pocket. He fished around a bit despite how shallow it was. Finally, his hand emerged, and he held up the ten of hearts. "Is that your card, miss?"

Miss Easton's eyes grew large, and she looked at Silas for an explanation as the crowd clapped and cheered.

Miss Fairchild hurried over to them, all smiles. "Did he put you up to that, Mr. Hayes?"

"He must have," Miss Easton said, still watching him carefully.

"I assure you," Silas replied, "that I had never seen that man in my life until five minutes ago and never spoken to him until he asked if I had stolen the card—which I had not." It was a good trick, he had to admit. The magician must have had the card hidden up his sleeve, then let it drop into Silas's pocket before pulling it out.

The other four began walking toward the market, chattering amongst themselves in an effort to determine how the magician had managed his feat.

"You may tell me the truth, you know," Miss Easton said in an undervoice as they followed. "I shan't tell the others."

Silas chuckled softly. "I was your husband the other night. Today, I am a liar and a coward. Miss Easton, I am positively on tenterhooks to discover what I shall be tomorrow."

"Who says we shall see each other tomorrow?"

"A terribly boring day it shall be if we do not." The comment was bordering on flirtatious, but Silas was spared whatever reaction she might have had by their arrival at the market stalls.

Covent Garden was a hive of activity, with shouts and conversation between the vendors and buyers creating a din amongst the rows of stalls piled high with wares. The scent of herbs and the earthy aroma of fruits and vegetables mixed with the smell of freshly baked bread and roasted chestnuts. A wooden flute played somewhere nearby, punctuated by the intermittent squawking of a parrot perched on a man's shoulder a few stalls away.

Miss Easton's head moved slowly as her gaze took in the scene, that same fascination in her eyes that was becoming familiar to Silas.

He leaned toward her. "Overwhelmed?"

She looked at him, then straightened slightly. "Not at all."

Silas suppressed a smile and looked around. "A dead bore, is it not?"

Miss Easton shot him a look that was half-suspicious, half-reproachful. "Not a bore, no."

"Bella," Miss Fairchild said, hurrying over. "Did you see the jewelry stand over there? Come. I am in dire need of a new pair of earrings, but you know how indecisive I am."

The two of them ambled off to the stand, followed by Mrs. Fairchild.

Silas and the others kept near the women, allowing them their freedom while ensuring their safety. Covent Garden drew a vibrant and varied crowd, and Miss Easton's intent perusal of wares made her a target for pickpockets.

Silas looked casually at a booth of snuffboxes next to the collection of knick-knacks the women were poring over in the next stand. He did not take snuff—the last thing his lungs needed was for him to be inhaling powder—and the vendor became so persistent trying to sell him a box that he moved to the knick-knacks instead.

He came up beside Miss Easton, who was fiddling with a

small tin music box, her eyes alight with interest. "Papa bought one of these for my sisters and me, but it was much larger. It is fascinating to see how small it can be while producing such beautiful music."

"A miniature wonder," Silas agreed.

She glanced up at him, as though only just realizing to whom she had been speaking. She set the box down.

Silas frowned as she moved farther along the stand. "Tell me, Miss Easton, what it is about my presence that seems to act as a jug of water over the fire of your amazement at interesting things."

"I cannot think what you mean." She picked up a gemstone and looked at it for a moment before setting it down again.

"Can you not? I have seen your eyes light up with delight at fireworks, in which you abruptly lost interest when you remembered my presence. The same thing occurred out there with the magician and again just now with that delightful music box. I can only conclude there is something about me that destroys your enchanting enthusiasm. The realization is a great disappointment to me, I assure you."

Miss Easton turned to him. "It is nothing to do with you."

"What is it, then?"

Miss Easton's lips pressed together, as though she was reluctant to answer. "It is my first time to London, sir, and I have a tendency to betray my lack of experience by what you refer to as my *enthusiasm*—"

"Enchanting enthusiasm."

"—which I have been assured marks me as unsophisticated."

Silas gave a little scoff. "If the mark of sophistication is for one to be bored by the world's constant and varied delights, may I never be accused of it." He picked up a pocket-sized spyglass and put it to his eye, directing his stare at Miss Easton, whose eyes were magnified through the lens.

They wrinkled at the corners, betraying her smile before the pretty laugh that followed it.

He handed her the spyglass. "Rest assured, Miss Easton, that in my presence, you may be as unsophisticated as you please. In fact, as far as I am concerned, the less sophisticated, the better."

Smiling, she put the spyglass to her eye and regarded him through it.

He clasped his hands in front of him and stood straight. "What do you see?"

There was a pause before she responded.

"Trouble on the horizon." She lowered the glass and revealed an impish gleam in her eye.

"The only kind of horizon worth chasing," he replied, picking up an oddity that was shaped similarly to the spyglass.

"Ahh," said the vendor, who had just finished selling a small almanac to a man. "You have found the most marvelous piece here, sir."

"Have I?" Silas shot an exaggerated look of self-satisfaction at Miss Easton.

"Yes indeed," the man replied, motioning for them to come closer as he took one of the same oddities in hand. "It is a marvel of modern science. They call it the *kaleidoscope*. You simply put it to your eye"—he demonstrated the manner of it —"then look through and turn it slowly."

Silas handed his kaleidoscope to Miss Easton, who followed the vendor's instructions.

Her mouth slipped open, and she drew in a sharp breath, then pulled the kaleidoscope away, looking at the man in awe.

The vendor beamed. "Enchanting, is it not?"

Her gaze flicked to Silas at the choice of word, and he smiled.

She looked through it again, the corners of her lips turning up at the sides with pleasure as she slowly rotated the kaleidoscope.

The vendor handed his to Silas, who put it to his eye. The most unique arrangement of colorful shapes met his view, fanning out from the middle in perfect, vibrant symmetry.

He turned the kaleidoscope, and the view shifted as the arrangement changed to something entirely new but every bit as beautiful. With each shift of the kaleidoscope, the view transformed until he finally dropped it from his eye.

Miss Easton was watching him, her own glass lowered. She smiled as their gazes met, and Silas felt that increasingly familiar tug toward her.

"Bella," Miss Fairchild said, coming up to them. "You must see these fabrics!"

"Have you seen one of these, Felicity?" Miss Easton asked, handing her the kaleidoscope.

Miss Fairchild glanced at it for a moment, her brow pulling together. "Is it a toy?"

Miss Easton's mouth opened as she seemed to consider this.

"Put it to your eye," the vendor instructed.

Miss Fairchild took the kaleidoscope and did as instructed, smiling at the view it offered. "Very pretty!" She set it down. "They have the most intoxicating bolt of purple satin. Were you not saying the other day that you wished for precisely that?"

Miss Easton's gaze went to the kaleidoscope for a moment, but she relented to her cousin's pull and was soon gone, following her to the stand across the aisle, which was piled high with bolts of fabric.

"Thank you, sir," Silas said, handing his kaleidoscope to the trinket vendor.

The vendor nodded politely, and Silas made his way to the others. Frederick and Mr. Fairchild were looking at pocket watches near the fabrics, and Silas took a place between them and the women, for he was curious about the fabrics as well.

Despite Miss Fairchild having pulled Miss Easton away from something she had been enjoying, Miss Easton did not seem to resent it. She was every bit as enthusiastic as her cousin.

A quarter of an hour later, she had purchased lengths of three fabrics, along with various ribbons and embellishments to complement them. Silas offered to carry the purchase, while Mr. Fairchild and Frederick carried those of Mrs. and Miss Fairchild.

"I have burdened you like livestock," Miss Easton apologized to Silas as the group continued down the lane of vendors.

"Nonsense," Silas said. "All I ask in return is that I be permitted to see the creations that come of it all. I must say, I approve of your choices."

She shot him an amused glance. "Do you?"

"I do. But given the way you are looking at me, I take it my opinion does not carry the weight it ought to."

She laughed. "I am willing to be convinced otherwise."

They stopped while Mrs. Fairchild insisted upon looking at a few rings. "Very well. The pink muslin you chose...it has a nice, tight weave but will still be light enough for summer wear, which I assume is a factor, given the time of year. The dye work is good too, which is more than I can say for the fabrics I noticed at the other stall we passed. And the satin... your cousin spoke truly when she said it was an intoxicating hue. If it was like any of the others I handled, it is a fine weave —smooth and consistent."

She looked at him with a bit of wonder. "You know fabric well."

"I made it my business to know," he said.

"How so?"

"I used to have investments in textiles." He turned toward the jewelry, for this avenue of conversation was unsafe to pursue.

A shimmering caught his eye, and he looked until he found the source. His lip curled up at the edge. "Look, Miss Easton." He picked up the small pendant and showed it to her.

Her eyes swept to his.

"A near-perfect match." Holding the gold loop the pendant was attached to, he used his fingers to gently twist it. The sunlight caught on the wings of a colorful butterfly, making the indigo and emerald shimmer, just as Miss Easton's mask, domino, and dress had shimmered at Vauxhall.

She touched the pendant with a finger, marveling, and he dropped it into her palm.

"We will take this one," Silas said to the jeweler, who nodded quickly and put out his hand for the pendant.

"Oh," Miss Easton said, ceding it to the jeweler. "I couldn't possibly…"

"Do not be ridiculous." Silas took a few coins out of his pocket and gave them to the jeweler. "That pendant might have been made with you in mind, Miss Easton. Consider it my apology for abandoning you the other night."

"You owe me nothing, Mr. Hayes," she said as the jeweler handed him the pendant, now hanging from a bracelet chain.

"It is the merest trifle," Silas said.

She hesitated, but her eyes looked at the butterfly hungrily as he dangled it in the air.

He waited a moment, then closed his fingers around it. "Very well. I shall wear it myself, for it deserves to be worn."

She narrowed her eyes as though she did not believe he truly meant it.

He draped the bracelet over his wrist in response. "Help me with the clasp, would you?" He held out his hand and waited.

When she made no move to assist him, he glanced up at her and raised his brows expectantly.

She gave a little incredulous laugh, then worked at the clasp until the bracelet was secured.

He shook out his wrist and tipped his head to the side to admire it. "Very fetching, I think. The colors complement my knuckles."

"You are the strangest man, Mr. Hayes," Miss Easton said, but her smile was wide and amused.

That alone was enough to keep the bracelet on his wrist.

7

ARABELLA

There was a knock on the bedroom door just as Arabella's maid put the finishing touches on her hair the next evening. The door opened, and Felicity's head peeked in.

"Finished?" she asked.

"Nearly," Arabella replied. "Am I late?"

"No." Felicity closed the door behind her and came to sit on Arabella's bed. She looked particularly beautiful this evening, despite the fact that they were spending it at home.

Arabella thanked and excused her maid, then opened the jewelry box on the dressing table, glancing at its contents. Her mind went to the butterfly bracelet Mr. Hayes had purchased, and she felt a flash of regret and guilt—regret for not accepting it and guilt for seeming ungrateful as a result.

She was simply unaccustomed to navigating interactions with young gentlemen.

"I just spoke with Mama," Felicity said, "and she informed me that Benedict and the others are joining us for dinner."

Arabella's gaze snapped to her cousin's through the mirror, her heart skipping a beat. "The others?"

"Mr. Drake, Mr. Yorke, and Mr. Hayes, of course. Benedict was complaining about the quality of food from their kitchen the other day, you know, and Mama was so taken with Mr. Yorke and Mr. Hayes yesterday that she sent one of the footmen over with a message inviting them."

"And they accepted?"

Felicity laughed. "Of course they did." Her eyes fixed on Arabella's, her smile perceptive. "You and Mr. Hayes spent a great deal of time conversing at the market yesterday."

Arabella broke her gaze away and selected a necklace from the box, focusing all her attention on fixing the clasp behind her neck, though it reminded her of doing the same with the bracelet around Mr. Hayes's wrist. "He was very attentive."

"And..."

"And kind," Arabella said, her fingers fumbling with the clasp.

Felicity stood and came up behind Arabella, taking the ends of the necklace and securing it with ease. She smiled at her through the mirror. "Do you fancy him?"

Arabella's cheeks grew warm, and she turned away, smoothing her skirts. "I hardly know him."

"That is precisely when one fancies a gentleman, Bella." Felicity took her by the hands and pulled her up. "There is no shame in it. I am sure I have fancied two dozen men since I first came to London. It makes the Season so much more enjoyable when one can look forward to seeing a particular face at parties and engaging in a bit of flirtation." She clasped Arabella's hands more tightly and smiled. "Mr. Hayes seems just the right sort of man for it. Handsome, amusing, easy to converse with."

"Felicity," Arabella said, her cheeks burning like a winter fire, "I am not here to pursue courtship."

"Courtship? We are speaking of harmless flirtation. Or do you mean to say that you feel *more* for Mr. Hayes?"

"No, no," Arabella hurried to say, embarrassed at her own naivety. The truth was, she didn't know how she felt. She simply hadn't the experience to describe it. She certainly felt an affinity for him, but she could not confidently say anything beyond that. "I merely do not wish for Papa to disapprove of my actions."

"And he shan't," Felicity reassured her. "Your father would not consider Mr. Hayes an eligible prospect as a husband for his treasured eldest daughter, but I imagine Mr. Hayes knows that as well as you and I do. That is when flirtation is safest— when both parties understand that flirtation is all it ever *can* be. If you come to doubt that with Mr. Hayes, you know it is time to put an end to things." She shrugged. "It is as easy as that."

Arabella let out a breath. "As easy as that."

"Come," Felicity said. "Let us go downstairs."

Arabella hardly knew what to hope for as they did so. She did not wish to *put an end to things* with Mr. Hayes, for she enjoyed his company and found conversation with him interesting and enlivening.

But Felicity was right—Papa would not approve of Mr. Hayes as a marriage prospect. Arabella had been raised with the knowledge that when she married, it would be to a man of Papa's choice, and that man would be titled or wealthy—likely both. Mr. Hayes was genteel, but he was not titled, and there was nothing to give Arabella to think him possessed of the sort of wealth Papa would expect. Papa had always sought the very best for her, and marriage would be no different.

But did she hope, then, that Mr. Hayes merely saw her as a

way to pass the time in Town? As an entertainment, much like Vauxhall or the opera?

Felicity might be content with such a thing, but Arabella found it a lowering prospect.

Perhaps what she wanted was a friend.

And perhaps it was naught but the novelty of having a new one that made her heart skip when Mr. Hayes arrived and then again when he smiled at her and bowed.

Whatever it was, Felicity seemed to have full confidence in Arabella's ability to manage a flirtation with him, for she arranged it so that he and Arabella were seated beside one another during the meal.

Mr. Hayes assisted Arabella into her chair. "I have been anxious to see you, Miss Easton," he said as he took the seat beside her.

Her heart flipped. "You have?"

He nodded. "I have come to rely upon you to tell me what I am—a husband, then a liar and a coward—and not having seen you, I had no choice but to continue being a liar and a coward. I find myself eager for a new role, so I trust you will tell me what I am today." He shook out his wrists and set them on the table.

Something glinted, and Arabella searched for the source until her eyes caught on it: the butterfly pendant, hanging from the chain around Mr. Hayes's wrist.

Her gaze flicked to his, which was entirely somber, belied only by the barest twinkle in his eye.

Arabella pulled at the fingers of her gloves to remove them. "Happily for you, I know precisely what you are today."

He shifted toward her with interest. "And what, pray, is that?"

She set her gloves on her lap and met his eye. "An incorrigible tease."

The edge of his mouth quirked up. "I think you will find me quite corrigible."

Their conversation was interrupted by the placing of the food on the table, and Arabella's mind was caught up trying to determine what Mr. Hayes's intentions were. He certainly enjoyed teasing her, which seemed to confirm Felicity's assertion that it was entertainment he sought.

Arabella disliked the way the thought bothered her.

"Take care," Arabella said as he served her a helping of green beans, "or you will sully your bracelet."

"It is not my bracelet," he said. "It is yours. I am merely caring for it until you wish for it."

She admired the piece of jewelry, which she liked even better than she had remembered. It was uncanny how well it matched her masquerade costume.

"Are you still pleased with your purchases from the market?" he asked.

"Quite," she said, leaving thoughts of the bracelet aside. "I have begun working on the designs."

"You design your own gowns?" he asked.

"I have done so for years."

"Did you design that one?" He indicated the dress she was wearing with a nod. It was made of silk—a dusky rose with small pearls adorning the neckline and matching the earrings and necklace she wore.

"I did."

His eyes ran over the dress, patent admiration in them. "You have considerable talent, Miss Easton."

A flush of pleasure coursed through her, warming her cheeks and her chest. "Thank you. It is easy to make beautiful garments with beautiful fabrics, and I have been fortunate to have had access all my life."

"And how comes that to be?"

"My father deals in textile imports."

His brows rose. "And do you guide him in this endeavor?" He asked the question as though it was the most natural thing in the world that a daughter would advise her father on such matters. She doubted Papa would agree. He did not solicit her opinion—indeed, he rarely spoke to her regarding matters of business.

"Given the keen eye you have for fashion," he clarified after her silence, "it would seem a great waste of talent if you did not."

"That is kind of you." She hesitated, glancing at him from the corner of her eye as she stabbed a green bean on the outer point of her fork. She had never spoken the desire she harbored, but given what Mr. Hayes had just said, he seemed a safe recipient of her confession. "I have often thought it would be enjoyable to curate the pieces on display in the shop Papa owns."

"And what is preventing you from doing so?"

She searched his face, then turned back to her food. "Papa would not approve."

Mr. Hayes watched her for a moment. "Have you put the question to him?"

"No," she admitted.

He returned to cutting his potatoes. "Perhaps you should. Life is too short to let important questions remain unasked."

Important questions. He thought her desire to curate the window display of Papa's shop important. Not silly or improper.

Papa was a talented businessman, and he had his hand in many a pie, but he was also conscious of what was owed his dignity, which meant that some of those endeavors—the shop, for instance—required a certain degree of distance to avoid sullying the family name.

But it was not as though Arabella wished to work in the shop herself. She would simply design the window display. What harm was there in that?

"Is that a bracelet you are wearing, Mr. Hayes?" Felicity craned her neck for a better view.

Arabella's eyes widened, but Mr. Hayes lifted his wrist without the least bit of embarrassment. "It is. It belongs to a friend."

Heat crept up Arabella's neck, and she forced her gaze to her food.

Felicity squinted and leaned forward for a better view. "It is a butterfly! It is very beautiful. Do you not agree, Bella?"

The pointed question was not lost upon her, and Arabella glanced reluctantly at the bracelet. "It is very pretty." She turned to Mr. Drake on the other side of her, leaving Mr. Hayes to speak with her aunt.

The conversation with Mr. Hayes lingered in her mind as she spoke with Mr. Drake on her left. What would Papa say if she asked to curate the window display?

He would refuse, she was nearly certain.

But what if he did not? Papa wanted her to be happy. He had always given her everything he could—everything within reason. Mama's death had made him overly anxious about anything that might put his daughters or their reputations in danger. But what if she convinced him there *was* no danger?

Sometimes, she wondered if he continued to see her as but fourteen. Perhaps his decision to allow her to come to London was evidence that he was growing more open and realizing she had left behind her schoolroom days.

If she never asked about the window display, she would always wonder.

Mr. Hayes did not tease Arabella again with the bracelet, engaging her in polite conversation and seeing to it that her plate always had what she desired until the women left to the drawing room.

Aunt Louisa went to fetch her knitting, and Felicity waited until the door was closed before coming over to Arabella.

"I saw that butterfly pendant at the market yesterday," she said excitedly. "He bought it for you, didn't he? *You* are the friend he spoke of."

"He only wishes to tease me," Arabella said.

"Then you should tease him back," Felicity said. "That is the art of flirtation, Bella, and when it is done right, it is simply delicious. Take Mr. Drake, for example. I am already impatient for the men to rejoin us to continue our conversation. Not that I shall let him know I am impatient, for that would entirely destroy the fun."

Arabella frowned. "What *shall* you do?"

Felicity shrugged a shoulder, her face full of happy mischief. "Ignore him for a time. Converse with Mr. Yorke, perhaps, to elicit a bit of jealousy."

Arabella could barely wrap her mind around such stratagems, much less execute them herself. Besides, she was hardly certain what she wanted from Mr. Hayes. It was strange for her to feel so naïve and uncertain, for at home, she was the eldest, and Mary and Catherine looked to her for instruction and wisdom.

Aunt Louisa returned presently, eager to discuss their guests. She was quite taken with all three of them, deeming Mr. Yorke *an able conversationalist acquainted with all the most important names in the Commons,* Mr. Drake *charming and handsome but a suspected fortune hunter Felicity and Arabella were not on any account to fall in love with,* and Mr. Hayes *an engaging and attentive gentleman who had the misfortune of being terribly obscure.*

"What did you think of Mr. Hayes's bracelet, Mama?" Felicity asked with a glance at Arabella.

"I thought it strange," Aunt Louisa replied. "I do not think I have ever seen a man wear a bracelet."

"And had you any other thoughts about it?" Felicity asked, a hint of amused impatience in her voice.

"It was pretty," her mother responded.

"And do you have any guesses as to the identity of the friend to whom it belongs?"

Arabella shot her cousin a look.

Aunt Louisa's mouth turned down at the edges. "How should I? I barely know the man, much less whom he claims as friends."

"Did it not remind you forcibly of Bella's masquerade costume?" Felicity urged.

Aunt Louisa looked up from her knitting, her gaze settling on Arabella for a moment. It shifted to her daughter. "Say what you mean, dear."

"What I mean is that Bella has her first admirer."

"You exaggerate, Felicity," Arabella said, her cheeks warming.

Aunt Louisa's knitting resumed. "She is bound to gain any number of admirers. You shan't let your head be turned by them, though, will you, child?"

"No, Aunt," Arabella assured her.

Perhaps Mr. Drake felt a similar impatience as Felicity, for the men did not linger over their port for long. True to her plan, Felicity paid him no heed, but contrary to that plan, it was Mr. Hayes she engaged in conversation rather than Mr. Yorke.

Arabella's heart pricked with jealousy, which she snuffed out like a candle by speaking with Mr. Drake.

For her part, she could not understand why Aunt Louisa

suspected him to be a fortune hunter. The designation had always brought to mind the image of a man with a devious grin and calculating eyes. Mr. Drake, on the other hand, had pretty manners, a ready smile, and seemed harmless enough. But perhaps this was yet another example of Arabella's lack of experience.

When Aunt Louisa rang the bell for tea, Arabella found herself seated next to Mr. Hayes again. Whether it was happenstance or something he had orchestrated, she did not know, but she was glad for it. Of all the people in the room, it was he she most enjoyed conversing with, and despite the amount of time they had spent together at Covent Garden yesterday, she had unfinished business with him.

"I have been meaning to thank you, Mr. Hayes," she said, stirring her tea.

"Have you?"

"Yes. For coming to my aid at Vauxhall."

His eyes flitted to hers. "It was my pleasure, Miss Easton."

She ignored the rhythmic pattering of her heart. "I also owe you an apology for being so reluctant to accept your help."

"You were being careful. I do not fault you for that. For what it is worth, though, I feel you would have managed well enough without me."

She smiled ruefully. "I am not so certain of that."

"And I respectfully disagree. You proved yourself capable of defending yourself."

Her brow furrowed as she thought back on that night. "When did I do such a thing?"

He chuckled. "Do you not remember when you struck my arm?"

She winced. She had forgotten when she had smacked his arm while chiding him for leaving his wife in the maze. In retrospect, it had likely been unnecessary, but there had been no time for thinking through her actions in the moment.

He smiled, and it was she who was struck now by the utter charm of it. "Do not worry your head," he said. "I am sure I deserved it."

She spun her teacup absently on its saucer. "I am becoming acutely aware of how life in the country has ill-equipped me for London Society."

He regarded her keenly. "You have good instincts, Miss Easton. You should trust them."

She raised a brow. "What of the instinct that led me to refuse your help?"

He smiled. "Let us think rather on the one that led you to trust me." His eyes held hers thoughtfully. "I would never hurt you, you know."

The feelings that swirled in Arabella's chest were so entirely novel and unfamiliar that it took her a moment to pull her eyes away. She cleared her throat. "And what of you? You hail from Devon, I believe."

"I do."

"And did you travel all this way alone?"

He looked at her for a moment, then his gaze dropped to his tea, and a slight frown appeared on his brow. "Yes. My parents dislike Town. My father needed business transacted and sent me in his place."

"Business," she repeated. "What sort?"

"Investments. He dislikes the hustle and bustle of Town, but he does *not* dislike the opportunities it provides for his pocketbook."

Arabella smiled, and a thought occurred to her. "My father is always looking for investors. Perhaps I could arrange for you to meet—if it is of interest to you and your father, of course."

His eyes warmed with gratitude. "Certainly. That is a kind offer."

"He should be in Town soon. Tomorrow or the next day, I expect. Perhaps Mr. Fairchild can help us arrange a meeting."

"I shall persuade him to do just that."

Mr. Yorke came up beside Mr. Hayes. "We should be going, Hayes. I promised Lady Broughton I would make an appearance tonight, and it is growing late."

Mr. Hayes nodded and rose from his chair. "I am being whisked away, Miss Easton, so I must bid you goodnight. I shall await word from you, though—or Fairchild will await it, rather."

"I will send it as soon as I can."

He bowed, then went to thank and bid farewell to Aunt Louisa and Felicity.

Arabella's gaze was drawn to him again and again—his smile and the ease with which he made others smile. When the four men left the drawing room, she was conscious of a sense of disappointment—emptiness, even.

Felicity went over to the window that looked over the street.

Arabella hesitated a moment, then allowed her curiosity to win and joined her cousin as the front door shut. The four men had come on foot and could be seen in the light of the gas lamp in front of the house, buttoning their coats and donning their top hats.

Her eyes fixed on Mr. Hayes as he said something that elicited a laugh from Mr. Drake, and she wished she knew what he had said.

A carriage rolled to a stop in front of the house just as the men began their walk away.

"Are we expecting anyone, Mama?" Felicity asked.

Aunt Louisa laughed. "I certainly hope not! Who on earth should we expect at this hour?"

Arabella squinted and drew her face nearer the window glass until the crest on the chaise became clearer. "It is Papa."

The postilion opened the carriage door, and sure enough, Papa stepped down, wearing his brown traveling greatcoat.

"We do not expect him for another two days, though." There was a hint of panic in Aunt Louisa's voice as she stood and made her way to the window.

"It is too bad the men just left," Arabella said, thinking of her promise to introduce Mr. Hayes to Papa. Not that she minded having a reason to see him again soon.

"Indeed," Aunt Louisa said, though she did not sound confident in her agreement.

Two minutes later, Papa strode through the door of the drawing room, and Arabella went over to him. Much as she was enjoying London, there was something about having him here that brought a sense of home. If only Mary and Catherine could have been here, her joy would have been complete.

Papa wrapped her in his arms and kissed her upon the head.

Arabella breathed in his familiar scent. "We did not expect you so soon."

"My business was transacted more quickly than I anticipated, so I thought I would surprise you. Have I done so?"

She pulled back and looked at him with a smile. "You might have done so more successfully had we not been at the window already."

His brows went up. "Because you were expecting me?"

"We had guests," Arabella said. "They left just as you arrived."

"My nephew," Aunt Louisa explained quickly.

"And a few of his friends," Felicity added.

Aunt Louisa gave a forced laugh. "Only listen to us keeping you when you are undoubtedly exhausted from your journey. You must be hungry."

"I am," Papa replied. "But I shan't force you and Felicity to linger when you have other things you wish to do. Arabella, on the other hand"—he smiled at her—"I would like to join me."

The servants were instructed to prepare something for Papa, and Arabella returned to the dining room with him. She felt the impulse to show him the way, only to remember that he knew this townhouse better than she, for it was his. She had come to think of it as Aunt Louisa's, for that was the only way Arabella had known it—with her aunt giving orders.

None of the staff had been familiar to Arabella upon arrival, but Papa addressed the footman who served him by name. It was strange to see him so at home in a place that had been foreign to her just a week ago. How many times had he sat at this table and walked these streets? She was accustomed to their life at Wetley, to thinking of it as both of their homes, but Papa spent nearly as much time here and at his estate on the outskirts of Town as he did at Wetley.

The realization sat strangely with her, making her own world, her own life, feel small and...inaccurate.

"Now," Papa said, settling into his seat and picking up his utensils, "tell me about your time in Town."

And so she did. While he ate a hearty dinner, she told him the places they had gone and the people she had met who had seemed so thrilled to make her acquaintance when they discovered she was his daughter.

"Most of them seemed not to know you *had* children," she said, stealing a glance at him as she fiddled with the tablecloth. The surprise so many had shown was another thing that had sat strangely with her.

"I have not spoken freely of you or Mary or Catherine," he

said. "I do not care to have your names bandied about amongst the *ton*."

"Ah," she said, a weight lifting from her shoulders. He was always acting with the interests of her and her sisters at heart, even when it sometimes seemed like his protective measures were excessive.

The furrow on his brow when she mentioned Vauxhall was enough to keep her from going into more detail about the night. She had no wish to lie to him, but neither did she desire to cause trouble for Aunt Louisa.

"And what of these guests Louisa mentioned?" Papa asked.

"One is Mr. Fairchild—Aunt Louisa's nephew, you know—and the others are his friends—the gentlemen he lives with."

"Ah." His expression was concealed as he looked down at the food on his plate, so she could not ascertain what he thought of this.

"Speaking of which," she said, "I offered to introduce you to one of them—Mr. Hayes—for he is in Town on business and searching for investment opportunities. What is more, he has experience investing in the textile industry."

Papa's brows went up as he chewed, a look of casual interest in his eyes.

"Now that you have come to Town early," she said, "you could accompany us to Lord Woodrow's party, and I could introduce him to you."

"I am agreeable, though that reminds me that I have some unwelcome news."

Her heart sank, her mind flitting immediately to the possibility that they would have to return to Wetley.

He grimaced and took her hand, squeezing it. "I must go to Dover next week. Not for long, of course, but it is inevitable, I fear."

She tried to conceal her relief. She would rather he be in

Town with her, of course, but having him leave again for a few days was far preferable to their leaving London entirely.

She offered a bracing smile. "We shall manage our best without you, but do not stay away longer than you must."

"Of course not. Duty will bring me back as swiftly as I may return, for I have both paternal and parliamentary duties here." He broke his hand away to pick up his fork again, and only the light clanking of his silverware on the china filled the room.

Life is too short to let important questions remain unasked.

Arabella's stomach tightened with nerves, but Papa seemed to be in a good humor at the moment. Now was as good a time as any, surely.

"Papa."

"Hm?" He gestured for the salt, and she handed it to him.

"Now that I have been in Town a bit and seen its fashions firsthand, I wondered if you would ever entertain the notion of my designing the window display in Burlington Arcade."

His gaze swept to hers.

"I have received more compliments on my attire than I can count," she hurried to say. "Aunt Louisa took us to see the shop last week, and the current display is well enough, but it could be so much more! I am certain I could help."

Papa regarded her for a moment, and she met his gaze, unable to hide the hope in her face.

"Would it not be beneficial for you to have the inventory sell more quickly, making way for new fabrics?" she asked.

The edge of his lip tilted upward, and he smiled at her. "A persuasive argument."

The hope within her bloomed. "If it proved to be unsuccessful, I would not press you further."

He kept his eyes on her for what seemed like an age. "Very well."

She grasped his hand impulsively.

"Provided"—he held up his other hand to check her enthu-siasm—"everything goes well for the next few weeks."

Arabella nodded, eager to show she understood what was expected of her.

"Acquit yourself well, as I know you shall—heed your aunt, be a credit to the Easton name—and you will be rewarded with this wish of yours."

"Thank you, Papa. I promise you I shan't give you any cause for concern or any reason to worry."

She embraced him again, her mind already teeming with ideas for the display.

8

SILAS

Silas sat in his bedchamber, spinning the kaleidoscope in his hand as he leaned back in his chair, his feet upon the dressing table. He had meant to give it to Miss Easton the other night at dinner, but he had not. Something had kept him from doing so. A sense that it would have been too much, no doubt. Miss Easton had not even accepted the little butterfly pendant, after all.

Why *had* he bought the kaleidoscope?

Mrs. Fairchild and Miss Fairchild had both expressed regret over things they had not been able to purchase, and he had not gone out of his way to buy anything for *them*.

The obvious answer was that he had begun to develop feelings for Miss Easton, but he refused to accept this explanation.

He put the kaleidoscope to his eye and watched the shapes and colors shift as he turned it. The memory of Miss Easton doing the same soon brought a smile to his face.

She had been both entranced and entrancing.

Since escaping to France two years ago, Silas had been focused on survival. In France, that had meant deprivation and fighting illness in whatever lodgings he could afford—or work in order to afford. Arriving at William's estate had been a welcome reprieve from such adversity, and yet even there, he had been obliged to remain hidden. If his presence had become known to anyone beyond his brothers and aunt, it could have meant the gallows.

Watching Miss Easton's appreciation of fireworks and magic tricks and kaleidoscopes was proving a needed reminder of all the marvels and beauties of life he had forgotten about and why his freedom was worth pursuing.

There was a knock on the door, and the front legs of his chair smacked down to the floor as he removed his feet from the desk. He slipped the kaleidoscope into the drawer of the dressing table just as the door opened to reveal Frederick.

Frederick looked around the room, frowning. "What were you doing?"

Silas raised a brow. "Is this the Inquisition? Or am I permitted to be in my bedchamber without being subjected to questioning by the brother whose leading strings I held?"

Frederick stepped inside and closed the door behind him. "Come off it. You are only two years older."

"Only someone lacking two years of life experience would discount the significance of such a difference." He clasped his hands in his lap and regarded his brother. "How may I help you, Freddie?"

"I am here to deliver a message from Fairchild."

"And what message is that?"

"That Miss Easton sent a note." Frederick watched for his reaction, which Silas made certain to keep entirely dispassionate.

He rose from his seat and made his way to the armoire, which he opened, burning with curiosity about the contents of the note but determined not to let his brother know it. "I felicitate Fairchild on the momentous occasion."

"Don't be daft," Frederick said impatiently. "The note was for you."

"Ah." Silas turned to his brother and put out a hand. "You have come to deliver it to me, then."

Frederick shot him an unamused look. "It was addressed to Fairchild, but the information within was meant for you, as you well know, for I heard you and Miss Easton discussing your plan to meet Mr. Easton the other night. She says her father will be at Lord Woodrow's party next week and that he is looking forward to making your acquaintance."

Silas rifled through his clothing in the armoire, refusing to ask the question that was in his mind: would Miss Easton be there, as well? She must intend to go, for if she did not, who would make the introduction?

The fact that this was the matter preoccupying him and not the introduction itself did not escape his notice.

"Thank you for relaying the message." Silas took out a fresh cravat and shut the armoire doors.

It remained quiet, but Frederick made no move to leave.

Silas shot him an amused smile as he turned up his collar and stepped in front of the mirror. "Go on, Freddie. Say it."

"Fine. I think you should not come."

Silas draped the cloth of the cravat around his neck. "You shock me."

"It is foolhardy, Silas."

Silas cocked a brow at him through the mirror.

"Hayes," Frederick amended with a hint of impatience. "You might be recognized."

"Is Drayton in Town?"

"He is not," he replied reluctantly.

"Then the danger is negligible. But"—he silenced Frederick's retort with a heavy emphasis on the word—"I do not at all know that I shall attend despite that."

Frederick stared. "You do not?"

"No." The disappointment that filled him at the thought of not attending was evidence enough that it was the right decision. He was becoming too attached to Miss Easton. Of course, not attending would mean missing a potential investment opportunity—the first since returning to England—but Silas needed to keep his focus where it was meant to be. There would be other investments.

"I cannot pretend to be anything other than relieved," Frederick said. "I was becoming concerned you were falling victim to Miss Easton."

Silas laughed. "Falling victim? Is she some scheming villain?"

"Of course not, but that does not change the fact that you are not in any position to be..."

Silas raised his brows, waiting to hear precisely what his brother accused him of.

Frederick stuttered a bit more. "...on the catch."

Silas snorted. "On the catch? You make me sound like a dashed loose screw."

"Well? What would *you* call toying with a woman's emotions under a false name?"

His words stung, but Silas forced a smile. "I assure you, Freddie, that I shan't toy with the emotions of Miss Easton, nor of any other woman, for that matter. I know why I am here, and I shan't let anything come between me and my goal."

Frederick met his gaze squarely and searchingly, then gave a nod, looking as though a burden had fallen from his shoulders.

A thought struck Silas as he made a knot with his cravat. "Will Bence be at Woodrow's party?"

Frederick's brows drew together. "He is good friends with Woodrow, so it is quite likely."

Silas tilted his head to regard his finished cravat in the mirror. "Then I retract my statement. I *am* coming."

Frederick grimaced.

Silas turned toward him and gripped him by the shoulders. "Fear not, little brother. I will take measures to ensure I am not recognized. Your political career is safe."

"You think my concern is my career?"

"Is it not?"

"No!"

Silas's mouth quirked up at the side. Their gazes held, Silas's amused, Frederick's mulish.

"Of course I do not wish for scandal to be attached to my name," Frederick finally said, "but such a consideration pales in comparison to the prospect of my brother meeting his end at Newgate."

"I have no plans to become acquainted with Newgate, Freddie. Nor shall I sully your name any more than I already have."

Bence would be key to both of those aims, however.

That was why Silas would attend the party. Not for Miss Easton.

He could explore investment opportunities with Mr. Easton and gain an introduction to Sir Walter Bence while maintaining a polite and shallow acquaintance with Miss Easton.

Those things were well within his abilities. They had to be. For if they were not, he stood no chance at all of clearing his name.

9

SILAS

Frederick shot Silas a look of distaste as they approached the door to Lord Woodrow's party. "Makes you look like a dashed frog," he said under his breath.

Smiling at his brother's disgust, Silas smoothed the beginnings of his mustache. "A very handsome frog, though, you must own."

"I must do nothing of the sort." Frederick handed off his hat to a servant. "It is not even a proper mustache. It looks like you fell asleep with your upper lip on the fire grate."

"Jealousy does not become you, Freddie. Just because *you* cannot grow hair on that cherubic face"—he gave his brother's cheek a quick squeeze—"does not mean you should resent the fact that I *can*." In truth, Silas had always hated how quickly his hair grew, but just now, it served his needs well.

"Besides," he said, "I owe this beautiful addition to *you*."

Frederick scoffed. "To me?"

"I—very uncharacteristically—lost a wager to you."

Frederick snorted. "I would surrender half my savings to

you on purpose before allowing you to lose if that"—he pointed to Silas's upper lip—"was the stake."

Silas chuckled. Privately, he agreed that the mustache looked foolish. But for all his assurances to Frederick that there was no danger in his attending this party, he felt a shiver of apprehension as they stepped farther into the townhouse. His face was not known in London, and he had it on the authority of all three of his brothers *and* Aunt Eugenia that his time in France had altered his appearance significantly. And yet, there was still the chance he might happen upon someone he knew, be it ever so slight.

It was that negligible possibility that had decided him upon allowing the mustache to grow. This was in addition to the other things he had been doing to alter his appearance: wearing his whiskers longer, styling his hair differently than had been his custom, and choosing more subdued colors rather than the more vibrant ones he had favored in the past.

The mustache was bound to draw a bit of attention, but losing a wager was an easy enough explanation for the oddity. There was the added possibility that Miss Easton would be repulsed by him because of it, and even though he hated the thought, there was no doubt it would be for the best.

They reached the door to the ballroom, and Silas's eyes searched the crowds and the set of dancers under the chandeliers. They dwelled on each young woman with honey-colored hair, but none of them was Miss Easton.

He forced his focus instead to the men, looking for Sir Walter Bence, though he had only a vague description of him from Frederick.

With the man's help, Silas trusted that someday soon, he might walk into a party like this one without the fear of being recognized.

And without a mustache.

"You will tell me if you see Bence?" Silas asked Frederick.

Frederick gave a nod, looking over the dozens of people in attendance. Unlike Silas, Frederick was well-known in Town and very well-acquainted. He had made it his business to be. If he intended to be elected to the Commons, those connections would be crucial, for he would need the support of the influential within whatever borough he sought election.

Silas felt a pang on his brother's behalf. Frederick's situation was made harder by the fact that his brother had been accused of murder by a man with as much clout as Drayton. It was essential for him to avoid more scandal, but for Silas to achieve justice meant courting precisely that.

It was not an easy position to be in—for either of them.

"There," Frederick said suddenly. "Seated in the corner, speaking with Mrs. Quinnell."

Silas's heart raced as he searched for and found Sir Walter Bence. He was in his fifties, with a head of wiry gray hair and a well-tailored suit. His right hand clasped the top of a cane.

"You will introduce me?" Silas asked, not letting Bence leave his sight. The silence lasted long enough that he glanced over at Frederick.

Frederick gave a nod, though his brow was furrowed. "Come. Mrs. Quinnell just stood."

She had indeed risen from the seat beside Bence, taking the arm of another gentleman and leaving Bence alone.

Silas followed Frederick through the crowds, a mixture of nerves and anticipation swirling in his stomach as they drew closer. Frederick had maintained that Bence was both amiable and reasonable. Silas was counting upon it. At some point, if he wished to obtain the information he needed, he would have to take Bence into his confidence. That was a terrifying thought, for no one in England, save his own family, knew he had returned from France.

Without information from Bence, however, he would be back at square one. He needed evidence to prove Drayton was the one who had killed Langdon.

"Sir Walter," Frederick said, executing a quick bow. "I am pleased to see you here."

Bence smiled and used his cane to help him stand. "The pleasure is mine, Yorke." He gave a shallow bow, and his gaze flicked to Silas.

"May I introduce you to my friend?" Frederick said. "This is John Hayes. He hails from Devon and is in Town on his father's business."

Silas bowed, hoping his mustache would not put the man off.

"Hayes," Bence repeated, narrowing his eyes in thought. "Where in Devon?"

"Near Exeter, sir," Silas replied, rehearsing the story he had invented for himself with William's help. "Do you know it?"

"Not well, but I have a cousin in Plymouth."

"Ah," Silas said. "On the precipice of civilization, before the wilds of Cornwall."

Bence laughed loudly. "Precisely what I have told him, but he insists upon remaining there."

"If you will excuse me a moment," Frederick said, his focus across the room, "I am being hailed by Walden."

Silas and Bence nodded, and Frederick locked eyes with his brother for a moment with a clear message: *be careful.*

"May I fetch you a drink, Sir Walter?" Silas asked once Frederick had left.

"Certainly," Bence said, looking pleasantly surprised at the polite gesture. "Some claret, if you would."

Silas fetched them both glasses, his eyes wandering for any sign of Miss Easton as he returned to take the seat on Bence's left. Still, she was nowhere in sight.

"Business brings you here, then?" Bence took his glass and raised it to his mouth.

"My father is looking for a new investment or two. I have come to find, however, that the difficulty in London is not *finding* investment opportunities but knowing which ones to pursue."

Bence chuckled softly. "Very true indeed."

"Do you invest, sir?"

"I do. It seems the only way to keep one's fortune intact these days, though a bad investment can do precisely the opposite."

"Quite so. My father is wary after an unfortunate experience, so he put me on my guard. According to him, London is full of men who can talk circles around the unsuspecting."

"A sad but true fact. Unfortunately, not even one's friends are always reliable in these matters. When a great deal of money is at stake, so, often, is the conduct one expects of a gentleman."

Silas regarded Bence through the corner of his eye. There was a pinched look to his lips that suggested his thoughts were not happy ones.

"I could not agree more," Silas said. His own predicament was a perfect demonstration of the truth Bence had expressed. Drayton's love of money had led him to abandon both his conscience and his word as a gentleman. The result had been not just loss of money but the death of Silas's friend and the destruction of Silas's reputation.

Drayton, on the other hand, was flourishing.

Bence smiled at a man nearby who seemed to be debating whether to come speak with Bence or leave him to Silas.

"I do not wish to keep you from friends, sir," Silas said, "but I would be interested in continuing this conversation if it suits you. I could use a bit of guidance, if I am being frank, and it sounds as though we may be of similar minds on the topic of investment."

Bence looked at him, an evaluative gleam in his eye, then nodded. "Dinner this week, perhaps?"

"With pleasure, sir." Silas conveyed his direction to Bence, then bowed and left him to the gentleman who was politely waiting for them to finish.

A sense of accomplishment and victory grew in Silas's chest as he walked away. There was no way of knowing for certain, but he was fairly confident that Bence's comments had been a reference to Drayton. Just as importantly, it seemed Bence had been genuinely taken in by Drayton, just as Silas had, though ostensibly with far less damaging results.

This boded well for Silas, for only a man with a strong conscience and sense of justice would be willing to help someone as unknown as Silas when Drayton was the target.

"Mr. Hayes!"

Silas turned and found Mrs. Fairchild, Miss Fairchild, and Miss Easton standing a few feet away. Miss Fairchild was the one who had said his name, but it was Miss Easton who drew his gaze.

She wore a dress of the most vibrant aquamarine taffeta, which glimmered alluringly in the candlelight. Small white rosettes lined the scalloped sleeves and squared neckline. Her soft honey curls were gathered at the crown of her head, and a golden comb with a few stones to match her dress glittered prettily at the base.

Silas tore his eyes from her and bowed to the three women. There was no sign of Mr. Easton. "I was beginning to think you would not come."

"My daughter would never have forgiven me," Mrs. Fairchild said, her eyes fixing on his mustache for a moment.

"Nor I," Silas replied with a teasing smile.

Miss Fairchild was looking at the new mustache warily.

Silas smiled but said nothing. "Shall I fetch refreshment for you all?"

"Thank you, but not just yet," Miss Fairchild said. "I would far rather dance, and I promised Mr. Drake I would do so as soon as we arrived. Look! Here he comes now."

Sure enough, Drake strolled toward them with his characteristic confidence. He greeted them all, then turned to Miss Fairchild. "I have come to claim the dance I was promised—if your mother agrees, of course." His gaze moved to Mrs. Fairchild.

She looked for a moment as though she might refuse. "Oh, very well. But just the one set."

"Of course," her daughter replied dutifully. "And Mr. Hayes and Bella may join us."

Silas opened his mouth to excuse himself, but Miss Easton was watching him with so much earnest but doubtful hope there that he bit back the words. "Gladly, if she will have me." He put out his hand.

Miss Easton looked to her aunt.

"Oh, go on, then, child," Mrs. Fairchild said with an indulgent wave of her hand.

Miss Easton placed her gloved hand in Silas's, her smile so radiant it could warm him as easily as the sun.

They took their places in the set, their eyes locking across the dance floor as the music began and they waited their turn to perform the figures.

It was perhaps fortunate that he had not seen her when he had first arrived, for whose thoughts could dwell on Sir Walter Bence when Miss Easton was in the room?

They approached one another, meeting in the middle of the dance floor. Their palms touched, and they rotated around one another, the scent of oranges enveloping Silas.

"May I trust you with a secret, Mr. Hayes?" Miss Easton asked.

"Without hesitation," Silas replied with a spark of curiosity.

She gave him an amused look, but before she could respond, they were obliged to separate again. The distance made him feel restless and impatient while they waited as the couples farther down the set completed the figures. Silas had never felt so out of patience with a group of perfectly pleasant and respectable strangers. They seemed to move with maddening sloth.

When they met for the next figure, he waited for Miss Easton to divulge the secret.

She did not.

"You hesitate," he said.

She smiled. "I am gauging your trustworthiness."

"Come now! I thought we had settled that matter at Vauxhall. What is tipping the scales against me tonight?"

She regarded him thoughtfully for a moment before responding. "Shall I be frank?"

"Always."

Her eyes danced. "It is your mustache."

A laugh burst from him. "I think it gives me a distinguished look."

She looked far from convinced of that fact but was too polite to say so.

"If it is simply too great a stumbling block, I have a proposal for you," he said. "I will tell *you* a secret. Perhaps then you will feel comfortable reciprocating."

She considered this, then nodded, but the dance took them apart. When they came together again, he allowed the silence to stretch as they danced.

"Well?" she finally prompted.

"Well what?"

She shot him a look that was meant to seem unamused but was unsuccessful, for her eyes twinkled, making his stomach swoop.

"Ah, the secret." He leaned in closer, then whispered, "I, too, hate the mustache."

She drew back, her eyes narrowed curiously. "Then why wear it?"

"For attention."

She laughed, and the sound seemed to filter through his entire body and make him feel light.

"Would you care for another secret?" he asked as they separated to opposite sides again.

She nodded from her place.

He stretched out his right arm and used the hand of his left to adjust his cuff, revealing the bracelet just long enough for her to catch sight of it.

"Mustaches and bracelets," she said when they met again. "I have always prided myself on being adventurous in my fashion choices, Mr. Hayes, but you make my attempts seem very dull indeed."

"You could never seem dull," he said.

He instantly regretted the comment. He was meant to be keeping his distance, not betraying his admiration for her.

"Besides," he hurried to say, "I do not think a mustache would suit you. I am not convinced a mustache suits *anyone*."

"I am inclined to agree, but"—she tilted her head to the side as she regarded him—"you manage it quite well."

He smoothed the mustache dramatically, but inside, the pleasure of the compliment filled him. "What say you? Have I earned a reciprocal secret?"

She considered this, her eyes sparkling as he waited and

they danced. "I suppose so." She hesitated for a moment, however, before offering it. "This is my first proper dance."

Silas's brows went up. "I see. And have there been many *im*proper ones?"

She laughed, dropping her gaze with a hint of pink on her cheeks. "That is not at all what I meant, Mr. Hayes."

"I know, but I find it impossible not to tease you just a bit."

"I do not believe you have stopped teasing me since we met."

He regarded her curiously. "Do you dislike it?"

"I suppose that depends why you do it."

He blinked. It was a valid question. Why *did* he tease her? He might say he teased everyone, for that was true...to an extent. But it was different with Miss Easton. He knew that.

Did *she*?

"If you had to guess?" he asked, taking the coward's way out by deflecting the question.

She took a moment to respond. "I have wondered if you perhaps find me naïve—an easy target."

His brows snapped together. "Not at all. I enjoy your smile, Miss Easton. That is the truth of it."

The dance took them to opposite sides of the set again, and the music faded to a close as she watched him as though trying to ascertain whether he spoke the truth.

He kept his gaze steady, determined she know he was not trying to poke fun at her—and wishing for a future where he could well and truly court someone like Miss Easton.

When he had come to Town under an assumed name, he had been so focused on seeking justice for himself and Langdon that he had not thought of all the people he might come to consider friends—or how he would manage things once he shed John Hayes for Silas Yorke.

"Perhaps we should go in search of Papa," Miss Easton

said. "He had a dinner to attend before this, but I imagine he has arrived by now. Or would you prefer to remain for the second dance of the set?"

"No, that is quite all right with me." One dance with her had been enough to make it clear he was *not* capable of maintaining a polite distance. A second might have more dire consequences.

She took his arm, and they walked away from the ballroom floor.

"Oh," she said suddenly, "I meant to tell you—I took your advice."

"Very wise of you. And, uh...what advice did I offer?"

She glanced up at him with that twinkle he so loved. "I asked Papa if I could design the display window."

Silas's brows went up. "And what came of it?"

"He agreed to it—provided, of course, that I prove myself worthy of such an opportunity."

"And how *does* one prove one's worthiness for such a task?"

"By acquitting myself well in Society..."

"There is no doubt at all on that score."

"And avoiding scandal."

Silas's smile flickered slightly. If there was a human personification of scandal, it would be indistinguishable from him—including the mustache.

He was saved the necessity of responding as they reached Mrs. Fairchild, who was conversing jovially with another woman.

"Will you not dance the second of the set?" she asked when they reached her.

"I promised Mr. Hayes I would introduce him to Papa," Miss Easton replied. "Have you seen my father?"

Mrs. Fairchild shook her head. "Not yet, my dear, though I

did see Mr. Lyle, and was that not the man with whom he had an engagement this evening?"

"Yes," Miss Easton replied, going on her toes to search the room.

"Mr. Hayes," Mrs. Fairchild said with a smile, "could I trouble you to fetch me a glass of ratafia? I find my ankle is still a bit unstable, and with all these people, it would be very like me to trip and injure it further."

"With the greatest pleasure. May I fetch something for you, ma'am?" he asked the woman beside Mrs. Fairchild.

"Just a little punch, perhaps," she said. Her rosy cheeks bore evidence that it would not be her first glass.

"And for you, Miss Easton?"

"Ratafia, please," she said with a grateful smile.

He gave a nod and went off to procure the promised refreshments. It would be a miracle if he managed to return with three glasses without spilling anything, for the crowds had grown thick.

The table that housed the drinks was surrounded by people with the same idea as Silas, and he was obliged to wait his turn.

He took the opportunity to look around for Frederick, but Frederick was not one for dancing. He would be in the card room, rubbing shoulders with MPs and discussing the latest bills. Fairchild would be with him, undoubtedly.

Mr. Drake and Miss Fairchild had remained for the second dance of the set and were conversing and smiling as they completed a figure.

The gentleman behind whom Silas waited gathered up the two drinks he had poured from the punch bowl and left, making way for Silas.

Silas could not move, however. He was frozen in place, his

gaze fixed, his heart stopped as he watched a familiar face move through the crowd.

Lord Drayton had not aged a day since Silas had last seen him two years ago. His clothes were impeccably tailored, his hair gray but still full, his gait confident as people moved aside for him.

He came to a stop in front of Miss Easton and, smiling widely, put his arm around her then leaned down and pressed a light kiss atop her head.

She returned a smile, then went on her toes to kiss him on the cheek.

"Sir?" Someone tapped Silas's shoulder.

He stepped away from the table absently, allowing the gentleman to take his place in the queue. His mind was still trying to grasp what he was witnessing.

There was no mistaking it, though. A dozen bits and pieces of conversation from the past week began to fall into place, confirming the impossible: Lord Drayton had returned to Town, and he was Miss Easton's father.

10

ARABELLA

Papa was introduced to Aunt Louisa's friend, Mrs. King, who exchanged a few polite words with him, then excused herself.

Arabella looked to the refreshment table for Mr. Hayes, but he was not there.

"Are you looking for someone, dear?" Papa asked, trying to follow her gaze.

"Mr. Hayes. The gentleman I told you of—the one who is looking for opportunities to invest."

"Ah, yes. Where is he?"

"On my errand," Aunt Louisa said. "He went to fetch us refreshments, for this room is on the verge of boiling over." She fanned herself.

Arabella searched the room, a little furrow on her brow, until she finally spotted him with a leap of her heart.

He was not making his way toward them, however, and his hands were empty. In fact, he seemed to be heading for the door, his gait quick and purposeful.

He reached it, then disappeared.

"He should have returned by now, surely," Aunt Louisa said, making her own search for him near the tables. She frowned, the perimeter of her hunt expanding. "I do not see him anywhere."

"Perhaps he went to give Mrs. King her punch," Arabella said, her stomach tight with emotions she could not put a name to.

"Mrs. King is over there," Papa said, indicating the woman a dozen feet away. "And she has no punch."

"Perhaps he was called away urgently." Arabella could hear the pathetic hope in her voice, even though she herself did not believe the excuse. Had he not done something similar at Vauxhall? He had not ever revealed why he had done it then, either.

I am an impulsive man.

That was all the explanation he had provided, and it was no explanation at all.

"If he cannot be troubled to make an appearance for an introduction," Papa said, "I have no interest in discussing investment with him. Shall I fetch your drink, Louisa?"

"Would you? And a ratafia for Arabella."

He nodded and went off, just as Mr. Hayes had done. But unlike Mr. Hayes, Papa returned.

Arabella's good humor was not quite as quick to do so, however. For a quarter of an hour, she found herself looking toward the doorway through which she had seen Mr. Hayes depart, hoping to see him hurry through it, full of excuses for his strange behavior.

But she looked in vain, and the effect on her was to make her feel low and confused. The longer he remained absent, the more her emotions shifted toward vexation.

"Why did you and Mr. Hayes not stay for the second dance of the set?" Felicity asked when Mr. Drake returned her to her mother's care.

"Mr. Hayes left," Arabella replied coolly, sipping from her glass.

"After you introduced him to your father?"

"He did not meet Papa. He simply disappeared. Again."

Felicity gave a little scoff. "How very curious of him!"

"I would rather call it infamous. One sudden disappearance might be excused. Two begins to take on the appearance of a habit."

Felicity threaded her arm through Arabella's. "Oh, Bella. You needn't be so upset. It is not as though you are courting one another. He is playing a game, and if you ask me, you should be playing it too. There is no feeling quite like beating someone at their own game."

"I do not at all understand, Felicity," Arabella replied in a defeated voice. "When I play games with my younger sisters, it is one we agree upon together, with clear rules and goals. How am I to play a game, to say nothing of winning it, when I have no idea what the aim is?" She simply could not understand what purpose Mr. Hayes's disappearances served except to confuse her and make her feel forgettable and easily discarded.

Felicity took both of Arabella's hands and smiled at her. "The only rule to a game like this is never to allow your opponent to believe he has bested you. Do not give him the satisfaction of even noticing he disappeared tonight. It is sure to drive him mad!" She looked positively joyful at the idea.

But Arabella had not thought of Mr. Hayes as an opponent. She had come to think of him as a friend.

Evidently, she had been wrong to do so.

But she would not be so taken in again. She would,

however, heed Felicity's counsel and not allow Mr. Hayes to know that his actions had bothered her.

The window of The Silk Room in Burlington Arcade was mostly clear, save a few smudges from hands which had pressed against it. Behind the glass, wooden racks held two dozen bolts of fabric, arranged in an orderly manner but with little rhyme or reason. Most of the fabrics seemed targeted toward gentlemen—grays, deep blues, browns, and blacks meant for tailcoats, with one crimson for a waistcoat, perhaps.

It was well enough, but Arabella could not help imagining how much better it might be with more artistry and vision. At Wetley, she had an entire room full of fabrics and ribbons and thread, and she had come to find how the arrangement of it all sparked her own desire to sew. If it grew disorganized, that desire faltered.

Might it not be the same for those passing by the shop window? What would more color, more embellishment, more imagination do?

"You think you can improve upon it?" Papa asked as they stood before the window.

He had agreed to allow her to accompany him to The Silk Room this morning before his departure for Dover.

"I do," Arabella responded with quiet confidence.

"Hm."

She smiled to herself. Papa would find it difficult to entrust her with such a thing. Not her only, though. He was a man who was accustomed to control. He did not merely hope things went his way; he ensured they did.

If he would let her have free rein, though, he would see

how a woman's touch could draw more customers, making way for new inventory and building a reputation for the place among the *ton*.

And he had agreed to entertain that possibility—thanks to Mr. Hayes's suggestion that Arabella pose the question.

A sliver of annoyance lodged itself in her chest. Gratitude toward Mr. Hayes was not what she wished to feel at this particular time, and yet she doubted she would have asked Papa if it had not been for Mr. Hayes's urging.

Well, she would not go out of her way to thank him this time.

The knock on the front door while Arabella read in the sitting room did not bring her head up, but the sound of Mr. Fairchild's voice in the entry hall did. She listened for any voice besides his, hardly knowing whether she wished to hear it or not.

But Mr. Fairchild was alone, a fact which was confirmed less than a minute later when he came through the sitting room door.

Felicity set aside the newest edition of *La Belle Assemblée* as though Mr. Fairchild had been precisely the excuse she had been wishing for to do so.

"I was passing by and thought I would stop in and see how you are getting on," Mr. Fairchild said.

"Terribly bored," Felicity said.

"Where is my aunt?"

"Resting. Have you any news?"

Mr. Fairchild frowned pensively. "It has been rather dull since I saw you last."

"We have not been alone in our boredom, then. But

perhaps we can change that now that Uncle Drayt—" Her gaze darted to Arabella, and she hastily added, "Never mind that."

Arabella suppressed a sigh. She wished Felicity and Aunt Louisa were not so intimidated by Papa.

He had left for Dover yesterday and was expected to be absent for a few days. There was no telling for certain when the shipment he was awaiting would arrive. Arabella's feelings upon his departure were mixed. On the one hand, she had been glad for his presence; on the other, there would be a greater degree of freedom without him, and wretched though it made her feel, she was not opposed to this.

"Have you come to extend an invitation to us?" Felicity asked. "Some party or other which would be unbearably dull without us, no doubt." Her eyes fixed hopefully on Mr. Fairchild.

"Erm, not exactly."

"Nothing?" Felicity said. "Not a single event of note?"

"There is an art auction on Friday. Silent, I believe. Proceeds to charity. That sort of thing."

Arabella set down her book, her interest piqued. "What sort of art?"

He shrugged. "Paintings and drawings done by members of the *ton*, as I understand it."

Felicity's nose scrunched. "Are they any good?"

"You will have to answer that question for yourself. But even if they are not, it is in the Egyptian Hall, which may be of interest to Miss Easton in and of itself."

"What is the Egyptian Hall?" Arabella asked, even more intrigued.

"Oh, it is the most curious building," Felicity said. "Only a few years old. The man who commissioned it had it built to display his own collection, but it is full of curiosities. You will adore it, Bella. What do you say? Shall we go?" Felicity's eager expression made it abundantly clear what answer she expected.

Happily for her, Arabella could provide it, for she was every bit as enthusiastic at the prospect. She adored art, and she was curious just how much talent would be on display. But the venue itself would have been enough to draw her in, for she had read a great deal about Egyptian civilization. "I would quite like that—if Aunt Louisa agrees, of course."

"She will," Felicity said without another thought. "And we may wear our new dresses."

"True," Arabella said, even further convinced that this auction was precisely what she needed. Papa would approve too, if he knew. There could be nothing untoward about a charity auction full of the *ton*.

"Will you accompany us, Benedict?" Felicity asked.

He frowned. "I told Yorke and Hayes I would go with them."

Arabella was already lost in thought deciding what gloves and jewelry she would wear to the auction, but this comment had the effect of unceremoniously pulling her from the pleasant endeavor. Mr. Hayes would be there?

"Never you mind, then," Felicity said to Mr. Fairchild. "We will see you there."

"Good," he responded. "If you have no commissions for me to fulfill, I shall be on my way. I will send Aunt Louisa the direction for the auction." He gave a small bow, then left them to themselves again.

"I do love an auction," Felicity said after the door closed. "It seems there is always a bit of awkwardness when someone does not win the item they wished for. I once saw two men nearly come to blows! Though perhaps the art will be too terrible for anyone to bid. It certainly would be if *I* were the one supplying it."

"Perhaps we should *not* go," Arabella said, hardly hearing her cousin.

Felicity's brows snapped together. "What? Why not?"

Arabella hesitated, grasping her fingers together absent-mindedly. "I do not wish to see Mr. Hayes."

"Oh, Bella," Felicity said, coming up to her. "Do you not see? This is the perfect opportunity to show him how little you care about his disappearance at the ball."

Arabella took a moment before responding, for the disappearance had preoccupied her ever since. She did not wish for this to be the case. She wanted to be as nonchalant as Felicity. Perhaps acting that way would help her feel it. She could not avoid Mr. Hayes forever, after all, and she could not let his poor behavior dictate where she went and how much she enjoyed London. "You are right."

"Of course I am," Felicity said. "You must have the most grand time there and converse with as many eligible young men as you possibly can."

"And ignore Mr. Hayes," Arabella said, feeling this detail needed to be added for clarity.

"No, no," Felicity said.

"No?" Arabella asked in bewilderment.

"Purposely ignoring him is simply another way of showing how much sway he holds over you."

"Oh," she replied faintly.

"Here is what you must do. You will treat him as any other young gentleman. If you pass him, you will smile"—Felicity demonstrated—"and offer him a kind greeting. And then..." She raised her brows, prompting Arabella to respond.

"And then...I...will..."

Felicity smiled as Arabella's response never came. "You will continue on your way to speak with someone else."

"That is precisely what I was going to say."

Felicity laughed. "It will drive him mad, Bella. Just you wait."

Arabella was not so angry with Mr. Hayes that she wished for *that*, but she did wish for him to feel just a bit sorry for what he had done.

Arabella gazed up at the Egyptian Hall as she waited for Aunt Louisa to descend from the carriage. The building façade was unlike any she had seen, with creamy stone, a flat roof, various trapezoidal windows, and two Egyptian statues standing guard over the entrance.

She had never seen anything like it.

They made their way inside and were soon in a hall lined with ornate columns covered in designs and hieroglyphs. The walls and ceiling boasted similar artwork, while a tall, domed window let in light from the sky. A violinist and cellist sat in the far corner, playing music for the people who roamed the tables covered in artwork.

Mr. Hayes was nowhere in sight.

Perhaps Mr. Fairchild had told him that Arabella would attend, and he had made his escape early.

"He is not here yet," Felicity said.

"Who?"

Felicity smiled at her. "Very good. Shall we look at this infamous artwork?"

They started at the nearest table, where a painting of a hunting party sat on a stand. In front of the frame were small squares of parchment and a polished wooden box with brass fittings, a keyhole, and a rectangular hole in the top. Identical boxes sat in front of all the pieces of art in the room.

Arabella gazed at the painting, impressed with the abilities of the artist, who had signed the bottom right corner in illegible script.

"That is enough for now, I think," Felicity said after the sixth painting. "Time for a bit of socializing."

As if on cue, Mr. Hayes, Mr. Yorke, and Mr. Fairchild came through the door, and Arabella's heart gave a responsive stutter.

"Do not look," Felicity said, slipping her arm through Arabella's and pulling her toward Aunt Louisa. "You are not even aware he is here."

"I am not," Arabella confirmed, focusing her gaze anywhere but on Mr. Hayes, though her body seemed ever-aware of him.

Aunt Louisa was speaking with a middle-aged man and, based on their resemblance, his son, who had sandy blond hair and a handsome face. Arabella and Felicity were introduced, and Arabella did her best to keep her focus on the conversation with the Lybberts.

When her gaze flicked to Mr. Hayes for a moment, she found him looking at her.

She immediately returned her gaze to the younger Mr. Lybbert, who had engaged her in conversation while Aunt Louisa and his father spoke. Felicity had disappeared—a talent she and Mr. Hayes seemed to share.

Should Arabella nod or acknowledge Mr. Hayes in some way? She seemed to have no sense for the right way to go about things. She was certain she should not have looked at him in the first place.

And yet, no matter what she did, her gaze gravitated to him. It was the need for comprehension that drove it. Of that she was certain. Some part of her hoped that, by looking at him, she might solve the riddle of him and reach some understanding of what drove him to tease her and make her feel like the only person in the room one minute, then to fade into the crowds and desert her the next as though he cared not a jot for her existence.

Would it be so wrong to simply ask him? To demand an explanation for his behavior?

She managed to go twenty minutes without allowing her eyes to veer in his direction, but that was only thanks to Mr. Lybbert. He must have been nearing thirty, but his age and time in Town had apparently not granted him the conversational skill one might have expected. Arabella was obliged to ask question after question to avoid awkward lapses in their exchange. The task required all her concentration, for Mr. Lybbert responded with short answers and never turned a question back to her.

It exhausted her and made her wish heartily for Mr. Hayes's teasing and easy conversation. Her eyes wandered the room until they found him standing in front of a painting. He stared at it, head tipped to the side in contemplation. His hands were clasped in front of him, pulling the sleeves of his coat taut over his back.

That was when she spotted it, dangling just below the cuff of his gray coat: the butterfly pendant.

Her gaze flicked to his face. What was this man about? He had not even been able to bring himself to bid her good evening after their dance or to fetch the drinks he had promised her and Aunt Louisa, and yet he insisted on wearing that bracelet—*her* bracelet, according to him. Beyond that, he had made no effort to seek her out here with an explanation for his behavior.

She could not see the reason in any of it.

Mr. Lybbert stared at her, apparently waiting for her to introduce the next topic of conversation, and Arabella suddenly felt tired. Tired of manufacturing conversation with this dull man, tired of trying to play the part Felicity had given her, and tired of playing a game she did not understand.

"Would you excuse me, Mr. Lybbert?" she asked politely.

"Yes," he said in his particular, bald way.

She curtsied, then, with a hammering heart, made her way over to Mr. Hayes for answers.

11

SILAS

The first sign Miss Easton was drawing near was the way Silas's body tensed and his breath came less easily. He braced himself for her to pass behind him. She did not.

She came up beside him, a choice marked by his heart beating twice its normal speed.

What was she doing? Why had she come to him like this when he had behaved so abominably toward her?

And since he was asking questions, why did she insist on looking so very beautiful all the time?

He should leave. It would be the wise choice. He should have left when he saw her here, and he nearly had. He had gone back and forth again and again on whether to come in the first place once Fairchild had mentioned that Drayton was in Dover. Fairchild had not *said* "Lord Drayton," though. He had simply called him "Miss Easton's father." If someone had even once mentioned Drayton by name when referring to him, this entire situation might have been avoided.

What dark and twisted sense of humor must fate have to see to it that, of all women in England, Silas was drawn to the daughter of his only enemy? The man intent on seeing him put to death?

"An interesting piece," Miss Easton said.

"Is it? I admit, I am struggling to determine whether the object in the corner is a cat or a dog."

There was a pause, and Miss Easton leaned forward for a closer view. "It is a tree."

Silas frowned. "Surely not."

She moved aside. "See for yourself."

Silas stepped forward and squinted, then tilted his head. "No, I am certain it is a cat. Or a dog. Or a very well-fed squirrel."

Miss Easton laughed, and the musical sound resonated in Silas's chest.

She did not hate him so much as he had feared, perhaps.

"Here," he said, taking a piece of parchment and the quill in the nearby instand. "I shall submit a bid on your behalf. Name your price."

"Mr. Hayes," she hissed. "I forbid you to do such a thing!" She put a hand on his to stop him.

She could not, however, stop his smile.

"Only think how much you will enjoy having this painting sit in your drawing room, where you can force your guests to debate the true identity of the dog-cat-squirrel-tree."

"It is a fox," said a voice nearby.

Silas and Miss Easton both turned toward it and found themselves facing a tall and lean gentleman in his middle age, wearing a somber expression.

Silas turned back to the painting to inspect the alleged fox. "How can you be certain?"

"Because I painted it." With a tight-lipped expression, the man stalked away.

Eyes wide, Silas looked at Miss Easton, who clenched her teeth. "Oh dear."

"Not a deer," Silas said. "A fox."

Miss Easton stifled a laugh behind her hand, attempting a reproachful look—and entirely failing at it.

"Perhaps we should move on to another painting," Silas suggested.

She looked at him for a moment, her smile weakening.

His breath suspended, for he was certain she was going to refuse.

She nodded, however, and with a suppressed sigh of relief, Silas led the way to the next painting. The painting itself was quite small, and the enormous ornate gold frame overshadowed it.

"A penny for your thoughts?" Silas said.

Miss Easton glanced cautiously over both shoulders before responding. "I think," she said carefully, "that the artist was right to put the focus on the frame."

Silas grinned. "My thoughts precisely."

She looked at him, and her smile dimmed again. "Are we simply going to pretend that nothing happened?"

His stomach tightened, and he shook his head.

Her gaze searched his. "Why did you leave? Again?"

Silas struggled for words. The full and unvarnished truth was the only thing that could truly rob his choice to leave the ball of offense, but he could not provide her with it. "I would that I could give you the full explanation. I assure you there *is* one. But I cannot."

"Why not?"

He lifted his shoulders helplessly. "Miss Easton, there are things in my life that I cannot divulge to anyone, much as I may wish to. Things that could put me and those around me in danger."

Her brow furrowed. "Danger."

He nodded.

She looked at him intently. "Am *I* in danger?" The words held no fear, merely curiosity.

He shook his head. Seeing Drayton act with such paternal affection toward her had been too strange for him to explain. That this man, who had so ruthlessly killed Langdon to cover up his greed and dishonesty and then blamed Silas for it all... that he could kiss his daughter's head and smile down at her in such a loving way had been troubling Silas ever since witnessing it.

Did she have any idea of what her father was capable?

"You are not in danger from me, Miss Easton," Silas reassured her. "I would never allow that."

Her forehead remained puzzled, but she said nothing for a moment. "Felicity will be disappointed in me for speaking with you."

"She will?"

"Yes." She smiled ruefully. "I had very specific instructions from her."

"To toss a glass of champagne in my face?"

Miss Easton laughed softly. "Nothing like that. I imagine she would say that would be incontrovertible evidence of how much your disappearance the other night had affected me. And I am not to betray *that* under any circumstances." Color crept up her neck, but she maintained eye contact with him.

He grimaced, his heart sinking. "I am truly, truly sorry, Miss Easton. I had no intention of hurting you. Please believe that I would not have left without good reason."

"Without a goodbye, even? I had thought we were friends."

"We are," he said. "That is, I certainly consider you a friend, but I have not given you much reason to consider me as such. I understand that. And, unfortunately, there may be other times when my actions seem strange to you. I beg you will believe me when I say that such situations are not a reflection of my true sentiments or wishes. They are borne of expedience."

She looked at him with such a mixture of confusion and earnestness that he wished to gather up her hands and force her to understand…somehow.

"You are a confusing man, Mr. Hayes," she said. "My cousin maintains you are playing a game with me and that I should play it too."

"I am not playing a game with you, Miss Easton," he said solemnly.

"But you delight in teasing me."

"I do," he said. "But that is not me playing a game."

"Then what is it?"

"It is…" He battled with his words again.

This was impossible. He wanted nothing more than to assure her of his regard for her, and yet, to what end? The admiration he felt could not be pursued. "It is my poor attempt, I suppose, at friendship with a woman I consider my superior in all respects."

Her gaze locked with his. If she looked long enough, she would see the truth, so he broke his eyes away and looked at her dress. "That is one of the fabrics you purchased at Covent Garden."

She looked down. "It is. I did promise you that you could see the finished product, did I not?"

"It is every bit as exquisite as I had imagined."

A woman came up beside them, bringing with her a heavy dose of perfume. It smelled of tuberose—or a whole field of tuberoses, rather, like an invisible, dense fog settling over them.

Miss Easton blinked a few times in succession at the strong scent.

Silas's reaction was far less subtle. He tried to take shallow breaths, but it was too late. He began coughing, and once he started, he could not stop.

"Mr. Hayes," Miss Easton said, setting a hand on his back as he doubled over. "Are you unwell?"

He shook his head, but he could not speak for coughing.

"I shall fetch you a drink." She hesitated a moment, then hurried off.

Even amidst the fit, Silas was aware of people's eyes on him, and he stepped away from the woman's cloud of perfume, struggling to regain control of his lungs.

By the time Miss Easton had returned, the coughing had begun to subside, but he took the glass of water with gratitude and drank the entire thing.

Miss Easton watched him with concern etched on her brow.

He cleared his throat and nodded at the small audience they had gained from his fit to assure them that he was well and they could return to their activities.

Gradually, they did so, leaving Silas and Miss Easton to themselves.

"Forgive me," he said. "I was overcome by..."

"Tuberose," she supplied, but she still looked concerned. "I have never seen such a fit of coughing."

"Nor have I smelled such a violent perfume."

She smiled briefly, but his attempt to make light of things fell flat.

"I am well, Miss Easton. It is merely the remnants of a bout with consumption last year."

Her eyes widened. "Consumption?"

"As you can see, I came out of the fight victorious."

"There you are, Bella," Miss Fairchild said, bringing Frederick and Fairchild along with her.

Frederick's gaze upon Silas communicated his thoughts with crystal clarity: *what are you doing?*

Silas could not blame him. Once Frederick had learned the identity of Miss Easton's father, he'd had a great deal to say on the matter, most of which was urging Silas to stay far away from her. It was all reasonable, of course.

And yet, Silas could not bring himself to do it.

If Miss Easton wished for his friendship, he would give it to her whenever it was possible—which would not be for much longer. Drayton would return from Dover, and then Silas would be largely confined to the townhouse.

Silas joined Sir Walter Bence at his address in Mayfair the following evening for dinner. Whatever his experience with Drayton, the business of investing seemed to be treating Bence very well indeed. Aside from his illustrious address, his apartments were furnished with the very best—the best paper hangings and furniture and case clocks.

He invited Silas into the dining room, which had only two places set. The meal might have easily fed Frederick, Drake, and Fairchild, as well. Silas made a mental note *not* to convey this information to them, for he happened to know that they would be dining on what was left over from the prior evening's dinner, for the kitchen staff had been given the evening off.

Bence had a brandy and wine collection to complement his fine lodgings, and he insisted on providing a bottle of each for the meal.

He lost no time in bringing up the topic of investment. Bence had a varied portfolio, including landholdings, canal construction, overseas trade, and even investment in the newfangled railways that were under construction.

Silas liked Bence. He was reasonable but intelligent and seemed to favor a balance of steady investments and riskier ventures. There was a thread of principle that shone through as he spoke.

"What of you?" Bence asked. "What sort of investments do you and your father seek?"

"We are open to ideas," Silas replied, cutting into the lamb on his plate. "We have a particular interest in textiles, though."

"Ah," Bence said.

Silas hesitated for a moment, taking note of the bland, one-word response. "Would you discourage us in that? I value your opinion, so I pray you will give it to me frankly."

Bence frowned and took a drink from his glass before responding. "Discourage? No. I simply have a bitter taste in my mouth after a poor experience."

"I quite understand. May I ask you something?"

"Of course."

"I was given the name of someone with connections in the textile trade—someone I was told might be able to direct me to valuable investments. Perhaps you are familiar with him if you have had dealings in textiles."

"It is reasonably likely." Bence cut into the leg of lamb on his plate. "What is his name?"

Silas paused a moment. Bence's response would tell him a great deal. "Lord Drayton."

Bence's cutting stopped, and his eyes flew to Silas's. His jaw tightened as he responded, "I *am* familiar with him."

Silas held his gaze but waited before speaking. "I gather you would not recommend him to me."

"I would not."

Silas nodded but did not press him. What happened next

would determine whether Silas chose to test the waters further.

Bence took another sip from his glass, then sat back, his expression growing pensive. "I am not wont to speak ill of people, Mr. Hayes, but I happen to like you, and I would hate to see you taken in as I was."

Silas's brow cocked. "As you were?"

"Unfortunately, yes. I was in business with Drayton for quite some time—years, in fact. He has a good head for business. Too good, one might say."

Silas smiled slightly. "I did not know that was possible."

"Oh, it is. If business and money are one's sole focus, you see, one can rationalize almost anything. Conscience and friendships take second place to loyalty to money. Atrocities and greed so readily go hand in hand."

"Atrocities?" Silas couldn't help himself. He had to know if Bence was aware of just how far Drayton had gone.

Bence nodded, slow and definitive, his gaze fixed on Silas.

"You mean the betrayal of friendship and conscience you mentioned?"

"Beyond that, even." He seemed reluctant to give voice to precisely what he accused Drayton of doing.

"That is certainly unnerving to hear," Silas asked. "Can he not be stopped?"

Bence smiled, but there was a bitter quality to it. "Stop Drayton? He has lured enough people into his schemes or managed to find unsavory information about so many that no one dares."

Silas leaned forward, his heart beating more quickly. "What if someone did?"

Bence's brow knit.

"What if someone dared to stop him?"

"They would have to be mad. Drayton's influence amongst the aristocracy is not to be underestimated, Hayes."

"But if what you say is true, surely there are a number of men who would gladly be given the opportunity to come out from under his thumb?"

Bence squared him with an evaluatory look. "I confess I am befuddled, Hayes. You speak as though you have some idea of how to bring about Drayton's downfall. Or perhaps I am misunderstanding you."

"You are not misunderstanding." Silas could barely hear over the sound of his heart beating in his ears.

Bence's gaze grew intent. "Do you have evidence against him?"

"Nothing but my own word yet." He shifted in his seat, drawing nearer to the table and resting his elbows upon it. "You have been frank with me, Bence. I wish to return the favor. I believe I may trust you, but if I am wrong about that, what I have to say has the power to put me in the gravest danger."

"You are not wrong," Bence said. "Your secrets are safe with me."

Silas stared at him. It might be folly to trust Bence, but what other option did he have? Bence was the person with the most experience with Drayton. If anyone could help Silas, it would be him. "My name is not Hayes."

A flicker of confusion passed over Bence's brow, but he did not otherwise react.

"Are you familiar with Drayton's dealings with the Yorke family?"

Bence scrutinized Silas, his gaze growing more intent. "Why do you ask me such a question?"

"Because what occurred between Drayton and the Yorkes concerns me."

There was a pause. "Concerns you how nearly?"

Now was the moment of truth. The moment *for* truth. "As nearly as it concerns anyone, save the man Drayton murdered."

Bence's wide eyes expanded.

"I am the only witness to that murder." Silas's eyes never left Bence's. "I am Silas Yorke."

12

SILAS

The ticking of the case clock punctuated the deafening silence.

"Silas Yorke is in hiding," Bence said. "He is in France."

Silas shook his head. "I returned months ago. Until I came to London, I was in hiding here in England."

"But..."

"I cannot hide forever, Sir Walter, and certainly not for a crime I did not commit."

Bence nodded grimly. "Who knows of your presence in England?"

"My family. And now you." His stomach clenched. Had he been wrong to tell him the truth? He hardly knew the man. And yet, he was confident he had not misjudged him.

"You do me a great honor by bringing me into your confidence," Bence said soberly.

"As you may imagine, there is a reason I have done so. I hope you will help me."

Bence took in a slow, deep breath, a hint of wariness entering his gaze. "What precisely do you wish for me to do?"

"Help me strengthen my case against Drayton. I have my own experience to share, of course, but I need more than that."

"You do," he replied. "The fact that your brother came into the dukedom is certainly a boon to your case, but without any evidence and testimony to corroborate your story..." He pulled a face. "It is your word against Drayton's, and—unjust as it may be—people will side with Drayton, if only to prevent angering him."

"Precisely. And there *was* evidence—evidence my brother Anthony went to great lengths to acquire. A journal. But Drayton destroyed it." Silas took a moment before speaking the next bit, for what he was asking of Bence was not only bold...it was dangerous. "You seemed aware of Drayton's guilt in Langdon's murder, Sir Walter. How?"

He spun his empty glass before responding. "Several months before Langdon's untimely passing, I became intrigued by Drayton's investment in textiles, for it seemed he was doing quite well. The returns were remarkable, and I wanted to be part of it. I approached Drayton with the intent to join the venture."

Silas's eyebrows rose.

"When I broached the subject, however, Drayton's response was...odd. He told me it wasn't the right moment and advised me to hold off. He hinted that a more lucrative opportunity was imminent and promised to include me when the time was ripe.

"At the time, I did not question it. Drayton and I had conducted business together before, and I trusted his judgment. Thanks to that history, however, I have contacts in the shipping industry, and I heard...rumors...whispers that

Drayton was covertly aligning with another company. A direct competitor."

Silas nodded grimly. "He was sabotaging us from within, preparing to shift his assets to our competition."

Bence grimaced. "When Langdon died and you were accused, I was uneasy, but I could not say why, for at that time, I had no reason to suspect Drayton capable of murder. I knew he had a temper—these things often make themselves known in business, as you know—but having a short fuse does not make a man a murderer. And yet, I was uneasy, all the same. Something did not sit right with me." Bence frowned, staring at the tablecloth. "I asked Drayton about it. Mentioned how tragic and untimely Langdon's death was. Drayton's response..." He hesitated, a shadow crossing his face.

Silas waited, his body crackling with anticipation.

"Drayton looked at me with an expression I shall never forget. It was...lazy. Unconcerned. And he said, 'An unfortunate business, certainly. But necessary, I fear.'"

Silas straightened. "He admitted it?"

"Not in so many words. But the implication was there. I could not help wondering—fearing—what had truly happened. And when Drayton moved his interests to the competitor and began to gain even more financially, I felt more certain he had been involved in Langdon's demise. I was in denial, of course, for I had begun to reap great benefit from my newest investment with him. But the seed had been planted, and from then on, I began to take note of the cold and calculating side of Drayton. I believe it was somehow precipitated by the death of his wife. He became obsessed with protecting his daughters and providing them with grand inheritances."

Bence rubbed his thumb along the base of his nearly empty wine glass. "Then there was an incident a few months ago. One of Drayton's ships was undermanned and ill-maintained

—an attempt to save money, of course. It wrecked in a storm, and lives were lost. The captain's widow inherited her husband's property, but Drayton coerced her into selling it to him at a price that was far from fair to her. He sold it at great profit not long after."

Silas's stomach roiled. His was not the only life that Drayton had ruined.

Bence's frown was deep and dark. "I could no longer turn a blind eye to his tactics. When I confronted him over it, he accused me of being lily-livered. He questioned if I was truly fit to invest with him and reminded me he is a widower with a family to support—as if his children are not amply provided for already."

Silas thought of Miss Easton and the way Drayton had acted with such paternal affection—the way *she* had regarded him with such devotion. The man was living a double life, and he was using his daughters to rationalize his depravity.

Bence shook his head. "I cut ties with him then."

There was silence as both men ruminated on the revelations they had made.

"Drayton cannot be permitted to ruin any more lives with impunity, Sir Walter," Silas said softly.

"I agree. But it is an easy sentiment to express and a difficult one to pursue."

"Difficult, but not impossible. Will you not come forward with me? Our testimonies together would be far stronger than they would be alone."

"They would. But do you not realize that I continued to do business with Drayton after knowing what sort of man he was? My own conscience is not clean, Yorke, and Drayton would use that to his advantage."

He was right, undoubtedly. Drayton had shown his colors

and the depths to which he would go to protect himself. They needed something more.

"We must find evidence," Silas said. "Are you willing to help me?"

Bence took in a slow breath, his chest rising as he considered Silas.

"You know Drayton far better than I—his habits, his weaknesses. All I need is for you to try to discover where we might find evidence of his wrongdoing. Can you do that?"

Bence's jaw hardened as he met Silas's gaze. "I will do my best."

13

ARABELLA

"Bella!" Felicity burst into the breakfast parlor, a piece of paper in hand and her eyes alight with excitement.

"Felicity," Aunt Louisa said with a look of long-suffering. "For heaven's sake, reserve your enthusiasm for a more suitable time of day."

"Yes, Mama," Felicity replied docilely as she took a seat next to Arabella and leaned in to whisper. "The penny post has just come, and look what arrived along with it." She handed the paper to Arabella, who set down her fork and took it.

"I am certain it is Benedict's doing," Felicity said, reducing the volume of her voice after a stern look from her mother, "for I was telling him the other day how much I wished for an invitation, and he said it would be the easiest thing to procure."

"Shall he be there?"

Felicity met her gaze, a little twinkle in hers, as though she knew Arabella's true question.

"I am certain *he* shall."

Arabella's returned her eyes to the writing. It was an invitation to attend a cruise on the Thames on Lord Dunsbury's private barge.

"A barge?" Arabella repeated.

"They say he has fitted it with dozens of lanterns and garlands of flowers so that it is the most beautiful vessel on the Thames. Everyone has been waiting to see if he will invite people aboard, for he first did so last Season, and I was positively green with jealousy of those who received invitations."

"If you insist on yelling in a whisper," Aunt Louisa said, "you may as well speak up." She infused her voice with chastisement, but there was curiosity in her eyes.

Arabella handed the invitation to her, and she looked it over, one of her brows cocking by the time she reached the end.

"Well," she said, "that is certainly intriguing."

Felicity beamed with satisfaction.

Arabella tended to agree with her aunt. The picture Felicity had painted was too enticing to refuse. Arabella had never been on a boat, much less one lit up and decorated as this one would evidently be.

The door opened, and Papa came through, dressed for the day. "Good morning."

They each greeted him as he took a plate from the sideboard and began to choose from the spread of foods.

Arabella rose and began to prepare his usual cup of tea.

"I have instructed your maid to prepare your things, Arabella," Papa said.

Arabella's eyes darted to Felicity, who looked alarmed.

"Prepare my things?" Arabella repeated. "Prepare them for what?"

"We are making a visit to Barrington Hall," he said, selecting a thick piece of ham.

Arabella opened her mouth, then shut it again.

"So soon?" Aunt Louisa asked. "But you only just arrived in Town."

Papa finished filling his plate and came to the table. "Some matters must be handled in a timely fashion, Louisa."

"What sort of matter is this?" Arabella asked.

Papa's gaze flicked to her.

"I only mean that I am enjoying my time in Town so very much. Must I go?"

He looked at her another moment. "May I have a word, Bella?"

She nodded and rose, then followed him out of the room, wondering at his reaction.

He closed the door behind them, then faced her. "I had hoped you would join me at Barrington. You have never been there, after all, and the purpose of the visit concerns you."

Arabella's brows rose. "Me?"

He nodded. "I may have found someone for you, my dear."

Arabella's heart clenched.

"It is no certain thing, of course, but I invited him to Barrington—not *only* him, of course—with the hopes of becoming better acquainted with him and his affairs. He is an earl."

Arabella forced a smile, trying to meet his obvious expectation. Whenever Papa had come to Town, she had always imagined him to be sitting in Parliament, listening to bills and casting votes, or perhaps conducting business across long tables with fellow investors. She had not imagined him leaving to Barrington to host parties or find suitors for her.

"I was not aware you were searching for...a husband for me."

"I was not. But when I met Lord Farnham, I was struck by his eligibility. And now that you have experienced Town, it has me thinking that perhaps the time for a match has come."

Arabella's stomach swirled, and Mr. Hayes's teasing smile swam before her.

"You are two-and-twenty, Arabella," Papa said.

She knew it quite well. It was simply strange to hear him say it as though she, rather than he, had been the one delaying things.

The thought of going to Barrington and meeting this Lord Farnham was almost as unappealing as returning to Wetley Abbey. Arabella wanted to be in London. She wanted to enjoy herself and experience more of what Town had to offer. She wanted to go on the barge with its lanterns and flowers.

She wanted to see Mr. Hayes again.

"What of your duties in Parliament?" she said, grasping at any excuse.

Papa waved them off. "They manage perfectly well without me."

"But are you not expected to attend?"

There was a flash of something like annoyance in Papa's eyes, but she must have imagined it, for it was gone as quickly as it had come. "You may safely leave the handling of my Parliamentary duties to me, my dear. Are you saying you do not wish to come to Barrington with me?"

"It is not that," she said, eager to reassure him. "Of course I wish to be with you. But..." She stepped toward him. "I am enjoying Town so very much."

Papa's gaze searched her face, his expression inscrutable.

Arabella pressed on. "Would it not be best for you to first spend time with Lord Farnham and see whether he is truly an eligible option?"

Papa watched her a moment longer. "Very well. You may remain. But"—he put up a hand to stop her gratitude—"if I do find him suitable, I expect you to be ready and willing for an introduction where and when I say."

"Of course." Arabella did not oppose meeting Lord Farnham. It was very possible, though, that Papa would learn more of him and decide he was not suitable. Papa was particular, so choosing a husband for her was bound to be a difficult task.

Arabella merely wished for more time...more time enjoying her new friendships before she was forced to consider matrimony in earnest. Not until coming to London had she realized how much she had been missing by being at Wetley with no one but her sisters for friends. Not that she did not love her sisters dearly, but it was simply not the same.

In fact, Arabella had found a little seed of frustration growing within her since Papa's arrival—frustration that he had kept her from the joys she was now experiencing. She knew he had only meant well, but that did not stop her from wondering how life might have been if she had been allowed to come to London sooner—at the age when most young women did.

But she was here now, and she hoped to make the most of it.

She hoped, too, that Lord Farnham was *not* as suitable as Papa hoped.

Arabella craned her neck to peer through the window as the carriage approached the dock. There were too many other equipages blocking her view, however, to gain a view of the barge. All that was visible was the glow of lanterns.

She was not the only one anticipating the evening. Felicity and Aunt Louisa, though familiar with London's attractions, had never attended a party on a barge. When the carriage came to a stop, Felicity sat on the edge of the seat, waiting for the door to be opened and the steps let down.

She had been fretting over the weather all day, worrying it would rain and the party would be canceled, but the gray clouds that had blanketed the sky had given way to a nearly cloudless evening with a pleasant breeze.

Felicity buzzed with chatter as they made their way toward the barge, where people were being assisted by servants across a short plank.

Arabella's eyes took in the scene hungrily, moving along the profile of the barge. Dozens of oil lamps and lanterns hung from lines across the deck, while a similar glow lit the windows of the covered section near the bow. The lights reflected in the dark water, glittering and shimmering on the surface.

The wooden railings that ran along the barge's edges were lined with greenery and white flowers. A string quartet serenaded attendees near the bow, completing an atmosphere Arabella found utterly enchanting.

Once she had seen the barge, she could not help but search for any sign of Mr. Hayes. Her heart jumped at the sight of Mr. Fairchild standing on the long deck of the barge, a drink in hand. Beside him were Mr. Drake and Mr. Yorke and two other men Arabella did not recognize.

Arabella, Felicity, and Aunt Louisa seemed to be among the last guests to cross over the short plank, for once they had done so, the servants on the shore and those on the barge began to communicate about removing it.

In her decisive way, Felicity guided them toward Mr. Fairchild, who greeted them jovially, then introduced them to the two strangers.

The bustle amongst the servants near the plank intensified, and still there was no sign of Mr. Hayes as the group conversed and Mr. Drake went to fetch refreshment for the women.

"Is Mr. Hayes here?" Arabella tried to keep her voice disinterested, but there was a knowing glint in Mr. Yorke's eyes as he responded.

"He could not come."

"Oh." Arabella's heart sank, but she forced a smile. "How unfortunate for him." But it was she who felt unfortunate.

A few minutes later, the rowers began to undo the knots that kept the barge ashore.

Arabella took in a breath, determined to enjoy herself rather than spending the evening missing Mr. Hayes. Surely, she did not require him for her entertainment.

"What in the world?" Mr. Yorke's brow furrowed as he focused on something behind Arabella.

All eyes turned in that direction, including the eyes of many not within their group.

Arabella's heart stuttered at the sight of Mr. Hayes on shore. He was in intent conversation with one of the servants, who was winding up a rope. The plank had been removed, however, and the servant shook his head.

Mr. Hayes sighed, then nodded, his shoulders sinking with disappointment as the barge began to move at a creeping pace with the river.

"He is too late," Felicity said sympathetically as he turned his back on the barge and began to walk briskly away from the Thames.

Arabella's impulse was to intervene and plead with the servants to stop the barge, but it would be useless. Worse than useless, in fact. Everyone would know how much she valued Mr. Hayes's company—including him.

He suddenly stopped and turned, and before Arabella had fathomed his intent, he was running at a diagonal toward the shore. When he reached it, he leaped.

14

ARABELLA

Arabella's hand flew to her mouth, and sharp intakes of breath sounded all around.

Mr. Hayes sailed through the air and over the water. He grabbed hold of the barge's railing, but his feet struggled to find purchase. One of them dipped into the water before settling firmly on the barge's edge. Without a moment of hesitation, he climbed over the railing, hardly taking note of all the people watching him with wide eyes and mouths agape as his boot dripped water onto the deck.

He nodded politely at his audience, then strode through the crowds, brushing his coat as though he had just stepped down from a carriage rather than bounding across the Thames onto a moving barge.

A chorus of silence and continued stares awaited him once he reached Arabella and the others, the way his chest rose and fell the only evidence of his exertion.

"Good evening," he said with a quick bow, then he took the glass from Mr. Yorke's hand and drained it.

"You," Mr. Yorke said, "are the most hare-brained and

ridiculous..." He fumbled over his words, apparently past the point of being able to pinpoint precisely what Mr. Hayes was.

Mr. Hayes smiled at him and handed him the empty glass, then grasped Mr. Yorke's shoulder with a hand. "Happy to see you too, Freddie."

The silence broke with incredulous chuckles from the others, and Mr. Hayes caught Arabella's eye just long enough to wink at her.

Her heart thumped with pleasure. Never had her mood shifted so drastically and so suddenly. She could not stop smiling. The beauty of the evening, already beyond her expectations, multiplied instantly with Mr. Hayes upon it.

The group soon migrated to the seats in the center of the vessel, and while Felicity sat beside one of the new gentlemen they had met, Arabella took a seat beside Aunt Louisa. She might have spared herself the trouble, for just moments after she sat down, Mrs. King took the seat on Aunt Louisa's right and engaged her in conversation.

"May I?"

Arabella glanced up and found Mr. Hayes looking down at her. He nodded at the empty chair on her left to indicate his intention to sit beside her.

"If I refuse," she said, "will you simply leap into the chair?"

His mouth spread into a grin. "You disapprove of my arrival, I take it. A bit too dramatic for your tastes?"

"Quite the contrary," she said, unable to stop a betraying smile. "It would have been far more impressive if you had done it from astride a horse."

He chuckled and took a seat beside her. "If only I had thought of it. Perhaps then I would not be walking around with wet socks." He looked down at his boot, from which river water continued to drip.

"A small price to pay, I think, for the attention you claim to love. Mr. Yorke said you would not be here, and yet now everyone is aware of your attendance."

"Provided *you* are aware of it, I am content."

Arabella searched his eyes, trying to determine the intent behind the words. He had told her his teasing was an attempt at friendship, but at times, his words hinted at more.

"It is fortunate, then, that I came," she said.

"Was that ever in question?"

"Papa wished me to join him at Barrington."

His smile flickered. "And you did not desire to go with him?"

"Not particularly." She hesitated. What would Mr. Hayes think to know she might become engaged soon? No doubt Felicity would encourage her to use such information to her advantage—to see if she could elicit some jealousy. But Arabella had no interest in arousing jealousy. She merely wished to understand what Mr. Hayes thought of her—or whether he *did* think of her when she was not present. "He wished to introduce me to a gentleman there."

Mr. Hayes's gaze held hers. "A gentleman..."

She nodded, watching him carefully, but she was too untrained to decipher his reaction.

"A suitor, you mean," he said.

"I believe so."

He nodded slowly. "What made you stay?" He watched her intently. Did he wish her to say she had stayed for him?

Had she?

Something within her responded with an unmistakable *yes*.

She ignored it. "I suppose I have not yet accustomed myself to the idea of...suitors or matrimony."

"But your father has," he offered.

"He wishes to see me provided for, as every father does."

He nodded slowly, his gaze never breaking from hers. "And what are your father's requirements for men who would presume to your hand?"

She smiled at the word *presume*. "Papa has high expectations. He always has. I can only imagine that will remain true in this case."

"Meaning…"

"Meaning," she said slowly, "that I believe he is set on someone in possession, as he is, of both title and fortune."

Mr. Hayes laughed and broke his gaze away, sitting back in his seat and folding his arms.

The reaction perplexed her. "You are amused."

"Oh, far from it."

She was quiet, and he turned to look at her again.

"For your sake, I sympathize with your father's stringent requirements, of course. But for my own sake, I regret them."

Her heart raced as they regarded one another, until finally, he spoke again, his tone casual. "And what of your requirements?"

"My requirements," she repeated, still trying to fathom the implication of what he had said. It was the first time he had said anything firm to give her to believe he had more serious intentions toward her.

"Surely there are things you wish for in a suitor, Miss Easton. Or perhaps you would be equally happy no matter whom you married. That man, for instance"—he indicated a tall, ruddy-faced man standing on the deck—"provided he has a title and a large fortune, of course." The gentleman gripped a glass in each hand, one full of wine, the other of brandy. He tossed his head back and laughed loudly at something, then took a sip from the wine followed by a sip from the brandy.

Arabella could not help drawing back at the sight. "I think not." The man reminded her of the drunkards from Vauxhall.

"Very well, then. What are your requirements?"

She let her gaze run over the variety of guests aboard the barge. It had never occurred to her to consider her own preferences, nor had she had the opportunity to develop them through association with eligible men.

Until recently.

"If it were entirely up to me," she said slowly, "I would wish for someone...kind. Someone who enjoyed my company and whose company I enjoyed. Someone with whom I could laugh—and perhaps even cry." She smiled slightly. "Papa says men cannot abide tears. I am not one to indulge in them often, but one of my only memories of Mama was when a storm blew down my favorite tree, and she held me while I cried. She took me out to see a new tree planted in its place just days later." She swallowed down the emotion that speaking of her mother elicited.

Mr. Hayes watched her, his expression inscrutable as he listened.

What would *he* do if she cried? Would he panic and feel embarrassed to be seen with her? Would he find an excuse to leave as Papa so often did?

The answer came to her with a surety.

He would not. On the contrary, she could imagine he might gently wipe her tears and speak reassuring words. He was far too kind to do anything else.

In fact, Mr. Hayes encapsulated everything she had mentioned. Did he realize that?

Perhaps she had revealed too much. "I know little of courting and marriage, though," she said. "I have only just begun to enjoy friendships."

It was quiet for a moment as they regarded one another.

"The value of friendship should not be discounted," he said with a smile. It had an almost sad quality to it.

"No, indeed."

He looked at her for another moment, then turned his focus ahead. "I hope you know you may rely upon me to help you fend off any unwanted suitors. It is the least an untitled, fortuneless friend could do." He shot her a quick smile.

"That is a kind offer, Mr. Hayes. And how do you propose to accomplish it?"

"Never fear. I shall find a way."

She laughed softly.

"Do you doubt me?"

"It would be the height of foolishness to doubt the ingenuity and determination of a man prepared to leap over the Thames."

"You would certainly be wrong to do so. When I set my mind to something, I find a way to accomplish it." The way he held her eyes made her heart race, though she could not say why. He had not said anything to elicit such a reaction.

But that was just it. Her heart behaved in strange ways when she was with Mr. Hayes.

He looked toward the other side of the barge for a few moments. "Would you care to join me in watching the river?"

She hesitated a moment, but there was no denying she *did* desire to join him there, so she nodded. If Papa had a mind to arrange her marriage, who knew how much longer she would be able to enjoy the company of Mr. Hayes?

She assured Aunt Louisa she would be within eyesight, then took his arm, and he guided them to the side of the barge.

A lamp hung above their heads, reflecting on the water flowing past. They had strayed from the lights of Westminster in their journey toward Greenwich, and the number of windows lit by candlelight or lamplight on either side of the shore had diminished, giving the impression that they were gliding along through the inky night.

"Is your father angry with me, Miss Easton?"

Arabella glanced at him. "Because you were not there to be introduced to him?"

He nodded.

She rested her hands on the railing. "He found your absence...off-putting." She grimaced. "I fear there is little chance of his agreeing to let you invest with him."

Mr. Hayes nodded, a rueful smile on his face. "I surmised as much. I am sorry to have made a poor impression."

She was sorry for it too. More sorry than she could say. She wanted Papa to like Mr. Hayes, but that ship had sailed.

Mr. Hayes leaned forward, resting his elbows on the railing, and she regarded him as he stared out at the view silently.

He was a handsome man, and yet his appearance did not fully account for the way her heart reacted to him. It could not explain why her eyes sought him wherever she went, or why her mind drifted toward him at every opportunity.

She had met other handsome men since arriving in London, but none of them made her feel what she felt in Mr. Hayes's presence. If Papa had taken any of *them* in dislike, it would not have bothered her the way it did to know he was forever prejudiced against Mr. Hayes.

She had referred to what she felt for him as friendship, but as she watched him fiddle with the sleeve of his coat, she knew in her heart that friendship did not fully convey what she felt.

Even her lack of experience in Society could not persuade her to believe it was mere friendship which made her wonder what it might feel like to run her hands through his hair, to have his arms around her waist, or to have his lips pressed to hers.

Mr. Hayes might be her friend, but what she felt for him went far beyond that.

She was falling in love with him.

And when her eyes caught on the bracelet his fingers fidgeted with and the thoughtful expression he wore as he stared out at the water, she had to wonder if he felt a glimmer of the same thing for her.

15

SILAS

So, Drayton intended to marry off his daughter.

Of course he did. He might love her, but that did not mean he would not use her to his advantage. He had essentially hidden the existence of his children from the *ton*, but now that it suited him, he intended to make use of her. Everyone was a pawn to be used and disposed of according to his needs and whims. Why would his daughter be any different?

The thought of Drayton choosing some ill-tempered, wealthy, philandering lord for Miss Easton was enough to send Silas's temper into a frenzy. It was simply unbearable.

He glanced at her as she touched a finger to the petals of the flower nearest her hand.

She deserved the best.

Silas wasn't fool enough to think he himself fell into that category. Even had Drayton not been intent on sending him to the gallows, he would not have stood a chance with Miss Easton. He had neither title nor fortune, as they had established.

She caught him looking at her and smiled perplexedly. "When you look at me so somberly, I fear I have displeased you."

He stood straight and forced a smile. "Never. I was merely lost in thought."

"That makes two of us." Her eyes flitted to his mouth. "Have you grown more fond of your mustache?"

His hand went to it involuntarily. "I fear that is an unlikely development." It had become a reminder of the captivity in which he lived, but it was a necessary evil. With Drayton flitting in and out of Town, he needed to adapt and protect himself and his family as best he could. It was his fear of meeting Drayton that had decided him against coming this evening. Then he had learned from William that Drayton had left Town again, and he had hurried to catch the barge, knowing Miss Easton would be here.

"Your need for attention outweighs your dislike of it, then?" She was clearly both amused and bemused by his choices.

"Precisely."

"Which is also why you chose to make such a grand entrance this evening."

"You know me so well, Miss Easton."

Her bemusement grew, and she studied him. "I do not believe you. If attention was the driving factor, you would be over there." She indicated a group of people at the stern of the barge, laughing and drinking. Amongst them was the man with the wine and brandy glasses. They were by far the most raucous group on the barge.

"Or perhaps I am merely selective in where I seek that attention."

Her eyes met his, questioning him over a set of rosy cheeks. Frederick's comment about toying with a woman's emotions came to him, and he felt a stab of guilt. He was not toying with Miss Easton. His admiration and affection for her were genuine. But what difference did that make when he knew he could not have her?

More than anything, he hated lying to her. He had never appreciated just how precious the truth was until he was forbidden from telling it.

"If you truly wish to know," he said, "I lost a wager to Yorke, and I am now condemned to look like a fool until midsummer."

"Well," Miss Easton said with an arch look, "we will all look forward to midsummer, then."

Silas's mouth broke into a smile, and he ran his fingers along his mustache. "Both I and my mustache take offense, madam."

"You agreed to be my friend by helping me ward off unwanted suitors, Mr. Hayes. I am merely trying to ensure *you* do not unwittingly ward off *wanted* ones."

"Ah, but do I wish for a woman who would be scared off by something as trivial as a mustache?"

"There is nothing trivial about it." The way her eyes twinkled at him robbed her words of offense, and Silas marveled at how he could feel so much joy in her presence while feeling simultaneous despair that he could never be more than a friend to her.

Silas's mustache was the constant topic of conversation whenever he went to see William, which made him wonder why he ever bothered to visit. But William's and Frederick's responses to it were nothing compared to Aunt Eugenia's.

Silas approached her in the entry hall of William's townhouse, intending to give her his customary embrace, but she drew back and prevented him from coming any nearer with the cane she had recently adopted.

"Get thee hence!" she warned.

Silas tried to suppress his laughter, feigning ignorance despite knowing full well to what she had taken such violent exception. "What sort of response is this, Aunt? I thought I was your favorite nephew." He took a few steps closer, and she matched them with her own steps away.

"Perhaps you were until you allowed what I can only assume is a dead squirrel to take up residence on your face."

"I have been told it is rather dashing," he said.

"He has not," William said. "Both Freddie and I have informed him, in no uncertain terms, that it is repulsive."

"And a fire hazard," Frederick added.

Aunt Eugenia walked around Silas, eyeing the mustache as though it might leap from his face and attack her at any moment. "I thought you were trying to be inconspicuous."

Silas followed her toward the parlor but was obliged to increase the distance he kept, as she continued to look over her shoulder at him with misgiving.

"I suppose it does keep people from wanting to be near you," she added.

"Nothing could do that. Besides, I think it quite romantic. Some have compared me to Byron."

Aunt Eugenia barked with laughter. "Byron? I hope you do not mean to ape his ways. Debt, scandal, and disrepute."

"Surely not all because of his mustache, though," Silas argued.

"Let us leave the mustache behind," William said. "If not in reality, at least as a topic of conversation. Freddie tells me you are in a scrape."

Silas looked at Frederick, who shot William an annoyed look.

"My entire life is a scrape, as you well know," Silas said.

"What scrape is he in, Frederick?" Aunt Eugenia asked baldly. "Pockets to let?"

"He is in love with Drayton's daughter," William said, his gaze fixed on Silas.

Silas scoffed, but there was little force behind it.

"Not so different from Byron after all, then," Aunt Eugenia said. "Are you mad as well, Silas?"

"Firstly," Silas said, "I did not know she was Drayton's daughter. I assure you, if anyone had mentioned his name in connection with her, I would have run the other direction. But no one did—including you, Freddie."

"I had no idea," he said defensively. "I thought Drayton had no children. How was I to know? The man never attends Parliament, and I certainly have gone out of my way to avoid him—for obvious reasons. William is the one with connections in the Lords. If anyone knew, it should have been him."

"I am not in the habit of interrogating Drayton about his personal life. He is infamously private, not to mention he is rarely to be seen in Parliament. Evidently, his duties there bore him. I had no notion his surname was Easton."

"You see?" Silas said. "There was simply no way for me to know."

"And yet," Frederick said, "now that you *do* know, you have not only run in her direction, you jumped across the Thames to be on that barge with her."

"What?" Aunt Eugenia exclaimed.

"Freddie loves a bit of drama, Aunt," Silas said. "I was invited to a party on a barge. I was late and did not care to be left behind, so I hopped"—he fixed his gaze on Frederick for a moment—"onto a *very* slowly moving barge as it was departing."

Aunt Eugenia's mouth drew into a lopsided smile. "You certainly have pluck! I only wish you had enough of it to pluck that horrid creature off your lip."

"Miss Easton was on this lethargic vessel?" William asked.

"She was," Silas admitted.

"And did you speak with her?"

Frederick snorted. "Spent the entire night in her pocket."

Silas shot him a look. But annoyed as he might be with his brother's tale-telling, he could not be angry with him. He understood his family's fears, and beyond that, he knew his friendship with Miss Easton was dangerous. He simply couldn't help himself—or perhaps it was that he didn't wish to.

William's eyes had settled on Silas and never once left.

"What?" Silas asked.

"You are being careless," William responded calmly.

"Oh, come, William," Aunt Eugenia said. "You had *your* romantic scandal. Anthony had his. It is Silas's turn."

Silas regarded his aunt with curiosity. He had not expected her to throw her support behind him.

"Not that he stands a chance with *any* woman if he keeps that furry atrocity," she said. "As long as he can clear his name and his upper lip, why should he not be able to choose the bride he wishes for?"

"I shall welcome whatever bride Silas chooses," William said. "My concern is entirely for his safety. Have you made any headway, Silas?"

"I took Bence into my confidence," Silas said. "He sent me a note just this morning. He is exploring various avenues and hopes to have promising news for me soon—evidence to use against Drayton."

"Let us hope he is trustworthy," William said.

"Bence is steady as an oak," Frederick said.

"And yet, he did business with Drayton."

"Something he sincerely regrets," Silas said. "He has no love for Drayton, William."

William nodded. "Then let us hope that he finds something we can use. In the meantime, I beg you to keep your distance from Miss Easton, Silas."

Silas suppressed a sigh, but he could not counter the sense of William's request. Drayton would return to London, and the danger in seeking her company once that occurred would simply be too great to seriously consider.

16

ARABELLA

Arabella had noticed something odd: she had begun to measure time in the number of days since she had last seen Mr. Hayes.

The count was currently four. Four long, interminable days. At Wetley, Arabella had become accustomed to spending weeks without anything of note taking place beyond a severe rainstorm or one of her sisters falling in the fish pond. This had never bothered her then.

Yet, here in London—the place she had dreamed of seeing for years—she found herself making visits to notable members of the *ton* and attending evening parties, then returning home at night feeling a sense of emptiness for no other reason than that she had not seen Mr. Hayes.

Her one consolation, if consolation it was, was that he had made an appearance in her dreams more than once.

On the first night since the barge cruise that they had not attended an evening engagement, Arabella sat down to dine at home with Felicity and Aunt Louisa. When the front door opened before they had even begun to eat, she cocked an ear, hoping to hear Mr. Fairchild's voice—and preferably Mr. Hayes's as well.

But it was Papa who said to one of the servants, "Set two more places at the table."

Aunt Louisa, who had been quite relaxed before, sat up straighter in her seat at the sound, while Arabella and Felicity exchanged curious looks.

Who was the second seat for?

They were not obliged to wait long to find out, for the door opened moments later, and Papa walked in, followed by a stranger.

The man was of average height and build, with hair of a reddish hue, except at his temples, where it had begun to gray. His eyes, an unexceptional shade of brown, flicked from Aunt Louisa to Arabella, then to Felicity, where they lingered for a moment.

He smiled slightly, and Arabella looked at her cousin to see whether she recognized him.

As she met his eye, however, Felicity wore an expression so distinctly unapproachable and unrecognizing that Arabella was hard-pressed not to laugh.

Papa came over to Arabella directly and kissed her on the top of her head, just as he always did after returning from a journey. "Good evening, my dear. I wish to introduce you—all of you—to Lord Farnham, who will be joining us for dinner."

It took Lord Farnham a moment to respond to this, for he seemed to be occupied with the realization that Arabella rather than Felicity was meant to be the subject of his interest.

He cleared his throat and smiled at Arabella, then approached her and put out his gloved hand in expectation. Her own hand was bare from having removed her gloves for dinner.

She glanced at Papa, then offered her hand to Lord Farnham.

He bowed over it, then placed a kiss upon the back. It was long and elicited a small shudder from Arabella, for it was— there was simply no other way to describe it—wet.

He released her hand and stood to his full height, and she suppressed the urge to wipe the back of her hand on her skirts. The moment she had taken her seat, however, she subtly removed the evidence of his greeting.

A footman set places for Papa and Lord Farnham, and Papa sat beside Felicity, while Lord Farnham took the place on Arabella's right.

Felicity caught Arabella's gaze from across the table, her own widening significantly.

"How was the journey from Barrington?" Arabella asked politely as Lord Farnham served her three heaping spoonfuls of peas, a food she did not at all care for.

"Happily without incident," Papa said.

"How fortunate," Arabella said with a smile. "And where do you reside, Lord Farnham?"

"Just outside of Manchester," he said.

"Ah," Arabella said politely, her mind returning to her own visit there and how much she had disliked it.

Lord Farnham was not put off by her lackluster response, however, and proceeded to speak about his estate and its convenient placement near Manchester for the next five minutes, with neither prompting nor interruption.

Arabella did her best to seem interested, but she found her mind wandering into more appealing avenues. Most of those avenues featured Mr. Hayes, she noticed.

Lord Farnham eventually finished his monologue, but he seemed to have taken all the words, as no one could find anything to respond beyond a polite "How nice" from Arabella and "It sounds lovely" from Aunt Louisa.

The silverware clanked loudly as the silence stretched on. Arabella nudged Felicity's foot with hers, hoping her cousin would shoulder a bit of the conversational burden.

Felicity shot her an unwilling look, but Arabella held her gaze speakingly.

Felicity sighed softly, surrendering to her cousin's distress signal. "Bella has plans to design the display window in her father's shop window in Burlington Arcade," she said brightly.

Lord Farnham had a spoonful of food halfway to his mouth, but it stopped, and his eyes flitted to Arabella beside him. He lowered the spoon. "Design a display?" he said, as though the concept was entirely foreign. Given how boring was his manner of dress, she was not surprised.

Arabella looked at Felicity for a moment to subtly manifest her displeasure with the choice of conversation, then responded to Lord Farnham. "I enjoy fashion very much and have been hoping to try my hand at something new."

Lord Farnham frowned. "Is that not the task of a shop-keeper or his assistant?"

Papa laughed, though there was a forced quality to it as he patted Felicity's hand. "My niece is getting a bit ahead of things. Arabella and I have discussed the display, but nothing is set in stone yet." His gaze flitted to her, and the way his eyes held hers told her this was not a topic he wished to pursue at the moment.

"Speaking of displays," Aunt Louisa said, "have either of you seen the one at The Royal Academy of Arts?"

The conversation turned, and soon Lord Farnham was speaking of a particular sculpture at the Academy.

Arabella listened with interest, for she enjoyed sculptures, but Lord Farnham somehow called that interest into question with the impressive length at which he spoke on the subject.

He was intelligent and well-spoken, and there was nothing unkind about him, and yet Arabella's mind took her to the evening she had spent at this same table with Mr. Hayes. She could have sat beside him for hours without tiring. Perhaps even more importantly, they could have sat in silence without the oppressive awkwardness that reigned when Lord Farnham's soliloquy expended itself.

Lord Farnham stayed for three days. Each morning in the breakfast room and each evening at dinner, he insisted upon kissing Arabella's hand in the same manner he had done upon their first meeting.

She took to keeping her gloves on at mealtimes.

"It is still wet," she said, showing the damp spot on the back of her glove to Felicity as they entered the drawing room while Papa and Lord Farnham had their port.

Aunt Louisa had retired for the evening with a headache—something she had become alarmingly prone to since Lord Farnham's arrival. She could not abide his long speeches.

Felicity regarded the spot with distaste. "You cannot mean to marry that man, Bella."

Arabella sighed as she took her seat. "Once he has left in the morning, I will speak with Papa and tell him how I feel."

Felicity did not look convinced that this would accomplish anything. "If you dislike Farnham kissing your gloved hand, can you fathom how it would be to be kissed by him—and only him—on the lips?" She gave a shudder.

Arabella suppressed one herself. "The prospect of sharing

such an experience with Lord Farnham is certainly not appealing."

"An understatement of immense proportions! If you must marry Farnham, at the very least you should experience a proper kiss. I cannot stomach the thought of you living the rest of your life without knowing what it should be like."

Arabella gave an incredulous laugh. "What exactly do you propose?"

"A kiss, of course," Felicity said impatiently. "Would you not like to kiss Mr. Hayes?"

Arabella stood abruptly, her cheeks burning, for just last night, she had dreamed of precisely that.

"Of course you would," Felicity said, rising to her feet. "And there is no question in my mind that he would very much like to oblige."

"Felicity," Arabella said censoriously, "you cannot be serious."

"I have never been more so! Surely you do not mean to pretend you have no feelings for him, Bella." Felicity stared at her challengingly.

"I...I do regard him highly," Arabella admitted, shuffling through music at the piano to occupy herself.

"Yet another understatement of immense proportions. I have seen you together enough to know that you have likely imagined kissing him at least a handful of times. Do not turn away, Bella. There is nothing to be ashamed of. I would be concerned if you had *not* imagined it."

Arabella reluctantly faced her cousin again, well aware that her face was as red as the beet soup they had eaten for dinner.

"Am I correct in my assumption?" Felicity pressed.

Arabella hesitated. "Perhaps..."

Felicity grinned, gripping her by the arms. "Then kiss him,

Bella! No one should have to marry without experiencing the joy of kissing a man who makes her heart flutter."

Arabella's heart was certainly doing that.

Felicity began to pace, a thoughtful hand at her lips. "You and Mr. Hayes will need the right opportunity, of course... plenty of time alone to—"

"Felicity," Arabella interrupted, her heart pattering at the picture her cousin was painting. "You speak as though my marriage to Lord Farnham is a foregone conclusion, but it is not. I will speak with Papa tomorrow, and then there will be no need for such plans or stratagems."

But as Papa and Lord Farnham joined them ten minutes later, kissing Mr. Hayes was all she could think about.

Lord Farnham departed late the next morning, leaving behind him a final—Arabella prayed—damp spot on her kid gloves.

She, Felicity, and Aunt Louisa were set to take a walk in the Park, but Arabella was too impatient to wait to speak with Papa until after, so she asked them to grant her ten minutes.

He was in the study, poring over a sheaf of papers, but when he heard her enter, he shuffled them together and set them in the drawer.

"Ah," he said, "I was hoping to speak with you."

"And I you," she said, feeling suddenly nervous.

"Have a seat, then," he said, nodding at the chair across from the desk.

She sat and clasped her hands in her lap, trying to gather her courage. It had felt much easier to express her sentiments when she had been speaking with Felicity yesterday.

"I think that went quite well," Papa said. "Farnham seems

very taken with you, my dear. Not that it is any surprise." He regarded her with a smile.

She looked down at her hands, glancing at the fading spot. It was enough to give her the needed resolve. "Papa, shall you be very disappointed if I do not wish to marry him?"

Silence met this question, and she brought her gaze up.

His brow was knit, his expression intent. "Why would you not wish for that? Farnham is an earl, Arabella, from an established family with considerable wealth. He could care for you in the way you deserve—in the way to which you are accustomed. What have you against him?"

"I have nothing against him," she said. "It is merely that I do not think..." She paused, trying to choose her words carefully. "I simply do not think we suit."

Papa's brows snapped together. "Suit? Of course you suit. What would possess you to say such a thing?"

"He is perfectly respectable, of course, and I am certain he will make some young woman very happy, but I do not think I am that young woman. We share no common interests."

"Arabella," Papa said with a hint of impatience, "you cannot comprehend the lengths to which I have gone for your happiness. For years, I have sacrificed and saved, putting my own interests aside for the sake of ensuring your education and your marriage portion so that I could be certain you would be properly cared for when the time came for you to marry."

She sat on the edge of her seat, eager to reassure him. "I quite understand that, and I am eternally grateful for it. Please do not think otherwise."

His deep frown lingered. "How can I not think otherwise when I provide you with the perfect match and you hesitate because of...what? A fear you do not share common interests with the gentleman I selected with utmost care and concern?

Do you expect that there are a bevy of earls and viscounts with a burning interest in dinner gowns and taffeta? Or that, if there were, they would be unmarried, with estates not leveraged to the hilt?"

"Of course not."

"Then please explain to me, Arabella: what interests do you expect to share with your husband?"

She met his gaze and swallowed. How could she possibly explain to him that it was not any particular defect in Lord Farnham that made the thought of marriage so distasteful to her? He might have had an obsession with fabrics or have known every issue of *La Belle Assemblée*, and she would not have wished to marry him.

Now that she knew what it was to converse so easily and happily with a gentleman, to search every crowd for his face, to see him when her eyes were closed as easily as she did when they were open...she did not know how to wish for anything less in the man she married.

Papa awaited a response, but she had none to give. She could not bring herself to tell him that, after everything he had done for her, the only person she could fathom marrying was the untitled man who had not even been able to bring himself to meet Papa.

"Arabella, you are young. It is natural for you to feel nervous at the prospect of marriage, but surely you understand that I want the best for you? I have decades of experience beyond yours. You must trust that I know what is right for you. Everything I do, I do for you."

Her stomach swam with guilt and dread, but she nodded.

"I trust this hesitation is not the doing of your cousin," he said with a hint of severity. "Felicity seems to harbor a great many romantic ideals. Do not make the mistake of prioritizing a hope of some silly infatuation over the things that truly matter in a marriage. Infatuation will inevitably run its course, and it so often turns to dislike."

Arabella still said nothing, for she was torn. Papa was right. She did not have experience. The entire world of friendship and courting was new to her. Perhaps her life *would* be most agreeable with Lord Farnham. Perhaps what she felt for Mr. Hayes was only infatuation.

And yet, could she ever grow to dislike him? It seemed impossible.

"Might I have time to...consider things?" she asked.

Papa's lips pursed. "What is there to consider? Do you not trust me?"

"I do," she hurried to say.

But did she? If she truly trusted him, would she not have let him guide her?

"Opportunities like a match with Lord Farnham do not come along often, Arabella. He is eager to move forward, and so am I. It will not do to make him wait."

Arabella's heart began to thud, and a sense of panic filtered through her. It seemed he meant for her to become engaged to Lord Farnham soon. "I simply feel...unready. It has all happened so fast."

Papa sighed, regarding her with concern. "It has certainly happened more quickly than I had anticipated. There is nothing to be done about that, however. I promised Farnham we would speak on the matter before he returns to Manchester. I would hate for us to be saddled with a lifetime of regret if he slipped through our hands."

Arabella's stomach swam. For her part, she was more concerned she would be saddled with regret if he did *not* slip through their hands.

Papa grimaced sympathetically. "Take a few days, my dear. I shall put him off."

A sigh of relief burst from her, and she laughed shakily. "Thank you, Papa."

He winked at her. "Anything for my Arabella."

There was a knock on the door, and Felicity's voice came through muffled. "Bella? Are you joining us?"

"Yes," she replied. "I am coming now." She looked at Papa. "We are going for a walk in the Park."

"The fresh air will do you good."

It certainly felt like liberty to inhale the fresh air at the Park, but she suspected part of that was due to the simple fact that Lord Farnham was gone.

The weight of the future hung over her like dark clouds in the distance, however. It felt as though her days were numbered—a melodramatic thought, perhaps, but she could not help how she felt.

Neither could she help looking for any sign of Mr. Hayes in the Park as they walked the varied paths.

She felt a sense of urgency about seeing him that she could not explain.

Why had he been absent at every recent party? She had been certain she would see him at one, at least.

There are things in my life that I cannot divulge to anyone, much as I may wish to. Things that put me and those around me in danger.

That was the explanation he had given her for why he had not stayed to meet Papa. Was it also why he had not made any appearances recently, despite Mr. Yorke, Mr. Fairchild, and Mr. Drake doing so?

What if she did not see him before she became engaged to Lord Farnham?

She grasped Felicity's hand.

Her cousin looked at her with confusion as they stood at

the edge of a pond, watching the ducks bathe themselves. "What is it?"

"Last night, you spoke of arranging...things for Mr. Hayes and me. Did you truly mean it?"

Felicity's eyes widened, then lit with sudden energy. "Every word. You may safely leave it to me."

17
SILAS

Silas had looked forward to his time in London with immense anticipation after being cooped up so long in his brother's hunting lodge, and yet he could not remember spending a more interminable week in his life than the past seven days.

The one thing those days had in common: he had not seen Miss Easton.

Bence had sent him word just once, and his message had been two-fold: he had an investment opportunity for Silas, and he was waiting for a final piece of information about a promising avenue to clear Silas's name.

Meanwhile, Silas had kept his promise to his brother to avoid Miss Easton and her father, but it was even more trying than he had anticipated. His desire to see Miss Easton did not abate, and yet, with each passing day, it became more apparent to him that he had been acting imprudently by seeking her company—even before he had known who her father was.

With a name beleaguered by scandal and a future over

which the gallows hung threateningly, he had nothing at all to offer.

Apart from not having seen Miss Easton for a week, Silas had been cooped up in the townhouse while Frederick and the others made merry and attended a number of events with the *ton*. It was simply too dangerous for Silas to tempt fate by joining them when Lord Drayton might be in attendance.

When he had been tempted to take that chance despite the risk to his life, he had been obliged to take drastic measures to prevent himself: he had shaven his mustache.

Kicking his heels inside a townhouse in London was a different sort of torture than being obliged to remain cooped up in a hunting lodge. At the hunting lodge, at least there was little to do. In London, there were any number of delights beyond the shut front door of the townhouse.

And yet, Miss Easton was the delight he most missed and wished for. What he wouldn't give to be transported back to Vauxhall or to spend another hour on the barge at her side.

It was a selfish wish.

Besides, who was to say that she was not already engaged to the man Drayton had chosen for her?

The thought was unbearable.

Instead of dwelling on impossible dreams and unpleasant possibilities, Silas took to playing the game he had come up with while shut away in the lodge: tossing crumpled bits of parchment into an empty brandy glass ten feet away.

It was far less amusing without his brothers playing too.

There was a knock on the door, and Silas tossed the last paper, which landed neatly in the cup.

He smiled in spite of himself. He might be a hermit with no friends and no future, but at least his aim was true.

"A message for you, sir," said the footman, a small letter in his hand.

Silas took it and thanked him, looking at the script on the front. It was the script of a woman, but it was not one he recognized. Could it be...?

He broke the wafer and unfurled the letter, his eyes darting to the signature on the bottom: Miss Fairchild.

His brows pulled together, and he read the short missive.

Dear Mr. Hayes,

I hope this message finds you well. I pray you will forgive the irregularity of it. Necessity required me to tiptoe past the bounds of what many would consider proper. I do it out of love and concern for my cousin.

Silas's heart skipped.

I beg you will find a way to be present at the orangery at Kew Gardens at noon tomorrow. Miss Easton has urgent need to speak with you.

I know we may rely upon you.

Miss Fairchild

Silas stared at the words, reading the few that had jumped off the page: *Miss Easton has urgent need to speak with you.*

He hardly knew how to feel upon reading that. Happy? Anxious?

When taken in combination with what had come before —*I do it out of love and concern for my cousin*—it made the matter seem ominous indeed. Was Miss Easton in trouble? And why did Miss Fairchild say it was urgent but then not request his presence until the next day—and at Kew, of all places? Surely, if it was truly urgent, it could not have waited until then.

No doubt Silas should send Frederick in his stead. Miss Easton could have no issue that required Silas specifically, and it would be unwise of him to go. The danger was that Lord Drayton might be at Kew along with her.

And yet, Silas *would* go. If Miss Easton needed him, he would do far more than leap onto a moving barge on the Thames to reach her.

He would have to take care not to be seen by Drayton. He would discover what Miss Easton needed, and then...he would try to help her understand that their friendship could not continue as it had been.

Heaven grant him the strength to utter those words, for no other power could.

"Freddie, I have hardly left this house for the past week. I made no complaint when I was left behind while you went to the prizefight nor when you attended Lord Rarington's party. You cannot begrudge me a stroll amongst the plants. What precisely do you fear? That I shall be recognized by one of the ferns?"

Frederick's unamused expression made clear what he thought of his brother's jab. "Since when have you cared to promenade amongst flowers?"

"Flowers?" Fairchild repeated, coming through the door just then.

"Hayes insists he is going to Kew Gardens today," Frederick said.

"Are you?" Fairchild asked Silas with only the faintest interest. He poured himself a drink from the liquor cabinet.

"You may see my aunt there. Or perhaps not. Kew is enormous."

Silas avoided his brother's eye, but Frederick was not to be avoided.

"I have a sudden desire to join you," Frederick said, his voice lifeless as he continued to stare at Silas.

"Do you?" Fairchild's brows rose, then pulled together thoughtfully. "Perhaps I shall join as well. A bit of fresh air would be welcome."

Silas opened his mouth to remind them both that he needed no chaperone only to close it again. Frederick could be stubborn as an ox at times, and the expression on his face made it clear that this was one of those times.

When the carriage reached the gates of Kew, Silas was the first to descend. He was followed by not only Frederick and Fairchild but Drake as well.

He sighed as the three of them gathered around him like chicks around a hen. As Kew had been his idea—or so they thought—they seemed to think him the leader. Frederick knew, of course, that Silas had never been to Kew, but when Silas pointed this out, he merely said, "All the more reason for you to guide us. You will help us to see it with fresh eyes."

But Silas had eyes only for the orangery. He had an inkling that Miss Fairchild had not intended for him to bring an entire entourage there, but what could be done?

He did his best to seem admiring of the gardens he had insisted he was so anxious to visit. In their defense, they were hardly to be sniffed at. Row upon row of flowering and leafy plants surrounded them as they traversed the paths. He had no idea such a variety even existed in the world, much less in a garden in England.

But amidst all the admiring of plants, his eyes darted around, looking for any sign of Drayton or Miss Easton.

"Is it everything you had hoped it would be?" Frederick asked after a quarter of an hour.

"Oh, quite," Silas said, stopping to inspect a cabbage rose. "I thought to see citrus fruits, however. I have always wished to see a grove of orange trees."

"Have you?" Frederick said with feigned curiosity and a sidelong glance.

"Anyone who has tasted an orange must surely share my same ambition."

"Even if there *is* a grove of orange trees, you would not be permitted to partake of the fruit. Or are you merely here to lust after something forbidden?"

Silas met his brother's gaze with reluctant appreciation at the subtle but pointed hidden meaning. "No doubt your constant and saintly presence will sustain me through my temptation."

Fairchild was looking at them as though he was beginning to worry for their sanity. "The orangery is this way, Hayes." He nodded at the path on their right, then started upon it.

"I have my eye on you," Frederick said in a low voice.

"And what of your other eye?" Silas asked. "Is it occupied persecuting someone else?"

"Not persecuting," he said as they followed Fairchild. "Protecting."

Silas brushed a flower with his knuckle as they passed it. "I am not a delicate blossom, Freddie. I can protect myself."

He jolted to a stop at the sight of a man ahead, but just as he was about to dart between the nearest bushes, the man's profile became visible, making clear it was not Drayton.

"What is it?" Frederick asked.

"Nothing," Silas replied, trying to slow his heart.

They reached the orangery shortly, and Silas's shoulders tightened as he surveyed the area. There was no sign of Drayton, only Mrs. Fairchild and her daughter hovering over something out of view.

"Ah," Frederick said, "what a surprise to see you all here—and at the orangery, of all places." He quirked a brow at Silas.

"Indeed," Silas said, noting the conspicuous absence of Miss Easton with a jolt of concern. A quick glance around told him that she was nowhere in the vicinity.

"Felicity has been stung," Mrs. Fairchild said.

"Stung?" Frederick repeated in alarm.

The gentlemen crowded around Miss Fairchild, and a debate soon broke out about what should be done to assist her.

"Go inside," Miss Fairchild whispered urgently to Silas as the others argued the seriousness and proper treatment of a bee sting.

Silas swallowed a dozen questions, and with a glance at Frederick, he slipped around the hedge toward the door to the orangery.

It was warmer inside and the scent sweet as he faced the walkway that ran through rows of citrus trees. He had lied to Frederick when he had said he had an ambition to see orange trees, but perhaps it was an ambition he *should* have had. The entire building was filled with plants not much taller than him, their deep green leaves full, punctuated by little pops of yellow, vibrant green, and orange.

He strained his ears for any sound—of Miss Easton, of course, but also of any other potential citrus enthusiasts. It would not do for the two of them to be seen alone together. It was quiet within, however, so he began to walk, glancing to the right and left each time he reached one of the smaller paths that intersected the main one.

The branches of one row intermingled with the adjacent ones, making it difficult to see but also unlikely that there was anyone *to* see. There was little space for a person unless they were keen to pick their way through branch after branch.

He was beginning to wonder whether he had been mistaken about what Miss Fairchild had said when he caught sight of something in one of the rows—a spot of blue. His gaze dropped to the ground, where there was less foliage obscuring his view. Blue skirts and a pair of half-boots paced the few feet available to them.

Silas's heart leapt into motion, and he threaded his way through the leafy branches until Miss Easton appeared, her hands clasped and her eyes wide as she looked at him.

"You came." There was patent relief in her voice as she came toward him.

He met her and gathered up her hands in his. "Of course I did. What is the matter? Are you well?"

"Yes." She looked up at him in a way that made his body glow with warmth. "But I wished to speak with you."

He nodded, delighting in the feel of her hands in his and having her so near. The past week had felt like an eternity without her, but that was nothing now that she was here with him. "What is it? Your cousin said it was urgent."

She let out an exasperated breath. "I assure you, I had no notion that Felicity intended to send you such a message. She told me nothing of her plans until a few minutes ago."

Silas lowered their hands, searching her face. "I do not understand."

"I told Felicity I wished to speak with you," she explained, "and she assured me she would arrange it, but I did not mean for her to go about it in such a way."

Silas did not respond, but he slowly released her hands. Miss Easton was *not* in trouble. There was nothing urgent which she required of him—indeed, she had evidently not even known he would be here until minutes ago.

Her brow knit, and she looked at him questioningly. "Are you upset?"

He shook his head quickly. "It is only..." His head whipped around at a sound somewhere in the vicinity. A door opened, then shut, then there was silence. "Is your father here?"

"No," she said, looking more confused than ever. "Why?"

"I should not be here." He had been a fool to come in the first place. He had let his selfish wishes overtake his reason. Who did he think he was kidding, coming to help Miss Easton? He could do nothing but bring her harm. "Neither should you be. Not with me."

"What do you mean?"

He did not meet her gaze, nor did he respond. What could he say to make her understand?

She stepped toward him determinedly. "What if I *want* to be here with you?"

He met her clear, stubborn gaze, and his heart twinged with want. "You should not want that."

She said nothing, her eyes searching his as they stood in silence, their faces but a foot apart until she finally broke her gaze away and looked down.

He shut his eyes in consternation, wishing she would look at him again and divine the truth herself so that he did not have to choose between telling it to her or keeping it from her.

Warm fingers wrapped around his hand, and he went still.

Her fingers glided along his fingers, then across his palm, leaving a trickle of chills behind, until they finally reached his wrist. She toyed with the bracelet, the tips of her fingers brushing against his skin as they did so.

She looked up at him. "I would like to claim my bracelet."

He grimaced. He had considered removing it every day since the last time he had seen her. He *should* have removed it, but he had not been able to persuade himself to. It had been his only link to her for the past week.

He shook his head.

"Did you not say I could have it when I wished?"

"I did," he admitted. "But I should not have."

"Why did you say it, then?"

She had so many questions—and rightly so—and the frustration at his inability to give her answers burst from him in a breathy, wry laugh. "Heaven only knows! When I am with you, I do a great many things I should not." His gaze fixed on hers. "And yet far fewer than I wish to."

Her eyes locked on his, her fingers going still on the bracelet. "What sort of things?"

There was silence as a dozen images flashed across his mind: tucking a stray lock of hair behind her ear, leading her by the hand through the gardens at Rushlake Hall, teasing her without restraint.

And then more dangerous things: his hand slipping around her waist, her body pressing against his, his lips covering hers...

He shook his head, trying to ignore the growing want such thoughts elicited.

She regarded him for a moment, a hint of pleading and frustration in her eyes.

When neither of them broke the silence, she brought her other hand to join the one at his wrist and began to undo the clasp.

"Arabella," he said, trying to gently pull his wrist away.

She stopped him and undid the clasp.

The bracelet fell from his wrist. Her eyes, intent and focused, locked on his, their blue piercing him to the center. "Papa has chosen a suitor. He means for me to become engaged."

Silas's stomach plunged.

"Soon." There was a note of blame in her voice, as though he could prevent this if only he had the nerve.

But it was not nerve he lacked. He would have spirited her away without a thought for anything else if he hadn't known that doing so would be the height of selfishness and dishonor. How could he make promises to her when she had no notion who he truly was—or his true name?

He wanted more than anything to tell her that now—to make her see that there was not a gentleman in England less fit than he to be the recipient of her precious affection.

When his silence continued, she swallowed, her brows knit with incomprehension and pain. She took a step back, and a blush rose from her neck and into her cheeks. "You know, I began to think you had been avoiding me this week. I convinced myself I was wrong. I *hoped* I was wrong."

His heart panged, but he said nothing, for the moment he opened his mouth, the truth would burst forth like evils from Pandora's box.

She took another step back, the bracelet clutched in her hand. "I had thought you..." She swallowed. "Never mind what I thought or hoped or convinced myself of. I can see I was mistaken." She turned away, but Silas caught her arm.

She did not struggle against him, but neither did she turn toward him.

"You *are* mistaken in me," he said quietly. "But not in the way you think."

She remained with her back to him for a moment.

"Arabella," he pleaded. "I am trying to protect you."

"Protect me from what?" She whirled toward him, her eyes wide and glimmering with tears.

"From *me*."

Her brows knit. "You said I was not in any danger from you."

"You are not. And I am trying to ensure it continues that way."

"Why will you not explain what you mean?"

He pressed his lips together, struggling with how to respond. "I cannot. I swear to you I want to do so more than anything! It is torture for me to keep the truth from you, and yet..."

"To keep the truth from me," she repeated. "Has everything been a lie?"

"Of course not," he responded. "My feelings for you are true, Arabella. But both you and I know that nothing can come of them. You said as much yourself. Your father has particular requirements of the man you will marry. I assure you, he would not choose me, for reasons both known and unknown to you. The specifics of those reasons matter not. Suffice it to say this: you would not want me if you knew the truth."

She shook her head, her chest rising and falling steadily as he stared at her, stupefied by her beauty and aching at the unfathomable knowledge that she wanted him. Fate's cruelty knew no bounds.

"I am sorry," he whispered.

She continued to stare at him, the only evidence she had heard him a small quiver of her bottom lip.

"Will you kiss me?"

His vision flickered. "What?"

"Will you kiss me?"

He could only stare at her, at a loss for both breath and words.

Her gaze was clear and intent. Stubborn, even.

"Arabella," he pleaded. "I cannot. I *should* not." And yet in his mind, his lips were already on hers.

"The night we met," she said, "you told me you would not kiss me unless I begged you to."

His heart thundered against his ribs like a battering ram, sending cracks through his resolve with each beat. "I remember."

She stepped toward him, lifting her chin to meet his gaze. "I am begging you to kiss me."

His determination splintered down the center.

"If I am indeed to marry, and if it cannot be you, I would like to know—just once—what it is like to be kissed by the man I love."

A thousand pieces of resolve crumbled onto the floor of the orangery, and desire burst through.

Silas stepped toward her and put a hand to her cheek. The other slipped around her waist, just as his mind had pictured minutes ago. But his vision had not prepared him for the feel of her body against his fingertips or the way she yielded so willingly to his touch.

He stared at her, hungrily taking in every detail. If he could only ever kiss Arabella Easton once, he would savor every moment.

She watched him, her eyes full of wonder and patience, as though she, too, wished to savor things.

But a man could only look at Arabella Easton for so long, surrounded by her sweet scent, his thumb stroking her impossibly soft cheek, before his lips begged for hers.

The moment she closed her eyes, he let his lips stray where they wanted, pressing softly against hers, as velvety soft as the petals of the roses.

And yet, not amongst all the flowers and exotic plants in

the gardens of Kew could one find a treasure like the one whose body gave a little shiver as he deepened the kiss, whose hands grasped the lapels of his coat and pulled him closer—as though he could even consider going anywhere else.

She may have begged him to initiate the kiss, but the depth of it required no urging. He would stay here in this precise place, holding her and showing her the way he longed for her —longed for a life with her—until time itself was extinguished.

His heart was hers, trapped inside his body and pounding against his ribs, beating toward her in a desperate attempt to reach the woman who possessed it. It beat with such force that it was not until the footsteps were upon them that Silas heard the rustling nearby and broke his lips from hers.

Frederick emerged through the branches and stopped short, staring at them in astonishment.

18

ARABELLA

Arabella had to blink a handful of times before she could fathom what her eyes were seeing.

But they were not deceiving her. Mr. Yorke was truly there.

Her heart and body were even slower to settle as she released the lapels of Mr. Hayes's tailcoat, one hand still clasping the bracelet, and he dropped his hands to his sides.

Mr. Yorke's lips pressed into a thin line. When he spoke, his voice was tight. "We must go, Hayes."

"Go where?" Mr. Hayes responded.

"Urgent business."

"What sort of—"

"Now," Mr. Yorke cut in unceremoniously.

There was a moment of silence as the men seemed to battle with their eyes.

"Miss Easton, your aunt is wondering where you are," Mr. Yorke said, the chastisement in his voice only marginally less evident than when he had spoken to his friend.

Arabella nodded, the heat the kiss had brought to her body filtering up to her cheeks. "Of course. I shall go to her."

Mr. Yorke held back the nearest branches for her in unapologetic expectation for her to leave.

Arabella glanced at Mr. Hayes, whose eyes were full of helpless apology.

There was so much more to say—so many questions to be asked—and yet none of it could happen in the presence of Mr. Yorke, so she held Mr. Hayes's gaze another moment, then walked through the branches and onto the main path, her heart still thumping against her chest.

What would Mr. Yorke do?

Would she and Mr. Hayes be forced to marry to avoid scandal?

The thought was far less unappealing than it should have been. She would have given anything to marry Mr. Hayes, and yet having him forced into it was far from what she wanted.

The thought of Papa learning of her indiscretion was enough to snuff out any remaining desire for such a train of events. It was not only that she would lose the opportunity to design the window display—she would happily sacrifice that for Mr. Hayes—but the disappointment and embarrassment it would cause him.

Aunt Louisa and Felicity were standing with Mr. Drake and Mr. Fairchild a dozen feet from the door of the orangery.

Aunt Louisa whipped around at the sound of the door, and her hand flew to her chest. "Thank heaven!" She hurried over and pulled Arabella to her bosom. "How *do* you manage to become lost in every garden we frequent, my dear child?" She pulled back and set her hands on Arabella's arms to look at her properly. "You are not hurt, are you?"

"No, no. I..." She glanced at Felicity, whose gaze was fixed on her, mad with curiosity. She nodded subtly, prompting

Arabella to go on. "I...thought I saw one of you go into the orangery, so I followed."

Aunt Louisa released her and smiled. "Bless you, dear! We have barely moved an inch from where Felicity was stung."

Arabella's gaze flicked to her cousin.

When they had reached the orangery, Felicity had claimed to have been stung by a bee. The scream she had let out had been deafening, not to mention the way she had waved her arms about yelling, "They are chasing me!"

Amidst the chaos of Aunt Louisa trying to fend off the supposed attackers, Felicity had hissed to Arabella to go wait for Mr. Hayes inside.

Arabella had been certain she had invented the entire story, but evidently, she had been wrong. There was no mistaking the raised white bump on her finger or the little prick at its center.

"We had better go home," Aunt Louisa said. "I would like to see a poultice put on her finger as soon as can be managed. We must pray the wound does not become more inflamed on the journey home. Come, my pet." She wrapped her arm around Felicity's shoulders and guided her away, assisted by her nephew and Mr. Drake.

Arabella glanced back at the orangery longingly and clasped the bracelet in her hand, but there was nothing for it. She had to follow her aunt.

That did not prevent her mind from reliving the glorious moments amongst the orange and lemon trees as they made their way to the carriage.

There was no chance for discussion in the carriage. Papa had returned by the time they arrived at the townhouse to dine, and Aunt Louisa was with them in the drawing room after dinner, her headaches having mysteriously ceased after Lord Farnham's departure. It was not until Arabella had dressed for bed that her door opened, and Felicity crept in.

She wore her dressing gown, and her forefinger had been wrapped in a white strip of cloth.

"Oh dear," Arabella said, striding over and taking her cousin's hand for inspection. "I had thought the bee sting was only a pretense."

Felicity merely laughed. "I considered pretending, of course, but if I wanted the diversion to last long enough, naturally, I had to provide evidence of a sting."

"How did you do it?" Arabella said, torn between wonder and horror.

Felicity shrugged as though it was the most natural thing in the world to plan to be stung by a bee. "It was easy enough. There were a number of bees on that hideous bat flower, so I caught one in my hand and shook it."

Arabella cringed. "Was it not painful?"

"Agony," Felicity said, though she was smiling. "Please tell me my sacrifice was not in vain. Were you able to...speak with him?"

The way she said the word *speak* made it clear she was talking about something far different from speaking.

The thought of the kiss sent a bloom of warmth through Arabella for the hundredth time that day. "I was."

Felicity did her best to suppress a squeal and pulled Arabella to the bed. "Tell me everything."

Arabella hesitated. Without Felicity, there would have been no kiss, and yet she was reluctant to attempt to describe just what had happened. There *was* no way to do so, and even if there had been, it felt...wrong.

The kiss was something she and Mr. Hayes had shared, and

she wanted to keep it that way. Their secret—and Mr. Yorke's, apparently.

Felicity regarded her curiously. "You do not *wish* to tell me." She smiled. "I should force you to, you know, for I went to no small trouble to ensure it was possible."

"Your poor finger." Arabella cradled it again.

"That is not the only trouble."

Arabella's head whipped up. "It is not?"

Felicity's eyes twinkled with amusement. "Did you truly think the orangery would be empty enough for a clandestine meeting?"

Arabella stared, remembering how she and Mr. Hayes had not heard so much as a footstep, apart from the door once opening and then closing immediately after.

"You kept people out?" Arabella asked.

Her cousin nodded, pleased as punch. "I warned everyone on their way in that there was a swarm of angry bees in the vicinity."

A little snort of laughter escaped Arabella and she covered her mouth, but soon, the two of them were laughing together, clutching their stomachs as their cheeks ached.

When the laughter had expended itself, Arabella sighed and let herself drop back onto her pillow. Felicity followed, letting her head press against Arabella's as they stared up at the bed hangings.

"What do I do, Felicity?"

"Dream of Mr. Hayes, I imagine."

Arabella smiled. She would welcome him in her dreams. But she wanted more than dreams of him. "I fear today was a grave mistake."

"A great deal happened today, Bella. You must be more specific. What was a grave mistake?"

Arabella's eyes fixed on the yellow silk above, but her mind was at Kew. "Kissing Mr. Hayes."

Felicity went up onto her elbow and looked down at Arabella. "You think it a mistake?"

Arabella turned her head to meet her cousin's eye. "How am I ever to be content with anything less than what I had today?"

Felicity's lips stretched into a smile, then she dropped back onto the pillows, and they lay in silence for a time.

All day, Arabella had been reliving the kiss, her mind and heart concocting ways she could have it again. She had gone so far as hoping Mr. Yorke would arrive at the door and tell Papa what he had witnessed. Surely Papa would demand Mr. Hayes marry Arabella.

"Perhaps Papa would let me marry him," she said faintly.

Whatever Mr. Hayes thought precluded him from being a proper match for her, it could not be so very bad, could it? He possessed all the hallmarks of a true gentleman, even if he did not have a title or fortune.

She felt Felicity's eyes upon her and turned. There was sympathy in her expression—or pity, perhaps.

"You do not think so?" Arabella asked.

"Oh, Bella," Felicity said, "Mr. Hayes is wonderful! But your father would not agree for you to marry him."

"Even if it ensured my happiness?"

Papa wanted her to be happy. She knew that. And while he had pursued a match for her when he had not known she held anyone in affection, perhaps he would change course once she made it clear that her heart was engaged.

The memory of his expression when she had told him she did not wish to marry Lord Farnham flashed across her mind, and her stomach tightened.

"Would he not come around to Mr. Hayes after seeing how happy he makes me?" Arabella asked.

Felicity's hand found hers and grasped it. "I would like to think so..." She did not go on, but it was clear there was more.

"But..." Arabella prompted.

"But your father is not known for being particularly tender-hearted, Bella. In fact, quite the opposite."

Arabella's brows pulled together, and she turned her body to face her cousin, resting her head on her hand. "What do you mean?"

Felicity's lip pressed into a line, as though she was reluctant to expound.

"Tell me, Felicity."

She matched Arabella's position, resting her head on her palm. "He can be so...exacting. Ruthless at times, even."

Arabella's stomach clenched again. "Ruthless is a terrible word. How can you think it of him?"

"Mama has told me plenty of stories. Perhaps you have not seen it because you are such a dutiful daughter."

A memory flitted into Arabella's mind of a maid named Sarah whom Papa had dismissed suddenly. His only explanation was that she had "been indiscreet and had to be let go." Arabella had later overheard a discussion between two of the other housemaids discussing that Sarah had seen something she had not been meant to see and had been dismissed without a reference.

Arabella had disregarded the conversation as servant gossip, but perhaps she had been wrong. Papa had certainly been more volatile of temper since Mama's death. But that did not mean he was ruthless.

"He is exacting, certainly, but that is only his desire to protect my sisters and me. He feels the weight of his responsibility keenly, and he has no one to share it with."

Felicity nodded, but she looked far from convinced.

It brought to mind how Mr. Hayes had looked when he had asked if Papa was at Kew. Perhaps it had been the prospect of being found with her unchaperoned, but Arabella could have sworn there had been another element to his urgent question.

"Why not tell your father how you feel?" Felicity asked.

Arabella suppressed the desire to swallow. The thought of revealing her true feelings was more frightening than she cared to admit.

But if there was any possibility it might lead to her ability to be with Mr. Hayes, was it not worth fighting through those fears?

It was late the next morning when Arabella found the opportunity to be alone with Papa.

Felicity had recognized the speaking glance Arabella had given and had asked Aunt Louisa to help her speak with the cook about a different poultice for the bee sting. The two of them had vacated the room, leaving Arabella and Papa alone.

"Quite an adventure you had at Kew," Papa said.

He had no notion...and she trusted he never would.

"A very unfortunate turn of events." Arabella's heart took up a quick pace as Papa returned his gaze to the newspaper, his brow furrowed in concentration. A moment later, however, he set it aside. "Well, my dear. It is time we discussed things, I think."

"Discussed...things?"

He smiled at her as though she was being coy.

Coy was not the right word, though. Reluctant, certainly.

Papa smoothed the paper beside him. "We agreed you

should have a few days to accustom yourself to the idea of marriage, and you have had more than a few—eight, in fact."

"Has it been that long? It feels as though it was just yesterday Lord Farnham was here." She gave an unsteady laugh.

Papa seemed unamused. "Do you mean to say you are still unready?"

Her heart pounded against her chest, but this was her opportunity to test the waters. "In truth, I do not know that I shall ever be anything *but* unready, Papa."

His jaw tightened and something flickered in his expression, and immediately Arabella thought of the word *ruthless*. But the ghost of whatever it had been was replaced by a smile. "What of your dream for the shop window? Have you forgotten it?"

In truth, it *had* drifted to the back of her mind. But that did not mean she had forgotten it or no longer wished for it. The truth was, she selfishly wished to have everything her heart desired: the shop window, Mr. Hayes, and Papa's approval. "No."

"We agreed, did we not, that fulfilling such a dream would come only if you proved yourself?"

Her stomach swarmed. Did he mean to say she would not be permitted to design the window unless she married Lord Farnham?

"Naturally, I wish for you to be able to do precisely that. Your happiness is of paramount importance to me, my dear. You cannot doubt that."

"No, Papa." He *did* care about her happiness. They simply disagreed on what would bring it about.

"We must work together to make a future with which you will be content. Am I thrilled with the idea of the shop window? Hardly. And yet, I have agreed to entertain the idea.

But what sort of father would I be if I allowed my daughter—one who is not yet wise to the ways of the world—to forego a blindingly brilliant match merely because she feels unready?"

He let that thought simmer for a moment before continuing. "No one is particularly *ready* for marriage, Arabella. It is a leap into an unknown which can only become known and comfortable through lived experience."

Her mind and tongue fought over a response. If what he said was true, why was the thought of marriage to Lord Farnham increasingly repulsive to her, while the thought of marriage to Mr. Hayes grew inside her like hunger?

"Lord Farnham is returning to Town tomorrow," Papa said. "I intend to write to arrange a meeting to discuss particulars. I will inform you once I have a response from him." He stood. "I must go fulfill my parliamentary duties." He came over and placed a kiss upon her head. "It is all for you, my dear."

Arabella stared blankly at the crumbs on her plate, and within moments, the door closed behind him.

All Arabella knew was that she needed to see Mr. Hayes again, and she knew who could help her arrange it.

Whether Mr. Hayes would agree to see *her* was a question that could only be answered by posing it to him. He had been so adamant that nothing was possible between them. When he had kissed her, it had been a result of her asking—nay, begging—him to do so. Not that he had seemed at all reluctant... He had been clear in both word and deed that he cared for her.

She had to hope those feelings would be enough to make him agree to see her again.

19

SILAS

S ilas picked at his food, unsuccessfully suppressing a look of distaste. He pushed away his plate and reached for his glass. "I shall be driven to drunkenness if I am obliged to eat much more of this food. I shall go to William's for dinner from now on, I think."

Frederick's only response was to cover his half-uneaten plate of food with his napkin. Fairchild and Drake had chosen to seek sustenance elsewhere, but after the events of the previous day, Silas had felt it incumbent to show some degree of penance by remaining at home.

He took a sip of his drink and stared at his brother. "Still punishing me, are you?"

"Someone certainly should." Frederick shot him a look of reproach, but despite the way he had been behaving since Silas had come to Town, the role of chastiser did not come naturally to the youngest in the family.

"You are suffering more than I, Freddie. You should have joined Drake and Fairchild. I give you my word I shall not leave this townhouse tonight."

"Unless you develop a sudden fascination with flowers, as you did yesterday?" He stared in challenge at Silas. "Just one particular flower, though, wasn't it?"

Silas tipped the little of his drink that remained, watching the candlelight catch on it. The corner of his mouth tipped upward. "*Arabella dulcis.*"

"You are unbearable," Frederick said, though there was a hint of a smile at one corner of his mouth. "You would have been wiser to kiss a bouquet of wolfsbane. What on earth possessed you to kiss Drayton's daughter? In public?"

Silas did not respond immediately. His mind was at the orangery. How long might he have kissed Arabella had Frederick not arrived and put a stop to it?

Forever, he imagined. He would certainly be thinking about it for that long.

That realization was both happy and lowering.

"Have you ever been in love, Freddie?"

"Who has time for love when they are occupied keeping their brother from the noose?"

"As I have told you a hundred times before, Freddie, you are not responsible for my choices."

Frederick held his gaze, his brow gently creased with worry.

"I am capable of taking care of myself," Silas said, "and I do not intend to allow anything more sinister—or less fetching—than this cravat to be tied around my neck."

Frederick smiled reluctantly. "Your cravat could hardly be *less* fetching."

Silas smiled in appreciation at this jab. "Focus your efforts on attaining that place in Parliament. I will manage, little though it may seem that way."

Frederick let out a sigh and sat back in his chair. "For what it is worth, I like Miss Easton. How a devil like Drayton came to raise such a daughter is beyond my capability to understand. What do you intend to do?"

Silas shrugged. "What I came to do. Clear my name. I am meeting with Bence tomorrow."

He hoped whatever news Bence had would be welcome.

Bence poured a drink for Silas. "It is in Town."

"What is?"

"The evidence you need."

Silas met his gaze fixedly, trying to control the hope trickling through his veins. "What evidence?"

He handed the glass to Silas. "A secret ledger Drayton kept. I saw it once on a visit, but I wanted to be certain it still existed."

Silas's heart beat more quickly. Was freedom truly within reach? The evidence was not, as he had feared, at one of Drayton's other properties or, heaven forbid, destroyed.

"Where?" Silas asked, trying to control the urgency he felt as he took a sip.

Bence met his gaze with the hint of a grimace. "In his townhouse."

"His townhouse." Silas thought of the night he had dined there before realizing who Arabella's father was. Just how near had he unknowingly been to the key to his exoneration? "Do you know where precisely?"

"No, but I know where I saw it last. And I know Drayton." He frowned. "That is less of a concern than how you intend to gain access to his townhouse."

But it wasn't gaining access that concerned Silas; it was living with himself if he did so—and not being caught by Drayton in the act. If he was, the same thing would happen to the ledger which happened to the diary when Anthony had been found searching for it: Drayton would destroy it.

"You are certain it is there?" Silas asked.

"As certain as I can be. I had it from a former servant of his."

Silas nodded slowly, taking in this information. But he was admittedly puzzled. "Why would he keep such an incriminating piece of evidence?"

"I told you, did I not, that Drayton has an obsession with amassing anything he might use against others if the need arises? That ledger contains leverage over his associates."

Silas watched Bence carefully. "Including you?"

"Do not concern yourself over that. This is an opportunity we cannot afford to forgo. I shall come about."

It did indeed seem the perfect opportunity. And yet, all night, Silas stewed over it. No matter how he reasoned, he could not feel anything but wretched at the thought of trying to elicit an invitation from Arabella or the Fairchilds to Drayton's townhouse.

But what, then, was he to do?

Was breaking in like a thief in the night any better?

When a letter arrived the following morning with the penny post, inviting them all to join the Fairchilds for dinner the following evening, Silas could only scoff at the way fate insisted on tempting him.

But dinner at the townhouse with Drayton present was out of the question.

"They offer a fine meal and a rousing round of charades afterward," Fairchild said, reading the note. "Miss Easton's father is in Brighton and will not be present, and he sends his regrets."

Silas laughed out loud.

All three of the others looked a question at him.

Silas cleared his throat. "Excuse me. I was thinking of something...else."

He had been thinking of how it felt very much like fate *wished* for him to steal that ledger—and of how Fairchild still insisted on calling Drayton "Miss Easton's father."

"I shall respond in the affirmative, then." Fairchild rose from his chair and made his way to the escritoire near the window.

"Not for me," Silas said.

Frederick's gaze whipped to Silas, who gave a subtle grimace in response.

"Nonsense," Frederick said. "Tell her that all of us accept her kind invitation."

Silas gave him a pointed glance with the slightest shake of his head, but his brother seemed not to understand. Apparently, the talk they had had last night had made an impression upon Frederick, and he was now determined to be supportive of Silas.

There was no way to make him understand with the other men in the room, however, so he said nothing when Fairchild said, "So be it."

When they left the room presently, Silas pulled Frederick aside.

"I cannot go, Freddie."

His brother gave an airy, incredulous laugh. "I tell you not to see the Easton girl only to find you kissing her. *You* tell me you can manage your own affairs, so I come out in support of you seeing her, and now you tell me you cannot. You"—he jabbed Silas in the chest—"simply take pleasure in being a contrarian."

"Undoubtedly. But that is not what this is about." He glanced around to ensure they were alone, then pulled Frederick into the window alcove nearby. "Bence confirmed that the evidence I need is at Drayton's townhouse."

Frederick's brow wrinkled. "Then surely that is the place you *must* go."

"How could I use Miss Easton or her family in such a way?"

Frederick grimaced. "Silas," he said softly, "you cannot let such scruples keep you from the freedom you deserve. Have you not said from the beginning that you would let nothing stand in your way?"

Silas met his eye but kept quiet.

"If Miss Easton is as wonderful as you believe her to be, she would not wish for you to remain captive to her father's malicious choices." He gripped Silas's arm tightly and stared at him intently. "You deserve liberty, Silas. Do not surrender this opportunity, for there is no saying you shall have another."

Silas held his gaze for what felt like hours. Finally, he let out a sigh. "You are right, much as I hate to admit it."

Frederick clapped a hand over his shoulder and squeezed. "Better accustom yourself to it. I am always right. That is what it means to be a politician."

Silas's heel bounced on the floor of the carriage on the ride to Lord Drayton's townhouse. At war within him were eagerness to see Arabella again, fear that Lord Drayton might unexpectedly be present at dinner, and an overwhelming anxiousness to lay his hands on the evidence and take it somewhere safe.

They were let in by the butler, and Silas's eyes darted around the entry hall, his ears alert for the sound of Drayton's voice.

"Thank you," Frederick said as the butler took his hat. "A pity Lord Drayton could not be here this evening."

"Indeed," the butler said in a formal, quelling voice.

Frederick smiled slightly and winked at Silas, as if he had known precisely what reassurance was needed.

"Mrs. Fairchild and the others await you in the drawing room," the butler said once the gentlemen had been divested of coats and hats. He led them up the stairs, and Silas's eyes fixed on the door to the study where Bence had told him to focus his efforts. When he would have the chance to make a search, he had no idea, but he trusted an opportunity would present itself. If not, he would have to create one. Frederick had agreed to help facilitate it if needed.

They reached the drawing room, and the butler opened the door to allow them to pass through. Fairchild and Drake went through first, then Frederick, and finally Silas.

His eyes found Arabella with neither prompting nor permission, and hers found him with equal swiftness. All thoughts of Drayton and the ledger faded as she smiled tentatively at him.

How was it possible he had been kissing her the last time he had seen her?

His mouth stretched into a smile, and hers grew in response, a hint of relief in her eyes.

He greeted Mrs. Fairchild and her daughter, then proceeded to Arabella as the others discussed Lady Fenton fainting at the opera the night before.

"Good evening, Miss Easton," he said in a calm voice belied by the response of his heart. He wanted to take her hand and kiss it. He wanted to kiss more than her hand, frankly, but he restrained himself. "How have you fared since I saw you last?"

Her eyes held his, and he knew she was thinking of their kiss just as surely as he knew he was more handsome without a mustache.

"Better now," she said, her eyes full of such patent affection and soft admiration that he did not notice he had been spoken to by someone until Frederick nudged him with an elbow.

"You remember?" Frederick asked.

"Remember what?" Silas asked.

"When that fellow fainted at that assembly?" Frederick asked with a hint of impatience.

The opportunity for further conversation had passed, and Mrs. Fairchild soon led them through to the dining room.

Silas couldn't help but appreciate how deftly Miss Fairchild managed things so that he and Arabella were seated beside each other. Aside from offering them desired proximity, however, with such a small number at the table, there was simply no way for them to converse between themselves on any meaningful topic.

Perhaps that was for the best. Silas's thoughts and feelings were a jumbled mess. He was reluctant to do anything to take advantage of her trust in him, but had he not already done that? He had masqueraded under a false name for the entirety of their acquaintance. He had kissed her under that false name, for heaven's sake.

What a cad he was. A selfish, lovesick cad.

"Miss Easton," Mr. Drake said, "this has been your first time in Town, has it not?"

"It has," she replied.

"And what do you make of it? Has it been everything you had hoped for?"

Her gaze darted to Silas and away again almost so quickly he might have imagined it. "It has. I miss my sisters, of course, but I can hardly imagine leaving London now."

"*Are* you leaving?" Silas couldn't help himself. She had said her father wished for her to become engaged soon. What if she was on the cusp of that and the plan was to spirit her away to the man's parish to be married post-haste?

"No," she said, "but Papa has been known to change his plans without warning."

"He certainly has made a habit of coming and going," Aunt Louisa said as the first course was laid before them.

Arabella pulled at the fingertips of her glove, and Silas caught a flash of the butterfly pendant.

His gaze flicked to hers, but she was too busy removing her other glove to notice. She fiddled with the bracelet, however, once both gloves were sitting upon her lap. She must have sensed Silas's eyes on her, for she looked up.

"Are you admiring my bracelet?" she asked in a low voice while everyone served themselves from the available dishes.

"I am," he said with a little smile. "Where did you come by it?"

"I was obliged to take it by force."

Silas's brows shot up. "Were you now?"

"Yes. Are you surprised?"

She was captivating. He could still remember how she had looked the night he had met her at Vauxhall, her eyes framed by that enchanting mask. Looking back, he was nearly certain he had already begun to fall in love with her then.

"What surprises me is that someone would find it possible to deny you anything you wanted."

Her clear eyes held his, a glimmer of intensity behind the amusement. "Anything?"

His fingers tightened around his fork, for her meaning was clear: she wanted *him*.

And gads, how he wanted her! But it was not in his power to give her what she wanted—or what she thought she wanted.

He broke his gaze away and reached for a platter of peas.

"Would you care for some peas?" He waited for her answer, mixing them together for an excuse to avoid her eye, for the choices he made when she was in his sight were not the ones he should be making.

She did not respond, however, and he was obliged to look at her.

"Did I speak amiss?" she asked in a soft, subdued voice.

"No." He glanced around to ensure no one was paying them any heed. "*You* have not said or done anything amiss."

This did not have the effect of reassuring her as he had hoped. Indeed, her brow knit more closely. "You mean to say that *you* have."

They were interrupted by Mrs. Fairchild, however, and had no further opportunity to speak before the women rose to go to the drawing room.

Miss Easton did so in a more subdued manner than usual.

Silas suppressed a sigh once the door closed behind the women.

The covers were removed and the port brought in, and Frederick pinned Silas with a speaking glance.

Now was the time. The moment he had been waiting for. And yet, there was a heaviness over him as he cleared his throat. "Will you excuse me a moment, gentlemen? I must attend to a private matter."

"Does the matter's name begin with a Miss and end with an Easton?" Drake asked with a wink.

"No," Silas said with less good humor than usual. He forced himself to offer a grimacing smile and put a hand to his stomach as he rose to his feet. "I feel a bit unwell." It was true enough. His stomach was swimming with nerves, his hands becoming clammy, and his heart beating at a clipping pace as he left the room.

The corridor was lit by a half-dozen sconces, but it was

otherwise quiet. The servants must have descended below-stairs, no doubt eager to partake of their own meal.

Silas made his way with soft feet toward the study and put his hand on the knob, turning it slowly. He pushed open the door, and the light from the nearest candle illuminated the otherwise dark room.

He looked down the corridor, then went to a table against the wall, took the candle, and lit it using the nearest sconce.

Protecting the flame with his hand, he hurried into the study and closed the door softly behind him.

The room was lined with shelves of books, their gold lettering glinting in the candlelight. He strode straight for the desk and set the candle upon it. There was a large drawer on either side of the tall wingback chair, and he gently pulled open the first one. A sheaf of papers sat on top, and after glancing at the first two sheets and finding them to be letters, he set them on the desk and continued searching. Beneath was a leather folio, and his heart skipped.

He pulled it out and eagerly flipped it open, his eyes searching the neat text.

His chest deflated. It was a ledger, but it seemed to be the one for the townhouse.

He flipped through it to see whether there were any abnormal expenses—or any mention of Seamark Trading, the competitor he had secretly helped, then joined. After a dozen pages and finding nothing out of the ordinary, he set the ledger down atop the papers on the desk to continue his search.

He was too late to catch the sealing wax stick as it toppled over, rolled, then fell off the desk.

He cringed at the sound, freezing in place and clenching his eyes shut until the ear-shattering sound had dissipated. Not moving a muscle, he listened for any other noise.

When none came, his shoulders slowly relaxed.

A sheaf of letters was beneath the ledger, and he gave them a cursory glance just as the door opened, and a silhouette appeared in the doorway.

20

ARABELLA

"Mr. Hayes?" Arabella asked in a faint voice.

When she had opened the door to the study, she had fully expected to see a servant dusting or fetching a forgotten item. Or perhaps an empty room with an open window and a breeze that had knocked something over.

She had certainly not expected to see Mr. Hayes.

He did not respond, though. He merely stared at her, eyes wide and alert. He had an eerie look about him, thanks to the candle casting shadows across his face.

Her gaze dropped to the papers in his hands, then to the other items on the desk, and finally to the open drawer.

"What are you doing?" she asked.

He was meant to be with the other men, enjoying a glass of port.

There must be an explanation for why he had wandered into this room and was going through Papa's desk.

But try as she might, she could not think of a satisfactory one.

"What are you doing, Mr. Hayes?" she repeated more firmly

when he did not respond. "Why are you searching my father's drawers?"

"Miss Easton." He put up a hand, as though pleading with her not to become angry with him. "There is an explanation. I swear."

This particular phrase had the effect of evoking a temper Arabella was unused to entertaining. Mr. Hayes was full of explanations he could not give but wanted her to believe were convincing.

"Is there?" she asked. "Let me hear it, then."

He swallowed, and no explanation came.

She let out an incredulous scoff. After his strange behavior at dinner, she had already been struggling against a feeling of rejection. She had all but confessed that what she wanted with him was…everything. And his response?

He had not even given one. He had looked away and offered her peas. She hated peas.

His lack of response *was* a response, in its own way. Even someone as unpracticed as she in the language of romance and love could decipher that.

"And so I am to simply trust you," she said, her wounded pride fanning the flames of a hitherto-unpracticed temper. "Trust you when you have acted in incomprehensible ways since the night we met and yet refuse to explain *anything* at all to me. And then I find you rifling through my father's personal affairs?" A thought occurred to her, and it sent a chill through her veins. "Is this why you came? Is it why you kissed me? To gain access to my father's belongings?"

"No," Mr. Hayes said firmly. He set down the papers in his hand, then walked toward her with slow, measured steps, as though afraid he might frighten her off if his movements were too sudden.

When he came within a few feet, she took a step backward, and he stopped.

"I swear it is not why I kissed you. Though I should not have done it."

The chill within her intensified, making the blood in her veins feel like ice. "You regret it."

"I regret it for your sake only."

"What does that even mean?"

"It means"—he took another step toward her, and she allowed it, if only to see his face more clearly—"that I am completely and utterly unworthy of you, Arabella."

She let out an incredulous breath and looked at the still-open drawer in the desk. "Because you rummage through people's affairs without permission? Or is there another reason? Ah, let me guess...you cannot give it to me."

"I have wanted to explain everything to you from the beginning. I swear it."

"Then explain!" She could hear the hint of hysteria in her voice, and with effort, she controlled herself. She took a determined step toward him, and when she spoke, her voice was taut. "I demand an explanation, Mr. Hayes."

He stared at her for a moment with an almost sorrowful glint.

She waited, determined to have information from him.

After what seemed an eternity, he spoke. "I am not Mr. Hayes."

It took her a moment to respond. "What?"

"My name is not John Hayes." He let out a long, slow breath. "It is Silas Yorke."

Arabella's vision flickered momentarily. Silas Yorke. He said it as though it should mean something to her. But what did anything mean? She could not fathom what he was saying.

"I once had dealings with your father," he said. "They ended...poorly."

"Poorly," she repeated.

He nodded, that same somber look in his eyes so at odds with his usual teasing smile. "My brother and another gentleman invested with your father—textiles, as I mentioned. But unbeknownst to us, your father was undercutting our investments, slipping information to a competing merchant. I suspected our other associate first—Langdon—for he was the one keeping the books. But it was not him." He looked at her as though waiting for her to understand.

But there was a strange echo in Arabella's ears, as though he was speaking through a wall.

"When Langdon and I confronted your father, he became furious." His brows drew together, deep, dark, and somber. "He shot and killed Langdon."

The room tilted, and Arabella shifted to stabilize herself. What on earth was he saying?

"He blamed me for it," he continued. "If I had not escaped, I would have been hanged. Instead, I spent more than a year eking out whatever existence I could in France, working to put a roof over my head and food on the table, coming close to death when I contracted consumption."

His brow furrowed at the memory, but he seemed to put it aside. "I returned to England some time ago, but I only came to Town recently to clear my name." He gestured toward the desk. "That is why I am in this room. To seek justice for myself and for Langdon."

It took time for the full weight of his claims to settle in and for Arabella to realize the audacity of the man.

He met her gaze, his own steady and intent, watching for her reaction to his revelation. Her reaction to the nonsense.

Disbelief and anger rose inside her. It was as though, now

that she had discovered her temper, it was prepared to make up for all the time it had lain dormant. "How dare you?" The words came out slow and soft, but each one shook.

He stared at her, silent.

The gall of the man was beyond the pale.

"You *used* me," she said, her voice shaking—whether with anger or hurt, she couldn't say.

He shook his head. "No."

"You used me," she repeated more loudly, "and now you stand here, besmirching the name of my father, who is twice the man you could ever be."

He shut his eyes. "Arabella, I swear, I had no i—"

"Miss Easton," she said. "I am Miss Easton to you." She swallowed the acrid taste in her mouth, remembering when he had first called her by her Christian name—before they had kissed.

It had all been a lie. A ruse.

"Miss Easton," he said obediently, "I swear I had no notion who your father was when I met you."

"And I am to believe this? When you said your express reason for coming to London was to find this evidence you speak of?"

"It may be incredible, but it is the truth. When we met at Vauxhall, I disappeared from your side—"

"A habit of yours," she interjected.

"I only did so because I saw the man I had come to Town to see—someone I thought could help me clear my name. The second time I disappeared, you will remember, was the night you promised to introduce me to your father. That was when I discovered precisely who your father was."

"My father the murderer," she said bitingly.

"I know it cannot be easy to hear," he said, his eyes alight with sympathy, "but—"

"Get out." Her teeth clenched together until her jaw ached.

He watched her fixedly.

"Get. Out." The tears were beginning to collect in her eyes, and the last thing she intended to do was allow this man—whoever he was—to see her cry.

He gave a curt nod. "Very well." He looked at her a moment longer, then passed by her on his way to the door.

She stood stock-still as his scent surrounded her, her body trembling, her eyes burning and full to the brim as she listened for his exit.

His footsteps stopped.

"I am sorry, Miss Easton," he said softly. "Truly and terribly sorry."

She grasped the bracelet around her wrist, then fiddled with shaking fingers until the clasp released. Turning toward the door, she flung it. It dropped just beyond the rug and slid across the floorboards, landing at his boots.

After a long moment, he stooped down and picked it up. He stood straight and looked at it for a moment, then closed his fingers around the bracelet and passed through the door, shutting it behind him.

Arabella drew in a shaky breath, then stopped fighting the tears that had been threatening.

21

SILAS

Silas had really only lost two things: Arabella and the chance to find the ledger.

But what else was there? Those two things were everything to him.

Frederick must have spread the word to the family about what had happened, for Silas had received invitations—no, summons—from both William and Aunt Eugenia to come dine.

He had ignored them both.

He would see them eventually, of course, but just now, he was not in the humor to discuss things with anyone. Instead, he had been taking all his meals in his room, sleeping a great deal, and spending the rest of the day tossing crumpled bits of parchment into the empty glass across the room.

There was a knock.

"Go away," Silas responded, slumped in his chair as he tossed a paper halfheartedly. It missed its target and fell amongst the others on the floor. He had only managed to make one crinkled paper fall into the glass. There was some grim satisfaction in the constant failure. It felt like a reflection of his own life.

"Aunt Eugenia is here to see you," Frederick's voice came through the door.

"I'm not at home to visitors," Silas said in a barely comprehensible, slurred voice, for his head hung lazily over his chest.

There was a pause, then Frederick's footsteps faded away.

Silas ripped another piece from the paper he held and crushed it with one hand. He tossed it, and it hit the rim of the glass before falling to the floor.

He had spoken with Bence the day after the fiasco at Drayton's townhouse. His response had been nearly as bleak as Silas felt. He had little hope they would find an avenue as viable as the ledger—and if Miss Easton had alerted her father...well, that was a possibility Silas did not care to dwell on.

The door swung open.

"Go away, Freddie," Silas said limply.

"I am not Freddie."

Silas's eyes widened, and he turned to verify that his aunt was indeed in his bedchamber.

"Aunt Eugenia," he said in a bewildered voice. "What are you doing here?"

"What do you *think* I am doing?" Her gaze ran over the room, and her lips turned down at the corners. "I have come to talk some sense into you."

Silas turned away and crumpled another piece of paper. "You should not have."

"And why not?"

"It is not...seemly, Aunt Eugenia. You should not be in St. James's at all. And certainly not in my bedchamber."

She barked with laughter. "My reputation has survived far more than a visit to my nephew in St. James's, I'll have you know." She covered his hand with hers before he could toss the paper. "Stop wasting paper. Stop moping. Pick up that mess and get ahold of yourself, boy! And for heaven's sake, find a razor and rid yourself of that vile mustache."

Silas frowned and put a hand to the lower half of his face. He hadn't meant to resurrect the mustache, but the rough stubble told him it was on its way to resurrecting—the natural result of not having shaved for the past two days.

Aunt Eugenia pulled the bell and ordered tea to be brought to the room. Whether she was ignorant of or simply unconcerned with the ill-concealed surprise on the servant's face at the sight of her in Silas's room, he could not tell.

It made him smile slightly, even amidst his despair.

"Now," Aunt Eugenia said, pulling him out of his seat and taking it for herself. "Speak."

"I would rather not." He went over and began to pick up papers resignedly.

"Did I ask what you would rather? I did not. Now, speak. And do not lie to me, boy. I always know."

"I believe you." He took the papers he had gathered up and tossed them into the fire grate. There was a small stool beside the armoire, and he walked over to it, sat down, and let out a long sigh, running his hands through his increasingly long hair.

He launched into the story of his interactions with Miss Easton, his hopes of vindication, and the crushing, untimely end of both.

Midway through, he was obliged to pause when the door opened and the tea was brought in.

Aunt Eugenia's face screwed up with the first taste of hers. "This is an affront to the name of tea. An abomination."

"Nearly everything from the kitchens is."

She cringed again and set down the cup. "How do you survive?"

Silas put out his hands to display himself in all his disheveled glory.

"Quite so," she said, taking his point. "Go on, then."

When his account reached the day at Kew Gardens, he tried to skirt around what had happened. He did not particularly wish to discuss the intimate details of the day with his aunt, neither did he relish the thought of being read a lecture.

"Kissed her, did you?" she said shrewdly, a little smile on her lips. "Good for you. Then what?"

Amused and a bit baffled, he finished by recounting the night at Drayton's townhouse.

When he finished, he half expected Aunt Eugenia to scoff at him and tell him he was a fool, that the solution to his problems was sitting in front of him, plain as the nose on his face.

Instead, she was quiet, a frown on her lips and brow. "You *have* made a bungle of it, haven't you?"

"And here I thought my life was exemplary," he said dryly.

She tossed one of the unused crumpled papers at his head. "I will tolerate none of your impudence, boy." She looked at him another moment, then rose to her feet.

Silas watched as she gathered up her things.

"Do not forget to shave," she said as she walked to the bedchamber door, "before you venture outside, which you *should* do."

"You are leaving?" he asked, baffled.

"As you see."

He blinked. "You came, then, for what purpose? To insult me, force me to recount my pain, then comment that my life is a shambles?"

She considered this, then nodded. "More or less, I suppose."

He gave an incredulous laugh, but she paid it no heed, opening the door and stepping out.

She paused on the threshold and looked to the side where the bell cord hung. "Shall I pull the bell for a razor? Or may I trust you to do so?"

He smiled in spite of himself. "I can manage."

"See that you do." And then she shut the door.

22

ARABELLA

Arabella pulled on her gloves and regarded herself in the mirror. A few weeks ago, her attire and appearance would have sent a flash of satisfaction through her: the dove-gray silk of her dress, accented with a bodice of lacework and intricate seed pearls—pearls she had spent the past three days working on in a desperate attempt to distract herself. The skirts featured a sheer overlay, which, when it caught the light, showed a delicate floral pattern.

Her hair had been pulled back into a loose chignon, with small lavender sprigs set around a silver comb.

She was satisfied with her appearance, but she could not find the same joy in the art of it as she had hitherto done.

She stifled a sigh, rose to her feet, and left the room, pulling on her gloves as she made her way downstairs. Her eye caught on the door to the study, just as it had every time she had passed it for the past four days.

Each time she did, a little voice inside told her to enter and see whether she could find whatever Mr. Yorke had been searching for, for once he had left that night, she had simply replaced Papa's things, taken the candle, and left the room.

She had refused to give credence to anything the man had said. It would have felt like a betrayal of Papa. And for what? Some silly, naive hope that Mr. Yorke was not the monster he had turned out to be?

If that were true, it would, by force, mean that Papa was the monster, and that she knew to be untrue. This was the father who had given her a magnificent home and everything her heart could desire, including this trip to Town. He had submitted to her silly whims and wishes when it came to fabrics and sewing. He had allowed her to choose the paper and the hangings in not only her own bedchamber but the salon and the drawing room.

He was not a heartless murderer.

She lifted her chin and passed the study, making her way to the entry hall, where Aunt Louisa and Felicity were waiting. Papa joined them shortly, and they went to the carriage awaiting them outside.

It was Arabella's first time at the opera—something she had been looking forward to since her arrival for the sole purpose of admiring the attire of everyone in attendance.

It was, indeed, magnificent when they arrived, with the swishing of different fabrics, the glitter and shimmer of jewelry, satins, silks, and taffeta. Why, then, did she feel a hint of dissatisfaction despite that?

"What do you think, my dear?" Papa asked as they reached their box.

"It is beautiful," she replied, trying to infuse her voice with an enthusiasm she could not feel.

He smiled at her. Was that the smile of a murderer?

The idea was almost laughable.

"Lord Farnham will be here," he said, "and promised to

visit our box this evening." The meeting Papa had mentioned —the one where he and Farnham would discuss the details of a marriage contract—had not yet occurred. Arabella had been too caught up in her own difficulties to ask why.

"Oh." She tried to make her voice sound pleasant, just as she had been working to accustom herself to the idea of marriage to him. What reason had she against it now? Before, much as it pained her to admit it, it had been her affection for Mr. Hayes that had made the idea of marriage to Lord Farnham so unpalatable.

But Mr. Hayes had been an illusion, a fabrication. The man she had fallen in love with did not exist, and all she was left with now was mortification at her gullibility and a heart aggravatingly resistant to accepting the truth about the man to whom it had attached itself.

"He wishes to pay his addresses to you, Arabella," Papa said, watching for her reaction. "Saturday."

She forced a smile. "It is very kind of him."

"Well," Papa said, "let us not forget how *he* benefits from such a match. He could not find a better wife than my little Bella."

Lord Farnham joined them a short time later, and Arabella forced herself to maintain a steady conversation with him and to notice every positive attribute he possessed. There were certainly several of them.

But after a quarter of an hour in his company, she felt exhausted—and just the smallest bit despondent at the thought of the future.

"Will you join me to seek refreshment, child?" Aunt Louisa asked her. "You look pale."

"Of course," Arabella replied, grateful for the suggestion. She excused herself to Lord Farnham and followed her aunt.

Felicity had gone to visit a friend in the box beside theirs and would likely not return for some time.

"That man is a chatterbox," Aunt Louisa said.

Arabella sighed but bit her tongue. It was impolite to speak ill of one's soon-to-be betrothed, which only made her wish to speak ill of him all the more.

They had reached the refreshments, and Arabella sipped her negus slowly, hoping to take all the time she could before returning to the box. She felt eyes upon her, and her gaze met that of a woman a dozen feet away. She had graying hair, fine attire, and a frank and curious gaze, which was directed at Arabella unflinchingly. Upon their catching eyes, the woman strode toward her.

"Miss Easton, is it not?" the woman asked.

"Yes, it is," Arabella replied with a hint of uncertainty. "Do I have the pleasure of knowing you, ma'am?"

"No," she replied, "and I trust you will forgive my disposing with formalities. I have a desire to make your acquaintance, and I was never particularly good at waiting for things to be done properly."

Arabella laughed in spite of herself. There was something about the woman's frank way she liked. It was refreshing and different. Familiar, even, though Arabella could not say why.

"I am Eugenia Ashby. You may not recognize the name, but you *are* acquainted with my nephews—Silas and Frederick Yorke."

Arabella's smile faded, and her voice was tight when she responded. "Only a little, ma'am."

Mrs. Ashby's eyes narrowed shrewdly. "Made you angry as fire, hasn't he?"

"I cannot think what you mean," Arabella replied.

"Of course you can. Do you claim, then, that you are *not* angry with my nephew?"

"I hardly know him to be angry with him."

"Well," she said, "I imagine you know him much better than you think."

"Do you?" Arabella did her best to sound quelling. She liked the woman, but she was not prepared to discuss Silas Yorke just now—or perhaps ever.

Mrs. Ashby smiled knowingly. "Unbearably forward, am I not? Well, I shan't force much more of my company upon you, Miss Easton, for nothing is worse than being obliged to listen to strangers prattle on about personal affairs, but I must say my piece before I go."

Arabella looked at her for a moment, then nodded.

"Heaven knows my nephew has made mistakes. All the most interesting people do so, you know. But the blame for the one he has been accused of does not lie with him. It lies with your father."

Arabella stiffened.

"Yes, I know. It is an unpleasant thing to have the person one loves accused of something terrible. There was a time when I believed the worst of my nephew, Miss Easton. I believed what everyone said of him, and I wish I hadn't. Your instinct to disbelieve ill of your father speaks to your character; it does not necessarily speak to his. Loving someone does not make them incapable of doing wrong. Your love for your father should not mean an innocent man goes to the gallows." She held Arabella's gaze. "I have never seen my nephew so abominably out of sorts as he is now. Some of that is, of course, due to the blow to his cause—a just cause, mind you. But even more so, it is the disappointment and despair of a man who fears he has lost the woman he loves."

Arabella swallowed, and the backs of her eyes stung.

It was silent for a moment.

"Does your father know the truth about him?" Mrs. Ashby asked.

Arabella hesitated. She had not told Papa of her encounter with Mr. Yorke in the study. Why she had not done so was a question to which she had no satisfactory answer. "No."

Mrs. Ashby nodded. "Though you may despise him for the lies he told, if you put yourself in his position, I think you will see that you would have done the same. Hate him if you must, Miss Easton, but do not let him take the blame for something he did not do." She gave a little grimacing smile, then turned and walked away.

Arabella watched, a bundle of conflicting emotions at war within her.

"Who was that?" Aunt Louisa asked, coming up beside her.

"I hardly know," Arabella said faintly.

"I assumed you knew her."

"She is the aunt of the Yorke brothers," Arabella said as Mrs. Ashby disappeared in the crowds.

Aunt Louisa's brows went up. "And what did she say?"

Arabella considered their conversation, and her eyes narrowed in thought. "She chastised me."

"Chastised you," she repeated, aghast. "The nerve!"

"Yes. I believe she has a great deal of nerve."

Chastising Arabella was not the only thing she had done, however.

It is the disappointment and despair of a man who fears he has lost the woman he loves.

Arabella thrust away the words. Her heart was too confused to inspect them without bias, and she could not allow herself to entertain any ideas about Mr. Yorke.

Her aunt led the way back to the box, from which Lord Farnham was mercifully absent. It was fortunate, as Arabella's mind was still occupied by the encounter at the refreshment table.

Mrs. Ashby, too, claimed Papa was a murderer. Having one person make such a claim was one thing. A second was more unsettling. And then there was everything Felicity had said about his ruthlessness.

Mrs. Ashby was Mr. Yorke's aunt, though. It stood to reason she would believe her nephew's account of things. She would resist the idea that he was a murderer, just as Arabella resisted the idea that Papa was one.

Yet, had she not already admitted that she had once believed the worst of her nephew?

Such confusing thoughts followed Arabella through the evening, preventing her from truly enjoying the opera as she had hoped to.

They followed her through the night and well into the next morning, until she felt she was going mad. Her mind could not fix on anything else, and finally, she came to a conclusion: she must ask Papa what had happened.

She would not tell him about Mr. Hayes's identity or that she had discovered him in his study—at least not yet. She would simply tell him she had heard gossip and wanted to hear the truth from his own lips.

Depending upon his answer, she would tell him about Mr. Yorke.

She set her sewing aside and went off in search of Papa, determined to set the matter to rest. When she reached the door to the library, it was ajar, and she reached for the handle, only to pause at the sound of his voice within.

"Been dashed near impossible on the topic," he said. "Silly female scruples, you know. Wanting a man who will kneel at her feet and worship her, I suppose."

Arabella's brows drew together. Of whom was he speaking?

"I had hoped that keeping her away from men of a marriageable age and other silly young women would prevent such absurd ideas from forming within her," he continued.

A man's laugh reached Arabella. "The female mind is simple, Drayton. It cannot deal in reason. It is all hysteria and emotion. And so many tears."

Papa laughed. "The tears are certainly abominable. But I think she is coming around to the idea of Farnham. I must hope she does so before his attention veers elsewhere, or I can say goodbye to the prospect of investing in Farnham's mill."

Arabella froze.

"Is that likely?" the man asked.

"I understand he has been paying more marked attention to Lady Beatrice. Arabella believes him ready to offer for her, but the truth is that I am finding it devilish difficult to get him to come up to scratch. My niece let something slip about this nonsensical idea Arabella has of arranging the window display in Burlington. It did more damage than I had realized. Farnham is a stickler when it comes to the proper place of women."

"And rightly so. I must admit I am surprised you would allow such a thing."

"Oh, she will not do the display, of course, but it serves my purposes to let her think otherwise for now."

Arabella swallowed the sick feeling in her throat, released the doorknob, and took a small step backward, hardly able to believe what she was hearing.

23

SILAS

Aunt Eugenia's visit, while somewhat baffling in its purpose, served as a sort of catalyst for Silas. As promised, he shaved his threatening mustache, cleaned up the remaining papers, and readied himself for the day.

What precisely he was readying himself for was unclear. Never had it been more dangerous for him to venture from the townhouse. Even being in Town was a risk, for if Arabella had told Drayton about him, he would know precisely where Silas was.

Every time there was a knock on the door or the bell rang, Silas hurried to the window to verify the identity of the guest, his heart pattering quickly in the event that it was a constable.

That fear began to dissipate as the days went by, however. If Drayton knew he was in London, he would have acted as swiftly as possible rather than giving Silas time to flee.

Being restricted to the townhouse made it difficult to pursue any possible routes toward securing his liberty—not that he had any ideas. Without tangible proof of Drayton's misdeeds, Bence was convinced any accusation against him would be quashed. Silas agreed, as did William.

Despite that, William was willing to use the influence he had garnered since coming into the dukedom to try to sway opinion against Drayton—or even launch the charges against him in public. But Silas had argued against this. If they had but one chance to take Drayton down, it needed to be done with confidence of success.

But what, then, was Silas to do without any evidence? Surrender to a life in hiding?

After the freedom he had experienced in London—freedom he had enjoyed with the woman he would do anything to spend his life beside—the mere thought of returning to France or even going into hiding was enough to make him wish to yank the window hangings closed, drop onto his bed, and allow his mustache to grow as thickly and wildly as it wished. Perhaps it would oblige him by consuming him entirely.

Three days after Aunt Eugenia's visit, he received a note from her requesting—nay, demanding—he come visit his "poor ailing aunt" at four o'clock that afternoon. Any refusal, she made clear, would have disastrous results.

Silas had no intention of refusing, however. He was impatient to leave the confines of the townhouse, and a visit to Aunt Eugenia was as safe as any outing could be. He took particular care for a close shave and to dress so that she would have no reason to criticize his appearance.

Hat pulled low over his head, he hailed the first hackney he came upon to avoid being spotted. He did not bother knocking when he arrived at Aunt Eugenia's. The presumption would gall her, but if she did not wish for him to do such things, she should not make it so amusing to provoke her.

"Aunt?" he called, shutting the door behind him and removing his hat.

"Jackanapes," he heard her mutter from the sitting room on the left of the entry hall. "In here!"

With a low chuckle, he hung his hat on a hook, smoothed his sleeves and waistcoat, then strode into the room with a smile on his face.

It disintegrated as he stopped short on the threshold.

Aunt Eugenia sat in a chair, sipping from her teacup, a distinctly self-satisfied glint in her eye.

Beside her, hands clasped in their laps, sat both Arabella and Miss Fairchild.

All of the bravado with which Silas had entered completely deserting him, he tore his eyes from Arabella and centered them on his aunt.

Her smile grew, and she set down her teacup. "I believe you know my guests, Silas."

"The question," Miss Fairchild said, "is rather whether we know *him*."

Aunt Eugenia laughed. "*Touché*." She stood. "Will you join me in the other room, Miss Fairchild? I believe you will enjoy one of the paintings there."

"Oh, yes," she agreed enthusiastically, rising to her feet.

Arabella grabbed her hand in a seemingly involuntary movement, and Miss Fairchild stopped, covering it with her own and offering a reassuring smile.

Arabella nodded and released the hand.

Aunt Eugenia waited for Miss Fairchild, then they proceeded toward the door where Silas stood.

He stepped to block their way. "Aunt," he said in a warning voice. If Arabella did not wish to speak with him, the last thing he wanted was for her to be forced to do so.

"She was the one who requested to speak with you," Aunt Eugenia said. "Now, out of my way, upstart."

Silas hesitated, then moved aside, and the two women passed through the door.

Aunt Eugenia turned back toward them, her hand on the doorknob, ready to pull the door closed. She pointed a stern finger at him, then at Arabella. "No funny business, you two. I do not aspire to start a brothel here."

Silas's eyes widened, but before he could remonstrate with her, the door closed.

He stared at it, waiting for the heat to dissipate from his neck and cheeks, but it lingered stubbornly.

"You will have to forgive my aunt," he finally said, turning toward Arabella. "She is a bit of an eccentric."

"I like her," Arabella replied. "She is refreshingly clear and frank. One knows one is hearing the truth when she speaks."

Silas made a pained expression, taking her point clearly.

"Let me be clear, Mr. Yorke," she said. "I am not here because I believe you. That is far from determined. I am, however, willing to listen. You have your aunt to thank for that. She sought me out at the opera and pled your case."

Silas's gaze fixed on her. "She did?"

"You mean to say you did not know?" She looked skeptical.

"Perhaps I should have expected something like that from her, but I confess I did not. She is easy to underestimate."

"A family trait, I think." From her clipped tone, this was not meant as a compliment in Silas's case.

He let out a little sigh. "I know you will find it impossible to take anything I say and believe it, but I must express my profound apologies despite that. I never meant to mislead you or hurt you."

Her lips pressed together. "Is that so?"

"Yes," he insisted. "It is. More than once, I have been on the cusp of telling you the truth—"

"And yet you did not."

"Your father is a powerful man, Miss Easton. To offer you the truth would have been not only to taint your view of a father you love but to put my very life in your hands."

She was quiet, her gaze fixed on his but her expression unreadable.

They stood across the room from one another, Silas unwilling to force his presence upon her. She was too angry with him to want such a thing, no doubt.

"I have been in hiding for more than two years," Silas continued. "Trust no longer comes naturally to me. My family are the only ones I know for certain I can rely upon, and even *that* has not always been the case."

Silence followed this confession for some time as they regarded one another from afar. How had it come to this? The woman he had once held and kissed, standing so far away like a statue?

"You say you were searching for a piece of evidence," she finally said. "What sort of evidence?"

"A ledger. Langdon kept the books for us, which is why I suspected him first. But your father was keeping his own private ledger."

The way her jaw tightened gave him to think she had not yet accustomed herself to slights against her father's honesty. He felt for her. Indeed, he wished he could cross the room, wrap her in his arms, and tell her how sorry he was that the man who had raised her was not the man she believed him to be.

But he kept his feet planted where they were.

"And what else do you know about this supposed ledger?" she asked.

"Precious little," Silas replied. "It should contain entries relating to Seamark Trading. That is all I know for certain, for they were our competitor, and after things fell apart following Langdon's death, your father joined forces with them."

Her eyes held his. It was strange to see the guarded sheen they had taken on since the last time they had been together. The change saddened him deeply, but there was nothing he could do about it.

He wasn't even certain why she was asking him any of these questions, for she had made it clear she did not believe him.

But she was here, and that was not something he took for granted.

Her gaze dropped to his wrist, then flitted back to his face.

He was not wearing the bracelet. It had felt wrong to do so given the change in her feelings toward him, not to mention that the bracelet was the reminder of her he never needed. But he had fiddled with it almost constantly for the past few days before setting it on his bedside table.

"I should return to my cousin," she said.

Silas nodded, though some primal part of him wished to guard the door and prevent her from leaving, for there was no knowing whether he would ever see her again.

She made her way to the door and reached for the doorknob, but his hand beat her to it.

He opened the door, and she looked up at him. For a moment, the guarded look retreated as they stared at one another from so near. Her eyes explored his, then she broke her gaze away suddenly.

"Thank you, Mr. Hay—" She stopped, her lips pressing together. "Mr. Yorke." She left the room without a backward glance, and all Silas could do was watch her.

24

ARABELLA

Arabella had hardly spoken to Papa since overhearing him in the library. He had asked her if anything was amiss the next morning at breakfast, but she had merely pleaded the headache, then returned to her room to write a note to Mrs. Ashby, asking for her help to arrange the meeting with her nephew.

Now that she knew what evidence he had been searching for amongst Papa's things, she could search for it herself.

And yet, she had not.

She had still not returned to the study since that fateful night she had found Mr. Yorke there. Perhaps she was afraid of what she would find.

Either way, one of the men she loved would not be the man she had thought him. In that sense, it was easier to delay seeking answers.

And yet, it was a different form of torture to sit with both possibilities.

She had underestimated just how difficult it would be to see Mr. Yorke again, to be in the same room. Her brain might have accepted that everything had changed between them, but her body and her heart still reacted to his presence. There was still the same kindness in his eyes, the same concern for her well-being despite the way she had treated him in the study.

As for Papa, she could not look at him the same way now. The sense of betrayal over his words to his friend ran deep within her. The one hope she had was that the conversation she had heard had not been an accurate reflection of his true sentiments and intentions. Perhaps he had simply said what he thought his friend wished to hear, though she tended to doubt it. Papa was a confident man. He was not the type to pander to his friends.

But in light of everything Mr. Hayes and Mrs. Ashby had said, and given what Felicity and Aunt Louisa evidently knew of Papa...it painted an alarming picture.

"Might we go to the shop again, Papa?" she finally gathered the courage to ask at breakfast the morning after her encounter with Mr. Yorke. "I had a few more ideas last night, but I want to ensure they are possible with the way the windows sit."

Papa took a moment before responding, a furrow in his brow. "I do not think so, my dear. The more I consider things, the more I feel certain that this idea of yours is simply not prudent. It is my job as your father to protect your reputation, and I fear the effect this would have if it were to become known."

Her heart clenched to hear him retract his promise. "Why should it?"

"Things have a way of doing so, my dear. This is London, after all. Not Wetley."

"But...I thought we had agreed that—"

"Arabella," he said, his voice sharp.

Her eyes widened.

His tone was softer as he continued. "Agreements must be adaptable as circumstances change, my dear. Surely you can understand that."

She said nothing. If she spoke, she might say something she regretted—or give something away she should not.

It was not as though he had confessed to the murder of which Mr. Yorke had accused him. And yet, in some strange way, it felt like that. She was seeing a different side of Papa than before. Had he changed? Or had she been blind and naïve?

"Do not be angry with me, Bella," he said cajolingly, reaching his hand over and patting hers. "We will find another way to satisfy your creative wishes."

But her creative hopes and dreams were far from her main concern now.

When Papa had left for the day, she ventured to the study.

Standing before the door, she took in a few long, slow breaths. Was she prepared for what she might find within? Could one ever be prepared to discover their own father was a murderer? She very much doubted it.

And what if she found nothing? What if she discovered Mr. Yorke had lied yet again? She would find it difficult to forgive herself for doubting Papa. He might have lied to her about Lord Farnham or the shop window, but that did not make him a murderer.

Whatever the truth was, she needed to discover it.

She squared her shoulders and opened the door. Hands trembling, she went straight to the desk and began with the drawer Mr. Yorke had been looking through. Her heart quickened when she opened the leather folio and found it full of entries with amounts beside them.

But they were household accounts with no sign of Seamark Trading, the name Mr. Yorke had mentioned.

There was nothing else of note in the entire drawer, so she proceeded to the other drawer, wondering if Mr. Yorke had simply been mistaken. By the time she was nearing the bottom of the drawer, she couldn't help asking herself if perhaps this was all a misunderstanding. Might not Papa *and* Mr. Yorke be innocent?

Her heart latched onto the idea, for that would mean she had not been mistaken in either of them.

Her hand met the wood of the drawer's base, and she let out a sigh of relief. She ran her hand along the bottom for good measure, and it caught on something.

She grasped the smooth leather, heart pounding. This folio was smaller than the other. She unwound the string that kept it closed and let it fall open in her hands.

Her gaze ran over the entries and numbers. It was certainly a ledger, and the expenses were related to shipping: repairs, provisions, dock fees. She ran her quivering finger along the list and came to a sudden halt on a large sum.

Her finger trailed from the number and across the page, where the name Seamark Trading was written, clear as anything.

"Are you unwell, child?" Aunt Louisa asked as they sat with their tea that afternoon. "You have been distracted for days."

Arabella blinked out of her reverie and met her aunt's eye, then looked at Felicity, who pulled a sympathetic face.

Felicity was aware of everything that had happened, including Arabella's discovery of the ledger. She had not been nearly as surprised as Arabella to find that there was indeed evidence of Papa's misdeeds. It was not direct evidence that he had murdered, but it certainly seemed to support Mr. Yorke's version of events.

Together with what Arabella had overheard Papa saying, it painted a bleak picture.

"Do you think my father ruthless?" Arabella asked suddenly.

Aunt Louisa's eyes widened in surprise, and she gave an uncertain laugh. "What a thing to ask, child! Whatever do you mean by posing such a question?"

"I wish to know your opinion of my father. Do you think him capable of being ruthless? Unprincipled?"

Aunt Louisa glanced at Felicity, as though hoping for aid, but Felicity regarded her expectantly.

"The truth, if you please, Aunt," Arabella said.

Aunt Louisa pursed her lips and was quiet for a moment. "I think," she said slowly, "that your father would do whatever was required to protect the things he cares about."

"Things," Arabella repeated slowly. "Not people."

"Both, no doubt," Aunt Louisa amended.

Arabella was quiet.

"He loves you, Arabella," Aunt Louisa said. "Of that I have no doubt."

Arabella blinked, pushing away the stinging in her eyes. "You believe he would do whatever was required. Does that include murder?"

Aunt Louisa's brow pulled together. "Why do you ask these things, child?"

"Please answer," Arabella said softly.

Her aunt took in a long breath. "If the threat was great enough, I suppose the answer is yes."

Arabella swallowed and nodded, the sick feeling in her intensifying. "Thank you."

The front door opened, and Papa's voice speaking to one of the footmen sounded.

Arabella rose. "If you will excuse me..."

Felicity nodded subtly, understanding her intent.

Arabella forced herself to breathe deeply as she left the room.

Papa had just removed his coat, hat, and gloves when she emerged into the entry hall. He glanced over at her and smiled. The smile faded slightly at the sight of her.

"May I speak with you?" Arabella asked.

A flash of something passed over his expression—worry, perhaps—but his smile grew again. "Of course."

Arabella led the way to the library, and Papa soon closed the door behind them.

He went over to the liquor cabinet. "What is it, my dear?"

Arabella took a moment before speaking. "What is your connection with the Yorke family, Papa?"

His hand paused, the decanter of brandy hovering over an empty glass. He turned to regard her. "That is a strange question. What brings it about?"

"I have heard things. Things that concern me."

His gaze was steady. "You must be more specific, my dear."

Her courage wavered. It was no small thing to ask one's father if he had murdered a man. Just what sort of horrors was he capable of?

But the question had to be asked. If there was any truth to her suspicions, she needed to know, not only for her own sake but for Mr. Yorke's. And if it was untrue, for Papa's sake. He did not deserve to be maligned any more than did Mr. Yorke.

"Did you sabotage the investments you had together?" she asked, forcing her voice to stay steady.

His expression flickered, then his brows drew together. "I beg your pardon?"

"Were you involved in the death of Mr. Langdon?"

A spasm of anger slashed across his face, and she felt a flash of fear. What if she had overestimated his affection for her? What might he do in anger?

"You dare ask me such a thing?" His voice was a near-whisper, but his cheeks trembled and flooded with color. She had never seen him look so forbidding, so...angry.

She suppressed the urge to draw back from him. "I want to know the truth, Papa."

"The truth?" he said in a voice dangerously calm. "You think you want the truth?"

She nodded and clenched her shaking hands, forcing herself to stand her ground as he took slow steps toward her.

"I have spent the last twenty-two years protecting you from the truth, Arabella."

"I do not wish to be protected from the truth," she said, but her voice broke with the fear increasing with every step he took nearer.

"You cannot know that. You have been cosseted and looked after your entire life—shielded from anything unsavory or painful." He looked at her intently, a harsh light in his eyes. "The truth would break you, Arabella. If you knew the things I have done to put those handsome clothes on your back and the finest roof over your head..." He stopped two feet in front of her.

Arabella regarded the man who had raised her, but she hardly recognized him with the expression he now wore. "What have you done, Papa?" she asked in a whisper.

Another flash of anger passed over his expression. "You think you can bask in the fruits of my labors, that you can reap the benefits of what I have sown out of love for you and your sisters, and then come down on me in self-righteousness?"

"I do not want handsome clothing or a fine home at the cost of your soul, Papa." Her voice shook with emotion.

"It is too late for that now. Everything I have done has been with your well-being in mind—Langdon included. We are finally at the culmination of my plans. Lord Farnham will be here tomorrow evening for dinner. Then your future will be secure."

Arabella shook her head and took a step back, unable to believe that he had ascribed the killing of Langdon to her well-being. "I cannot marry him, Papa."

"I am losing patience, Arabella. We have discussed this. Countless times. You *will* accept Farnham's proposal. Things are already arranged."

She stared at him, trying to comprehend how he could stand here and lay the blame for his actions at her feet, saying he had done atrocious things for her benefit, and then demand she marry a man she knew she would be unhappy with.

The only reasonable explanation for it was that her marriage to Farnham was not truly for her benefit but for his—for the good of his investments.

But she would not be a puppet in his plans. Not anymore. And she would not allow him to ruin the lives of people like Mr. Yorke with her as an excuse. When she spoke, her voice trembled with a mixture of fear and determination. "Agreements must be adaptable as circumstances change."

Papa's brow snapped together as he recognized his own words being used against him. His face contorted with rage.

With every limb trembling, Arabella turned on her heel and left the room just as Felicity emerged from the parlor. She looked at Arabella questioningly.

Arabella, whose eyes were full of tears, shook her head, unable to speak.

Felicity's face crumpled with sympathy, and she hurried

over, wrapping an arm through Arabella's and following her to her bedchamber.

Through tears and with Felicity's hand holding hers tightly, Arabella recounted what had happened. The horrible truth.

"Is this my fault?" Arabella asked once she had finished, her cheeks wet with tears.

"What on earth do you mean?" Felicity asked incredulously, wiping the tears with her thumb. "Of course not!"

"Perhaps if I had not been so...worldly, Papa would not have felt obliged to—"

"No," Felicity said firmly. "It is entirely normal for a father to wish and seek the best for his children, Bella, but plenty of fathers do so without resorting to murder."

Arabella saw the sense in this, and in her heart, she knew her father's actions were not her fault, but it made her sick to think that *he* might see it that way. That he should kill a man and use her as justification—it was unthinkable. And yet, it was true.

"You need to go out, Bella," Felicity said. "You need distraction—a reminder that there is good in the world."

She *did* need that reminder. But what she truly wanted was to see Mr. Yorke.

"There is a musical soirée this evening," Felicity said. "You will come, won't you? Music always soothes *my* agitation."

Arabella considered the prospect. It felt wrong to seek entertainment when her mind was weighed down with such heaviness. But what good would it do to sit all alone with her unhappy thoughts at home? And what if she was obliged to dine with Papa?

She could not face him. Not yet.

"We will only stay as long as you wish," Felicity reassured her. "I swear it."

Arabella smiled sadly at her cousin, grateful to have someone who understood her, someone who was so eager to support her and buoy her spirits. "I fear I shall ruin an otherwise pretty evening."

Felicity grasped her hands tightly, her mouth pulling into a pretty smile. "You could never do so. You shan't regret coming —I promise."

Arabella chose her plainest dress for the evening, one she had made plans to add to and embellish but had not yet managed. It felt wrong to put on display the things that had been bought with money Papa had gained through such unsavory means.

Felicity and Aunt Louisa were pulling on their gloves in the entry hall when she came down the stairs. Felicity's gaze ran over the dress Arabella was wearing, and she gave an understanding smile.

"Just in time," Aunt Louisa said. "I believe that was the carriage wheels I just heard outside. Come, child."

Papa emerged from the nearest room, and Arabella stopped short a few feet from her aunt, her heart thumping.

He was dressed to go out, wearing gloves, a coat, and his hat. His brows rose. "Where are you going?"

"To a musical evening," Aunt Louisa said. "We shall not stay out too late, though. I am quite tired already."

"You may stay out as late as you wish, Louisa, but my daughter will not be joining you."

Everyone's eyes darted to Arabella.

She stared at Papa, and he met her gaze calmly.

Her nostrils flared, and she looked at Felicity and Aunt Louisa.

There was mutiny in Felicity's eyes, whereas, Aunt Louisa looked torn between a sense of injustice and the knowledge that she had no right to challenge a father's orders for his daughter.

"Go on," Arabella said to them.

Felicity hesitated a moment, but after a nod from Arabella, she followed her troubled mother to the front door.

The echo of the door closing reverberated through the entry hall.

Arabella stared at it, not meeting Papa's gaze.

"I have arranged for you to return to Wetley on Saturday."

Her head came around, her eyes wide. Saturday was but four days away.

"You expressed such strong feelings about my methods of keeping you in a life of comfort," Papa said, "that I can only conclude you will be happier without all the entertainments afforded by our ill-gotten wealth." His eyes dared her to counter him.

She gave a stiff nod, still not meeting his eye. "Very well." She gathered her skirts and made her way to the stairs.

"Arabella?"

She stopped on the second stair but did not turn.

"If you leave, I will know."

She stayed a moment longer, and then, when she was satisfied he had said all he wished to, she continued up the stairs and to her bedchamber, a fire burning within her as the front door closed behind Papa.

25

SILAS

"Nothing from Miss Easton?" Frederick asked as Silas watched him tie his cravat.

"No." He'd not had a word from her since their tense exchange at Aunt Eugenia's, days ago, and he was not fool enough to think that boded well for him. And yet, there had been no visits by the constable, indicating she had not told her father of his presence in Town.

It was puzzling, to say the least.

Frederick adjusted the knot at his throat, then turned toward Silas. "No news may be good news."

"Perhaps," Silas said doubtfully. Anything short of Arabella forgiving him and Drayton taking the blame for his actions would not seem *good*.

Frederick pulled out his pocket watch and checked the time.

"Time to go?" Silas asked.

Frederick, Drake, and Fairchild were attending a lecture that evening.

Explaining why Silas insisted on remaining at the townhouse each night rather than joining them had become a difficult task, and he was running out of excuses. One could only have so many headaches and urgent letters to write, after all, particularly when one had no correspondents.

"I have a few minutes," Frederick said. "You know how long Drake takes to dress."

"Everyone but Drake knows how long Drake takes to dress," Silas retorted.

There was a knock on the door, and Frederick went to open it. A servant stood there, but his gaze shifted past Frederick and landed upon Silas.

"This was just delivered for you." He held out a parcel wrapped in brown paper and tied with string.

Frederick reached for it, but the servant withdrew it from reach. "Forgive me, sir," he said with sincere apology, "but I was given very particular instructions to place it directly into Mr. Hayes's care."

Silas rose with a puzzled brow and went over to receive it. "Thank you."

The servant bowed and left, and Silas stared down at the package.

"What in heaven's name is it?" Frederick asked.

Silas did not respond, for he had an idea, but he was too afraid to give voice to it. He turned over the package, but there was no note or writing to provide a clue as to who had sent it.

He strode over to Frederick's dressing table and set it down, then pulled at the bow and began unwrapping it.

Between the first and second layer of paper laid a small note. He picked it up, but his eyes had already devoured the message.

Forgive me for ever doubting you,
A

Silas tore the second layer of paper away, and just as he had hoped and suspected, a leather ledgerbook sat beneath it.

"Is that...?" Frederick asked.

Silas nodded and picked it up reverently, his heart pounding like war drums. He opened the ledger as Frederick stepped up beside him to watch.

Silas's eyes and finger ran over the entries hungrily, and his heart threatened to leap from his chest at the sight of the first entry for Seamark Trading.

"There," he said, pointing at it.

"By Jove," Frederick said with awe.

"And there again," Silas said, indicating another instance.

The more they looked, the more they found. Tangible, physical proof that Drayton had been working in secret to undercut his own investments with their main competitor—the competitor with whom he had later gone into business.

"It is enough, isn't it?" Frederick asked, his voice full of restrained energy.

"It is more than I had even hoped for," Silas said, his heart racing with anticipation.

Frederick grasped him by the shoulders excitedly, then pulled him into his arms.

Silas responded with gusto, only to draw back suddenly. "Careful!" He pulled the ledger book from being crushed by their exuberance and set it aside.

Frederick laughed at him, and Silas's heart was so full of joy he couldn't help but join, and they were soon embracing again.

"What do we do now?" Frederick asked once their laughter had subsided.

"Protect it with our lives," Silas said, running a hand over the soft cover. The truth, however, was that he had been so focused on obtaining the evidence that he had not truly thought through what precisely he would do with it once he had it.

It needed to be brought to light—and by someone they could trust, someone who was not in Drayton's pocket and might be tempted to alert him or even destroy the evidence to stay in his good graces.

"William will know what to do," Frederick said.

Silas nodded, flipping through the pages again to see the entries, as though perhaps he had imagined them before. But they were still there.

"William is the only person I would trust with this. And Bence, perhaps. The information here will ruin Drayton, Freddie. Once its contents are known, the people he has been blackmailing—half of London, from what Bence says—will be able to come forward, as well. It will finish him."

He gave a little sigh. "Poor Miss Easton."

Silas's gaze shot to his. "What do you mean?"

Frederick shrugged. "If what you say is true, it is not only Drayton who will be ruined. His family will be disgraced."

Silas stared at his brother, his thoughts racing.

How had he never considered what his own freedom would mean for Arabella? How had he been so single-minded to neglect considering what her father's downfall would mean for her or her sisters?

"Silas," Frederick said, a warning in his voice, as though he was following the train of his unspoken thoughts.

Silas did not respond.

Frederick took him by the arms and rattled him. "Silas, you

cannot throw away your chance at freedom. You are *innocent*! Drayton is guilty. Justice requires that he pay for what he did."

"And what does justice require of Arabella? That she be sacrificed for something she had no hand in? Is my innocence, my liberty, my future of more value than hers?"

Frederick had no response for this, but he shook his head in frustration. "What do you mean to do?"

That was the question, indeed.

The one thing Silas knew for certain was that he needed to return the ledger to Arabella, and he needed to do it in person. How he could arrange for such a thing was less evident. But there was one option.

"You think I have nothing better to do than arrange clandestine visits?" Aunt Eugenia barked.

Silas opened his mouth, intending to placate her, but she interrupted him unceremoniously.

"Because I don't," she said. "Leave it to me. I will summon you when it is arranged."

Silas smiled, took her by the hand, and kissed the back of it.

She yanked her hand away. "Save that for the Easton girl."

This had the effect of wiping the smile from his face, for there was no prospect of sharing any such intimacy with Arabella. Both of them knew now that anything between them was an impossibility.

The best he could do was to assure her he had no intention of turning her life on its head in his quest for justice.

Just what he *did* intend was less clear, for he could not live in hiding forever.

Perhaps he could assume a new identity and move to Bath or Brighton or somewhere Lord Drayton was unlikely to venture. It was not a particularly happy prospect, but he was not convinced that a future without Arabella *contained* any happiness, whatever the circumstances.

Silas's heart thudded with force as he opened a note from Aunt Eugenia just before five o'clock.

> *A meeting here is impossible. Her father is keeping her home like a prisoner. He has plans to return her to their estate in Staffordshire soon.*
>
> *Naturally, this has only increased my determination. He shan't win. Miss Fairchild and I are in contact and will find a way.*
>
> *Await word from me.*
>
> *Aunt Eugenia*

Silas didn't know whether to laugh or cry. Drayton was keeping Arabella like a prisoner? And he meant to send her home?

The words brought a sort of panic in their wake.

And yet, he knew his aunt and he knew Miss Fairchild. They would, indeed, find a way.

He had been pacing for nearly an hour in his bedchamber, wishing Aunt Eugenia had specified what *soon* meant so he would know when exactly Drayton meant to send Arabella home, when a servant brought another note.

He tore it open and looked over the exceptionally brief note in Aunt Eugenia's script.

> *Vauxhall. Ten o'clock. Entrance to Dark Walks by the Chinese Pavilion.*

Silas's brows snapped together. They had set up a meeting at Vauxhall? How in heaven's name would Arabella manage to visit a place like that when her father would not even allow her to visit Aunt Eugenia?

He pulled out his pocket watch.

Half-past eight. It was just enough time.

26

SILAS

Most visitors to Vauxhall gardens did not arrive with a parcel in hand, but Silas gripped the ledger, rewrapped in the paper Arabella had sent it in, tightly between his arm and body as he passed into the gardens.

His eyes were wide and alert as he strode with purpose toward the Chinese Pavilion. He searched the area for any sign of Arabella as he approached the set meeting place, but there was no masquerade tonight, so no one was masked.

It was Miss Fairchild he first spotted and her mother beside her.

His heart dropped. Arabella was nowhere to be seen.

"Where is—"

"Follow me," Miss Fairchild said, her eyes flitting to the parcel he held. "I will take you to her."

Her mother grasped her arm, keeping her from turning away. "You belong at Bedlam if you think I intend to let you go into the Dark Walks without at least two sets of eyes on you, child. We will both show him the way." She turned back to Silas. "Your aunt is with her."

Silas nodded, then followed with a thumping heart while the two women led the way into the hedged paths. They turned right and then left, left again, then right. Just when Silas was beginning to wonder if Miss Fairchild had forgotten the way, she stopped and turned to him.

"We required help from the servants to spirit her away, but we managed. She is just around that corner." She pointed to a place just ahead where the path split.

"Thank you," he said, then brushed between Mrs. and Miss Fairchild and made his way toward Arabella. When he turned the corner, Aunt Eugenia spun around.

"There you are," she said.

Silas barely heard her. His eyes were on Arabella. She wore a gown made of the pink satin she had bought at the market at Covent Garden. She took his breath away, and immediately, he knew he had made the right choice to come. Was there anything he would not sacrifice if it meant her happiness was possible?

Aunt Eugenia looked at Arabella, then made a sound of aggravation. "I can see it is an exercise in futility to speak to either of you." She picked up her skirts and swept past Silas, then around the corner and out of sight.

They stared at one another for a few moments of silence.

"I am so sorry," she said. It was dark, but her eyes glistened even in the dim light.

He shook his head and took quick steps toward her. "You have no reason to apologize. *I* am the one who should be doing so."

It was her turn to protest with a head shake. "You did only what was required for your survival."

He reached for her hand. "I wanted to tell you. So many times."

She nodded and squeezed his hand. "The way I reacted when you did only proved your hesitation warranted."

"How could you *not* have doubted me when you found me in such suspicious circumstances?" He released her hand and took the parcel from under his arm. "I cannot tell you what it means to me that you would give this to me, Arabella. But I cannot take it." He held it out to her.

Her eyes widened at the sight of it, but she refused to take it. "You *must* take it."

He shook his head, then took one of her hands and placed it gently but firmly around the bound edge of the parcel.

"Why?" she asked, looking at him with a puzzled brow.

"I promised I would never hurt you. I have already broken that promise by my dishonesty. I will not break it again." He released his hand slowly, leaving the ledger in her hands. "I love you too much."

Her gaze flickered as she stared at him. She stepped forward, tipping up her chin to meet his gaze. "Do you love me enough to run away with me?"

The silence echoed in Silas's ears.

"Papa means to send me back to Wetley," she said. "I cannot go, Silas. I cannot leave you. I love you."

To hear his true name on her lips, followed by such an admission...the truth of it washed over him, infusing him with warmth and a need too great to be ignored.

He took her face in his hands and pressed his lips to hers.

Gone was the statuesque austerity from the last time he had seen her. She melted into his arms, her lips forming perfectly to his as though two halves of one whole. He had never thought to have the chance to kiss her even once; to do so a second time, and to do it without the weight of dishonesty hanging over him, made him feel weightless and free in a way the ledger never could have.

She broke away. "Is that a yes?" she asked breathlessly.

He cupped her face between his hands and looked into her eyes—the most beautiful eyes in the world. "You truly wish for me to run away with you?"

She nodded.

He kissed her again, softly this time. "I would go anywhere with you, Arabella. But I cannot let you sacrifice everything on a whim."

"It is not a whim."

He smiled slightly and brushed a hand along her cheek, reveling in its softness. "And just how long have you been planning to run away with me?"

She laughed and held his hand with hers. "An abrupt change from when I tried to run *from* you the night we met."

"You mean the night you called me your husband?"

Her smile grew. "I did call you that, didn't I? I had forgotten."

"*I* had not. I have been wishing you would call me that in earnest for some time, all the while knowing it was impossible."

She shook her head. "It is my greatest wish."

His smile wavered. "Arabella, have you truly thought this through? I am a wanted man. Wanted for murder."

"Not with this." She held up the ledger.

He shut his eyes, for the temptation she presented was almost more than he could bear. "*I* would gain my freedom, yes, but you..."

She covered his cheek with her hand, forcing him to meet her gaze. "Do you mean to say you would not want me once my name is sullied by the contents of that ledger?"

He took it, set it at their feet, then pulled her into his arms and kissed her. He kissed her and kissed her until he was satisfied there could not be so much as a shred of doubt left in her mind of the strength, depth, or breadth of his feelings.

He pulled back and fixed his gaze on hers. "I permit no one to question the constancy of my love for you."

"Not even me?"

"Especially not you. Express such doubt again, and I will be forced to take more extreme measures."

"Hardly a deterrent, is it?"

They laughed softly until Silas gave a sigh.

"Does this mean you will not run away with me?" she asked.

"No," he said. "But I *will* marry you. I am not strong enough to deny you such a wish, for it too perfectly aligns with my own. But it must be by special license."

"How would we acquire such a thing?" The question was warranted, for a special license would give them permission to be wed anywhere of their choosing. It was both expensive and could only be granted by the Archbishop of Canterbury himself.

Understanding dawned on her face. "Your brother."

Silas nodded. "He will manage."

"But if I return tonight, Papa will know I have disobeyed him and will ensure I am sent to Wetley without delay."

Silas considered this for a moment. "You may stay with Aunt Eugenia until we have the license."

"Will she allow that?"

Silas chuckled. "She will be ecstatic to be involved in such a way."

Arabella smiled. "I like her."

"And she you."

Arabella stooped and picked up the parcel with the ledger inside. "And what of this?"

"That is yours to do with as you will. The contents affect you most nearly. The decision must be yours."

"Silas," she said incredulously. "This is your freedom."

"And it is your father's life, Arabella. It is your reputation. Your sisters' reputations. I cannot be the one to make that choice."

His words seemed to have hit home, for her forehead puckered.

He ran his thumb along the lines to smooth them away. "I am already living the life of a wanted man, and I can continue to do so. I have nothing certain to offer you beyond my love, sure and unwavering as it might be. Take the time to consider the future while you are at Aunt Eugenia's. If you decide this is all too much, there will be no blame in my heart for you. If you wish to live life with me as a wanted man, I will take you happily and carve out the best life for us of which I am capable."

"And if I choose to make the contents of the ledger known?" she asked.

"Then," he said, looking down at her tenderly, "I will be here to hold you and cherish you—and to shield you and your sisters as best I can."

She let out a slow, trembling breath.

"Take the time you need," he said softly. "And know that my love is sure, whatever you decide."

27

ARABELLA

For a woman who was so forthright and frank, Eugenia Ashby was surprisingly compassionate. Whether Silas had told her of the decision Arabella faced or she had simply deduced as much on her own, Arabella did not know. She was simply grateful for Mrs. Ashby's kindness and consideration in allowing her to remain at her townhouse, providing enough conversation to distract her but also giving her the time and space to be with her own thoughts.

Of those, there were plenty. The depths to which the disappointment and hurt from Papa's duplicity and depravity took her were only countered by the heights to which the joy and ecstasy of Silas's love and constancy brought her. She cried many tears—tears for the man she had believed Papa to be, tears for the pain he had caused the man she loved, and tears for the life he had taken.

Felicity and Aunt Louisa had chosen to stay with friends rather than return to the townhouse and risk Papa's ire, for none of them doubted he would interrogate them regarding Arabella's whereabouts.

Arabella tossed and turned and tossed as she faced the dilemma of which road to take. Life without Silas was an option she dismissed immediately. When she pictured the future, the only certainty within it was him.

If she loved him, how could she ask him to live a life without freedom? And yet, the alternative required a great sacrifice indeed of her sisters.

And then there was Papa.

She loved the version of him she had known, however incomplete or false it may have been. Knowing he had murdered a man in cold blood did not erase the moments of kindness and affection they had shared, but it tainted them irrevocably. That did not mean she wished for him to be subjected to the fate he might face for his terrible crimes: death. And for her to be the one to condemn him to that fate... the thought made her sick.

Justice must be done, but was there not a way to achieve it without leaving even more pain and destruction in the wake of the pain and destruction he had already caused? Her sisters surely did not deserve to be punished for the sins of their father.

Silas had promised to see that they were cared for, and for that alone, her love for him expanded past the bounds she thought possible.

While she had been doubtful at first of the necessity of a special license to wed, the more she considered it, the more she grew to understand. A trip to the border might well be stopped by Papa, while any attempt to wed in one of their parishes could be met with danger on Silas's end or reluctance from the priest at Wetley. If he knew he was marrying Papa's daughter without his approval, he would undoubtedly refuse to perform the ceremony.

She sincerely hoped the duke was able to help them obtain

the license. If anyone had the necessary connections, it must be he.

Arabella went still, a thought occurring to her.

After a moment's reflection, she sat up, whipped the covers off, and left her bed.

She knew what she needed to do.

"I hope you will forgive my wife joining us," said the Duke of Rockwood, taking a seat beside the duchess in their sitting room. "She is far wiser and intelligent than I, as you will no doubt see, and I value her perspective."

"Of course, Your Grace," Arabella said, her hands clasped tightly in her lap as she smiled at the duchess.

"How may we be of service?" the duke asked.

Arabella took the parcel beside her and set it on her lap. "I have quite a large request to make of you, Your Grace. I realize it is entirely presumptuous of me to do so, as we do not know each other, but as it concerns your brother, I hope you will consider it despite that."

The duke's eyes rested on the parcel for a moment before returning to her. "We are all ears, Miss Easton."

She launched into an explanation of the decision she had been struggling over, coloring up as she referenced her feelings for Silas, then fending off tears as she explained how impossible it all felt.

She did not even manage to voice the request she had come to make when she was obliged to take a moment to breathe through her emotions.

"We quite understand, Miss Easton," the duchess said kindly. "You are in the most difficult of positions through no fault of your own."

"Indeed," her husband echoed. "Is that the ledger?"

Arabella nodded.

There was a moment of silence before he spoke again. "Would you like for me to take it off your hands?"

Arabella stared at him. That was precisely what she had come to request, though she had not yet said as much. It felt like the height of presumption to arrive at the house of a duke and ask him to help the man who had falsely accused his brother of murder and sent him into hiding.

The duke smiled at her reaction, then looked at his wife. "As we discussed the situation the other day, my wife pointed out that, given both the position you are in and the affection you and Silas share for one another, it would be difficult for either of you to do what was necessary with that ledger. I, on the other hand, am fortunate enough to have the connections to do so in a manner which is less...messy. I believe I can bring about a conclusion to things that will result in my brother's freedom and the least amount of pain for you and your family."

Arabella sat forward, heart beating anxiously. "You do?"

He nodded calmly. His entire demeanor was at odds with his brother's infectious energy, but it couldn't help but inspire confidence. He wore the dukedom well.

"I will present the ledger directly to the Prince Regent," he said. "I cannot say for certain what he will decide—I doubt anyone could claim to know such a thing when it comes to Prinny—but I believe this will lead to a better outcome than to make a spectacle of things in the House of Lords." His brow furrowed. "Please understand, Miss Easton, that I can make no promises regarding the end result, but I intend to do every- thing I can to minimize the repercussions for you—and to see to it that your father, while held accountable for his actions, does not face death."

She could hardly breathe. "You would do that?"

The duke's eyes grew kinder. "If there is anything the Yorke family has learned over the past two years, Miss Easton, it is the unmatched value of familial relationships. You intend, we hope, to become part of this family."

The duchess smiled warmly at her.

The tears that had been threatening spilled over onto Arabella's cheeks, and she gave a breathy laugh as she dashed away at them.

She loved the Yorke family already.

28

SILAS

Silas's pulse thrummed as he entered the confines of the enormous St. James's Palace. After more than two years of ensuring no one knew of his presence in England, setting foot in the residence of the monarch under his true name seemed like an act of madness.

He was putting every ounce of his trust in William and the note he had received that morning, summoning him to the palace.

He had not seen Arabella since Vauxhall three nights ago, though Aunt Eugenia insisted she was doing well. He had not wanted to exert any pressure on her by coming to visit or asking questions. He wanted the decision to be hers, for she would have to live with it for the rest of her life.

But the uncertainty of what his future held was beginning to take its toll. He could only assume that uncertainty was about to be laid to rest. Just how desirable that rest would be was the question.

He was led by a liveried servant through a series of corridors, their steps echoing on the flagstone floors and giving an almost eerie feel to the grand but impersonal palace. The eyes in the paintings that lined the walls seemed to follow him, executing judgment upon him in a way that made his stomach knot with nerves.

William would not have told him to come if there had been any real danger, surely. But what if William was mistaken? He was a duke, but Drayton's influence was far more established.

The servant led him into an antechamber, a dimly lit room with two tall, thin windows draped with heavy velvet curtains. On the far side was another door of ornately carved wood, giving the impression it led somewhere equally as impressive.

"Wait here, if you please, sir," the servant said, and without waiting for confirmation, he left Silas alone in the room.

He stood for a moment, then made his way to the window, eager for something to distract him from trying to anticipate what lay ahead. The rippled glass of the window pane gave the view outside an almost dreamlike quality, blurring the lines between the cobbled stones of the courtyard.

A door opened, and Silas turned. William emerged from the carved wooden door, his expression somber until he noted Silas.

"William," Silas said, hurrying over to him. "What is happening?"

Arabella emerged from the same door, her expression similarly somber, and a little *v* carved into her otherwise smooth brow.

Silas's heart came to a halt just as her feet did the same.

Her mouth stretched into a smile, and she let out a sigh of relief as she came over to him, her hands out to receive his.

He took them eagerly and brought them in turn to his lips. "What are you doing here?"

The joy in her expression wavered just as Lord Drayton emerged.

Silas went rigid, his wide eyes fixed on the man who had done his level best to destroy his life.

Drayton looked paler than usual, but his chin was high, his shoulders straight. His gaze moved to Silas, then to Arabella.

Silas shifted in front of her protectively, but she pressed his hand to reassure him as two servants appeared behind Drayton—escorts, it seemed.

"You have nothing to fear from him anymore," William said in a low voice.

"You dare to shield my own daughter from me?" Drayton said. "Who do you think has protected her all these years?"

"You protected yourself," Arabella said, stepping forward while keeping her grip on Silas's hand. "You betrayed my sisters and me by manipulating us for your own purposes. You kept us away from the world and called it love to soothe your own conscience."

The vein in his head pulsed. "I protected you from the realities of a vicious world."

"A world made more vicious by *you*. If there is one thing I have learned, it is this: if you use love toward one person to justify hatred and evil toward another, in the end, you will find the hatred has expanded to consume everything its path, down to your very soul." She looked up at Silas, her eyes bright with emotion. "I choose love."

The fire he had been feeling inside at her words swelled, and he pressed a kiss to her hair.

"Except toward me," Drayton replied with a sneer.

She shook her head. "I do not hate you, Papa. I pity you. You were so intent on having everything that you lost it all."

He stared at her for a moment, then turned his gaze to Silas. "You do not deserve her."

"I do not. But I will spend my life cherishing and protecting her, Drayton."

Arabella's hold tightened on his hand.

"He is no longer Drayton, Silas," William said. "He is simply Mr. Easton."

"Come along, sir," said one of the servants, urging Mr. Easton forward.

He gave Silas one last look of disgust, then followed the servants from the room.

Silas turned to Arabella, whose eyes were on the door as it shut. He regarded her with concern.

"I am sorry," he said.

She shook her head and met his gaze. "It would be dishonest of me to say that I am unaffected, but he is unrepentant, and justice must be done."

"What will become of him?" Silas asked.

Another liveried servant appeared at the door. "Please enter, Mr. Yorke."

Silas nodded, then looked at William questioningly. Any hint of what he would hear when he stepped through that door would be welcome.

"I gave Prinny the evidence yesterday," William said, understanding his desire, "but he wished to consider things before making any decisions. Evidently, he has made them. Mr. Easton has been removed from his position. They will begin the search for the nearest male heir to take his place. Meanwhile, he agreed to voluntary exile—in France. He has been made to understand that any repetition of his choices here will result in his being returned to stand trial here."

Silas's brows shot up. He had a thousand questions, but the servant cleared his throat significantly.

"You will both come?" Silas asked his brother and Arabella.

"Of course," Arabella said. "If you wish us to."

He did. Whatever the result was of this audience, he wanted to be surrounded by the people he loved.

The door behind them burst open, and his brother Anthony came striding through, breathless.

He was followed shortly by Frederick. "You cannot simply burst into the reigning monarch's residence, Anthony."

Aunt Eugenia, Clara, and Charlotte brought up the rear. Anthony and Charlotte must have ridden post-haste from the small estate they had been renting near Charlotte's family.

"Are we too late?" Anthony asked, eyes wide and urgent as he regarded Silas and the others.

"No." Silas smiled at the sight of his brother. Anthony had been the only one who had believed him from the beginning. He had sacrificed a great deal in pursuit of Silas's freedom. He *and* Charlotte, in fact. Though their efforts had not been successful, he would never forget what they had done.

The servant cleared his throat even more loudly this time so that the sound reverberated throughout the antechamber.

Everyone turned toward him.

"I take it you all intend to come?" he asked with evidence of worn patience.

"Of course we do, you fool," Aunt Eugenia said, making her way toward the door.

"Aunt!" Frederick cried, no doubt fearing his political aspirations were about to be obliterated by the behavior of his family.

The servant's mouth twitched at the corner, then he put out a hand to indicate that they should all pass through.

With Arabella's arm in his, Silas led the way, his heart swelling as the footsteps of his family shuffled behind him. Whatever happened here, he was a fortunate man indeed to have the support of so many.

Dark wood paneling and arched windows framed the room they passed into. A long table stretched from the front toward them. It was surrounded by tall chairs upholstered with rich damask and brass studs. At the head sat two unfamiliar men, one with a quill and parchment at the ready.

"Please have a seat, Mr. Yorke," said the man at the head of the table, indicating the seat at the end of the table opposite him. "And, er"—his gaze shifted to the others, though his head did not move—"family."

Silas helped Arabella into the chair nearest him, while William took the one on his other side.

"I am Lord Turlington and am representing His Royal Highness today. The Prince regrets that he could not be personally present. He was unavoidably detained by a pressing matter of State."

Silas's gaze flitted to Anthony, who cocked a skeptical eyebrow at this. Frederick shot Anthony a severe glance, as though it was blasphemy to doubt the importance of whatever had kept Prinny away.

"Something to do with the acquisition of a pair of Arabian stallions," said Turlington, "which required his immediate attention, as you can understand."

Silas cleared his throat, and a small spasm near the edge of Frederick's mouth made it clear that even he was struggling to see this as a matter of greatest urgency.

"Rest assured," Turlington continued, "that His Royal Highness has entrusted me with the full authority of the Crown as I conduct this meeting." He turned to the scribe, who handed him a piece of official parchment. He cleared his throat and read, "By the authority vested in His Royal Highness, George Augustus Frederick, Prince of Wales and Prince Regent of the United Kingdom of Great Britain and Ireland, acting in place of His Majesty King George III, and in consultation with the Council of State, the following proclamations are hereby made known and declared.

"Firstly, it is decreed that Mr. Silas Yorke, of the family

Yorke, is hereby cleared of all charges and accusations previously laid against him. The evidence presented before the Crown has been deemed irrefutable, proving beyond doubt that the allegations were the result of falsehoods and malicious intent.

"As such, Mr. Yorke is to be restored in full to his rightful status and standing as a gentleman of unimpeachable character and honor. The stain upon his name is removed, and all rights and privileges due to him are hereby reinstated."

Silas swallowed the emotion rising in his throat as Arabella's hand found his under the table.

She beamed at him, her eyes gleaming with joy.

"Secondly," said Turlington, "as restitution for the harm caused by the machinations and deceit of the man known as Mr. George Easton, it is further ordered that all unentailed lands, properties, and holdings under his name be transferred to Mr. Silas Yorke, who has suffered greatly as a direct result of Mr. Easton's actions and is deemed deserving of restitution."

Arabella's hand gripped his, but Silas stared unblinking at Turlington, certain he had not heard correctly.

"High time!" Aunt Eugenia said loudly, conveniently forgetting that, at one time, she, too, had thought Silas guilty of murder.

Rather than chiding this outburst, Frederick clapped, and the others joined so that the room echoed with applause.

Lord Turlington waited for the applause to subside, then continued. "Thus concludes the proclamations of His Royal Highness, the Prince Regent. Let it be known that these decisions are final and bear the full weight of the Crown's authority. Justice has been served." He looked up from the document and set it on the table before him. "You will be contacted shortly by a representative from the office of the Lord Chancellor." There was another pause. "Mr. Silas Yorke, you are free to go."

Silas let out a shaky laugh, still struggling to believe or understand that not only had his name been cleared, he was now the possessor of...what precisely? He hadn't any idea what of Drayton's fell into the category of unentailed.

There was no time to dwell on the question, however, for he was surrounded by family embracing and congratulating him.

Arabella had moved aside to allow the familial celebrations to proceed without her interference, but Silas was ever-aware of her, his gaze meeting hers as he embraced Aunt Eugenia.

Arabella smiled widely at him and dashed a tear away.

"The best part of this, of course," Aunt Eugenia said as she pulled back, "is that the mustache need never make a reappearance."

"You take too much for granted, Aunt," Silas said, his cheeks aching from smiling.

"And here *I* thought the best part was that Silas inherited unspeakable wealth," Anthony said.

"What *have* you inherited?" Frederick asked with curiosity.

Silas lifted his shoulders, for he hadn't any idea. It was entirely possible that the extent of the material benefit he would receive would be a case clock. Not that he would sneer at such a thing, for any case clock would be a case clock he had not possessed before.

He looked at the Lord Turlington, but both he and the scribe were gone. They must have left amidst the chaos of celebration.

"Barrington Court and the London townhouse."

All eyes turned to Arabella.

"They are unentailed," she explained. "As, of course, are Papa's holdings in shipping and textiles. Those holdings are...

significant." The corners of her mouth drew up slowly as she looked at Silas. "You *have* inherited a great deal."

He regarded her for a moment. Without taking his eyes from her, he said, "Might I trouble you all to grant me a moment of privacy with Miss Easton?"

"I am not at all convinced we *should*," Anthony said, a hint of teasing in his voice. "You have just regained your reputation, Silas. It seems a bit cavalier of you to play fast and loose with it so soon after."

"*You* can stay, Anthony," Frederick said, moving toward the door with purpose. "I have already been witness to the sort of privacy Silas desires with Miss Easton, and I have no desire to repeat the experience."

Silas smiled vaguely, his focus still on Arabella, who met his gaze with her own twinkling one.

"Shoo," Aunt Eugenia said, pushing Anthony toward the door with the help of his wife.

The group shuffled out, and soon the latch clicked into place, echoing in the room.

"Quite a day for you," Arabella said, still standing a dozen feet away.

Silas nodded, searching her face for any sign of the thing he feared. "Even more so for you, I think. How do you...feel?"

She took in a breath. "I feel..." She took a step toward him and smiled. "Happy."

He watched her intently, then took his own step toward her. "You do?"

She nodded, then took another step.

"Is it not difficult," he asked, his skin tingling as he matched her progress with his own, "to think that I am now in possession of two of your father's properties?"

Her smile grew as she took the final step to close the distance between them, looking up at him with a glint of mischief in her eye. "Why do you suppose I wish to marry you?"

Silas let out a shaky laugh of relief and threaded his arms around her waist. "Do you mean to say you have an ulterior motive in accepting my offer of marriage?"

"Who says I *have* accepted it?" she asked, pulling his lips down to hers.

It was the seal upon an impossibly joyful day. How could a man go from losing everything to gaining everything so swiftly?

They pulled apart, Silas's body and heart afire. "I do not think an acceptance is necessary."

"Oh? And why is that?"

"You claimed me as husband the night we met."

Her head fell back as she laughed, and he took the opportunity to press a kiss to her exposed neck. It was warm on his lips, and he couldn't resist trailing more across the soft skin.

A throat cleared loudly, and their heads whipped toward the source.

The servant who had first ushered them into the room stared at them austerely from the doorway. "If it is not an inconvenience to you," he said dryly, "we have other declarations to make today."

"Can a man not have a few moments in private with his betrothed?" Silas replied teasingly.

Arabella took his arm, and they walked toward the door his family had passed through. "We will have to content ourselves with the bit we have enjoyed. Your family wishes to celebrate with you, no doubt."

He opened the door, but his family was not in the antechamber. "Apparently, one room was not enough distance for Freddie." He gave the servant a nod, then shut the door.

"You deserve it all, you know," Arabella said when they were alone again.

"That is debatable." He ran his finger along her hairline tenderly. "I would give it all up if it meant I could have you, you know."

Her expression warmed. "I know. But thankfully, you needn't do so. You have me, and you always will."

He took her face in his hands and brought his lips just shy of hers. "I shall hold you to that. Mercilessly."

"I am counting on it," she replied, any further response stopped by his kiss.

EPILOGUE
ARABELLA

"For all the work you put into them," Silas said, guiding Arabella through the throngs in front of the shop in Burlington Arcade, "it is dashed difficult to see the shop windows."

Arabella merely smiled. While she was ineffably proud of the displays she had created, she was even more proud of the crowds they had attracted.

The *ton* was ever anxious to see what changes would appear in the windows of The Silk Room every other Wednesday. Her sister-in-law Charlotte had given her the idea to make it a bi-weekly occurrence, thanks to the past success Charlotte had experienced doing so with her drawings. As it was Thursday and the newest items had only just been put on display yesterday, it was difficult to find room to step—or breathe.

Arabella held tightly to both Silas's hand and to the hand of her sister Mary, who in turn held Catherine's hand. Shortly after the summons to St. James's, Silas and Arabella had gone to Wetley to bring them to London. While the first week had been particularly trying as they dealt with the drastic changes in their lives, they had since settled in—and become quite enamored of their new family. Frederick, in particular, was a favorite.

There had been inevitable talk amongst the *ton*, of course. As the initial shock of the situation settled, confirmation from various quarters arose of the depravity of Easton sister's father. The fact that most people had not even been aware of their existence led to a great deal of curiosity, and the majority of gossip took the form of sympathy rather than judgment. That they were now so closely connected to the Duke of Rockwood only helped their standing in Society, of course, and no one came to their defense more readily than Aunt Eugenia.

Silas was a determined guide, and he saw Arabella, Mary, and Catherine through the throngs and into the shop. He wore a forest-green tailcoat and a copper-colored silk cravat with gold-threaded stitching at the edges—incontrovertible evidence of two things: firstly, that he was married to Arabella, and secondly, that he was a good husband, for he never complained about the little embellishments she made to his garments. Indeed, he wore them with pride.

Her hand in his, he looked around the shop, which was full to the brim with customers inspecting fabrics and vying for the attention of the two men cutting lengths for them.

"There," Silas stated, nodding to indicate a place across the shop. "Freddie and Drake are over there."

They shouldered their way toward the two, Mary and Catherine beaming at the sight of them.

"It is a madhouse," Frederick said in smiling exasperation. "Well done, Arabella. As for you"—he cocked a brow at Silas, then held up something small and furry-looking—"I can only assume this was strategically placed for my benefit?"

Silas grinned. "You found it, did you?"

"Found and removed," Frederick said.

"A public service," Arabella said, though she shot an amused look at her husband.

Using wax as adhesive, Silas had taken to slipping fabric in the shape of a mustache onto the dress forms Arabella had acquired to display examples of what could be achieved with the textiles sold in the shop.

"This is the most handsome superfine I have ever seen," Mr. Drake interrupted, his hands on the fabric. "What do you say to a reduction in price for a dear, dear friend?" He put his hand over his heart in dramatic fashion.

"Don't you have a coat of that precise fabric already?" Frederick asked.

Mr. Drake narrowed his eyes and inspected the fabric. "I suppose I do. But one can never have enough well-made coats." He put the fabric aside despite this. "Well, I am off to Blackstone's now. Pleasure to see you again, ladies." He bowed to Arabella and her sisters, nodded at Silas and Frederick, then left.

Frederick watched him leave with a frown.

"What is Blackstone's?" Silas asked.

"His club," Frederick replied. "It exists solely for those who have been blackballed by other clubs."

"Drake was blackballed?"

Frederick shrugged. "Must have been. He keeps things close to the chest, you know, but I heard something regarding fortune hunting. I have been wondering if he is in a scrape."

"Silas says you wished to take us to Gunter's, Uncle Freddie," Catherine interrupted, apparently unmoved by Mr. Drake's situation.

Frederick shot a look at Silas to inform him what he thought of this proxy promise, then returned his gaze to

Arabella's sisters and smiled. "More than anything. What do you say? Shall we leave this wild place?"

The girls nodded, and he shepherded them toward the door.

"Ah, Freddie!" Silas called, bringing him to a halt. "I wanted to tell you—Henry Brightmoor's uncle is expected to die soon."

Frederick stared at him, uncomprehending. "My condolences to him—whoever he is."

"Freddie," Silas said with an amused smile. "Brightmoor's uncle is Lord Westvale. Brightmoor is his heir."

Frederick looked none the wiser for this offering of information.

"Brightmoor has been the MP for the borough of Haverton —with a mere twelve voters—these twenty years. His seat will have to be filled."

Arabella suppressed a smile as Frederick's eyes widened and understanding dawned. This could be just the opportunity he had been waiting for—a chance for election.

Any opportunity to pursue the topic was prevented by Catherine pulling insistently on Frederick's hand, however, and he and the two girls were soon swallowed by the crowd.

"You really mean to leave him to their mercy?" Arabella asked.

"We will join them soon enough. But first, I have something to give you."

Arabella cocked a brow. "You do?" He delighted in telling her he had something to give her, but without fail, it was a kiss he pressed to her lips.

Silas smiled conspiratorially and guided her out of the main area, then into one of the back rooms.

They had been married for two months now, but the fluttering in her stomach had not abated whenever she found herself alone with him.

He shut the door behind them, and the din of the shop became muffled.

She waited impatiently for the kiss, but Silas turned away from her and searched behind a few bolts of surplus fabric before bringing out a rectangular box tied with string.

"I have had this an age," he said, handing it to her, "but it was misplaced when we moved to Barrington. It turned up the other day."

She took the box with wonder and looked at him for any clue.

"Open it," he urged.

Obediently, she tugged at the string, which he took so she could manage the box.

She fiddled with the top until it gave way. It was too dark to see within, so she carefully turned it on its head and let the contents slip into her palm.

Her gaze shot to Silas, who was looking at the kaleidoscope with the ghost of a smile.

"I bought it for you that day at Covent Garden, you know," he said. "I wanted to give it to you, but I feared it would seem too pointed, particularly after the way you resisted the butterfly pendant." His eyes flitted to the necklace she wore, from which the pendant now hung.

She smiled at the evidence that he had admired her from so early on in their acquaintance, then put the trinket to her eye. The vibrant shapes stared back at her in their orderly but beautiful array of color. She turned the kaleidoscope, and the view shifted.

"It reminds me of you," Silas said.

She lowered the kaleidoscope to look at him.

"Constant but ever-changing beauty," he said. "You not

only reminded me of the beauty in life, you brought it back yourself. And now you are sharing it with all of London."

"It is only thanks to you I am able to do so." She set the kaleidoscope aside to free her hands for more important work, threading them together behind his neck. He was the greatest champion of her ideas, the most fervent supporter she possessed. "I love you, Silas. More each day than the one before."

"And yet, somehow never as much as I love *you*," he said, bringing his mouth near hers.

He guided her until her back came up against the wall, then he reached around her. His lips smiled against hers as the privacy lock clicked into place. "Freddie will simply have to manage on his own for now."

THE END

OTHER TITLES BY MARTHA KEYES

A Chronicle of Misadventures

Reputation at Risk (Book 1)

Secrets of a Duke (Book 2)

A Reckless Courtship (Book 3)

The Donovans

Unrequited (Book 1)

The Art of Victory (Book 2)

A Confirmed Rake (Book 3)

Battling the Bluestocking (Book 4)

Matchify

No Match Found (Book 1)

Sheppards in Love

Kissing for Keeps (Book 1)

Just Friends Forever (Book 2)

Selling Out (Book 3)

Hail Marry (Book 4)

Sheppards in Love-Adjacent Titles

Host for the Holidays (Christmas Escape Series)

Solo for the Season (Gift-Wrapped Christmas Series)

Summer Tease (Falling for Summer Series)

Tales from the Highlands Series

The Widow and the Highlander (Book 1)

The Enemy and Miss Innes (Book 2)

The Innkeeper and the Fugitive (Book 3)

The Gentleman and the Maid (Book 4)

Families of Dorset Series

Wyndcross (Book 1)

Isabel (Book 2)

Cecilia (Book 3)

Hazelhurst (Book 4)

Romance Retold Series

Redeeming Miss Marcotte (Book 1)

A Conspiratorial Courting (Book 2)

A Matchmaking Mismatch (Book 3)

Standalone Titles

To Hunt an Heiress (Bachelors of Blackstone's Series)

A Suitable Arrangement (Castles & Courtship Series)

Goodwill for the Gentleman (Belles of Christmas Book 2)

The Christmas Foundling (Belles of Christmas: Frost Fair Book 5)

The Highwayman's Letter (Sons of Somerset Book 5)

Of Lands High and Low

Mishaps and Memories (Timeless Regency Collection)

The Road through Rushbury (Seasons of Change Book 1)

Eleanor: A Regency Romance

ABOUT THE AUTHOR

 Whitney Award-winning Martha Keyes was born, raised, and educated in Utah—a home she loves dearly but also loves to leave for stints of world travel. She received a BA in French Studies and a Master of Public Health from Brigham Young University.

Her route to becoming an author was full of twists and turns, but she's finally settled into something she loves. Research, daydreaming, and snacking have become full-time jobs, and she couldn't be happier about it. When she isn't writing, she is honing her photography skills, looking for travel deals, and spending time with her family.

ACKNOWLEDGMENTS

Writing often feels like a solitary endeavor, and yet, when you finish a book and look back on the process, you realize just how many people were instrumental in making it fit to see the light of day.

I couldn't do any of this without my husband, Brandon, whether it's running the show at home, talking through character emotions, or catering to my many and varied wishes. He's a true keeper, and I will definitely be keeping him.

My kids have grown up with a mom whose mind is often in other (imaginary) worlds, but there's nothing better than living in the real one with them.

Thank you to my critique partners and dear friends, Kasey, Deborah, and Jess. Couldn't do this gig without you, and I certainly wouldn't want to.

Thank you to my beta readers: Brooke, Melanie, Heidi, Karen, Cory, and Nan. Your feedback was instrumental in getting this story into shape, as always.

Thank you to my editors, Jenn and Carolyn, for helping make sure this book was fit for public consumption.

Thank you to all my readers who make it possible for me to continue writing stories. I will forever be grateful to you for spending your precious hours on my books!

Printed in Great Britain
by Amazon